D0370296

ILL Conceived

Book 1 in the
Aimee Brent Mystery Series

by

L. C. Hayden

Cover Jacket Design by
Maritza Jáurequi-Neely

ISBN-13: 978-1491215760
ISBN-10:1491215763

Angel's Trumpet Press

Printed in the United States of America

What Readers Are Saying About *ILL Conceived*

In *ILL Conceived*, the past and present converge as Aimee Brent tries to solve the murder of young Lauri Evans and comes smack up against the secret of her own mother's brutal death. The surprise ending is a shocker. Great suspense!

Mike Befeler
Award Nominated Author of The V V Agency and Care Homes Are Murder

ILL Conceived is a good suspense thriller. Thoroughly enjoyed reading it. Recommend it for anyone who wants to escape for a weekend.

Rosemary Staley from Indiana

Comments on *When the Past Haunts You*, a Watson Award Finalist

L.C. Hayden keeps me up at night. Seriously. *When the Past Haunts You*, her latest entry in the Harry Bronson series, has all the ingredients you'd expect to find in an L.C. Hayden book: lots of action, interesting characters, oodles of suspense, and a surprise ending. I loved it all. Highly recommended.

Valerie Stocking
Author and Playwright

Comments on *When Death Intervenes*

When Death Intervenes is thoroughly engrossing with no dull moments in this page turner mystery. L.C. Hayden has created an intriguing plot with a storyline that leaves the reader guessing to the very end. Her characters are daring and diversified revealing her talent and skillfulness in her plot, setting and storytelling. Do not miss this winner!

Connie Gregory
conniesreviewsblogspot.com

Comments on *Why Casey Had to Die*, an Agatha Award Finalist for Best Novel

Drawn in from the first page, I was reluctant to put the book down until the very end. Hayden has created a suspenseful tale full of interesting characters that will keep readers guessing. Every twist and turn adds depth to this well crafted story. All fans of whodunit mysteries will find a new series to devour. I am already anxiously awaiting the next Harry Bronson mystery.

Lisa Kisner
Reader Views

List of L. C. Hayden's books

Aimee Brent Mystery Series:
ILL Conceived
Coming soon: *Vengeance in My Heart*
Throw Away Children (working title)

Harry Bronson Mystery Series:
When the Past Haunts You
When Death Intervenes
Why Casey Had to Die
Novels featuring Harry Bronson:
What Others Know (Part 2)
When Colette Died (Part 1) (Bronson not
featured)
Where Secrets Lie
Who's Susan?

Inspirational:
Nonfiction: *Angels and Miracles Abound*
(coming fall 2013)
Angels Around Us
When Angels Touch You
Fiction: *Bell-Shaped Flowers*

Children's picture books:
What Am I? What Am I?
Puppy Dog and His Bone (coming soon)

Paranormal:
The Drums of Gerald Hurd

Writing Advice:
Help! I Want to Write

Contributed to
A Second Helping of Murder (a cookbook)
Haunted Highways
   (a collection of haunted places in Texas)
Edited and compiled
   Breaking & Entering: The Road to Success
      (a   Sisters in Crime how-to guide)

Dedication

To my critique group
You make my writing so much better

Dick Schwein, retired FBI Special Agent in
 Charge; author of the Ben Douglas series.
Thanks, Dick, for the advice on proper police
procedure and all the other suggestions that took
this story to the next level.

The Fatal Four:

Donnell Belle, author of *The Past Came Hunting*
 and *Deadly Recall*
Mike Befeler, author of the Paul Jacobson
 Geezer-Lit Mystery Series and the
 VVAgency, a paranormal PI mystery
Annette Dashofy, author of *Circle of Influence*
 (March 2014)
Fatal Four,
 Your advice has been beyond helpful. Thanks
for all the time you devoted to my novel.

Kristen Weber, awesome editor
 Your suggestions, your comments, and your
advice have taught me so much about writing.
Thanks a million. I'm so glad our paths crossed.

Beta Readers:

Debbie Carroll, Leslie Connell, Joan Huston, Lynn Rhodes, Pat Tracey
You're wonderful Mystery Babes and great friends. Thank you for being part of my first readers.

Carol Aspinwall, Charlene Tess, and Bobbye Johnson, Don Moss
Still another set of readers and dear friends I'm indebted to. Thanks for your time, your comments, and your suggestions. You're the best.

Grammar Checker

Valerie Stocking
Thanks for doing such a super job and for giving my book top priority so that I could meet my deadline.

Acknowledgements

Lots of kudos goes to the people who honor me by bidding to be characters in my book: Dolphine Birescik, Louise Dietz, and Tom and Marie O'Day. I salute you and thank you from the bottom of my heart.

Other folks who are behind the scenes include Maritza Jáurequi-Neely who designed the gorgeous, eye-popping cover. I'm in awe of her talent.

A big thank you to the folks at the Meyers Visitor Center, especially Pam Ross and Launa Craig. I called them a million times requesting specific information about the area. Each time, they were not only gracious and courteous, but extremely helpful.

Last, but not least, a million thanks goes to all my readers. Without you, I wouldn't have a reason to write. I appreciate your support and loyalty. I couldn't make it without you.

Please feel free to drop by my website and leave a message: www.lchayden.com. There, you can sign up to receive my newsletter or contact me through my website.

Attention, book club readers, for your convenience, I placed on my website a group of discussion questions for *ILL Conceived*.

If you're on Facebook, please befriend me. Lc Hayden will lead you to my fun page while Lchayden takes you to my author page.

Find me on Twitter: @LCHayden1

As always, a special thanks to my honey, my love, my life, my husband: Richard Hayden.

Lots and lots of love to my grandkids. Their laughter and love lights up my life. You rock my world.

Chapter 1

The bright sun had begun its descent when Lauri Evans first opened her eyes and wished she hadn't.

The world spun around her. She rubbed her eyelids, hoping to clear her vision. Tall pine trees came into focus and a cluster of aspens stretched toward heaven. Beneath her, a carpet of grass and pine provided a somewhat uncomfortable cushion.

A bird chirped nearby. Fifty yards down the hill, the crystal blue waters of the lake sparkled in the sunlight. She recognized Lake Tahoe Basin.

She gasped when a throbbing ache exploded somewhere in her chest and shivered against the cold that came from within her.

She wiggled into a sitting position, ignoring the raw pain that screeched through her body. She ran her hands over her chest and torso, taking inventory. Something felt sticky and warm--blood.

"Oh, God," she whispered.

Glancing around, she searched for anything that would give her hope. She struggled to her feet. Thoughts of her mother, her baby sister, and Gary, sweet Gary, who deserted her when she needed him the most, invaded her mind. Somehow, she needed to get down the hill, find help, and tell them what happened.

Or more people would die.

* * *

Aimee Brent stopped at the red light. Briefly, her gaze drifted to the police report that she and her reporter friend, Dolphine Birescik, had picked up at the police station.

Lauri.

A complete stranger but still only a teen. Someone who should be looking forward to prom. Her first kiss. Graduation. Starting her life.

Lauri Evans. Where was she?

South Lake Tahoe's population hadn't reached the twenty-two thousand mark yet, but it was still large enough to swallow Lauri in its shadows. The woods that surrounded the area certainly didn't help.

Aimee rolled down the window. A breeze blew in, ruffling Dolphine Birescik's fiery red hair. Aimee touched her own wavy, brunette mop and envied her friend's vibrant color.

The light turned green and Aimee eased off the brake, accelerating through the intersection. "What if Lauri is dead?"

Dolphine squeezed Aimee's upper arm. "Don't go there. All we know is that the police listed her as a runaway. It's their job to find her.

2

Not ours. We're just reporters."

True, but what if a piece she wrote helped to find Lauri? Maybe even save her life? "Have you read the statistics on runaways? A significant number of them end up dead or involuntarily hooked on drugs and alcohol. Eventually, the females end up as prostitutes." Aimee focused on the heavy traffic. "Do you know that 1.6 to 2.8 million teens run away from home each year in the U. S.? They think they're escaping their problems, but instead, they flee into an abyss of dangerous predators which will propel them into a life of crime and abuse on the streets."

"Sounds like you've been considering writing this piece for a while."

Aimee nodded. "Before, it was just something brewing on the back of my mind. But now with Lauri, maybe if I wrote an exposé on runaways, citing Lauri as an example, someone will read it, spot her, contact the police, and she's saved." Even though the possibility seemed slim, Aimee wanted to pursue the piece. "She's just a kid, barely fifteen."

"I know, but I don't think Rich will want a story on runaways. There's not enough meat there."

"Under normal circumstances, you're right. But since Lauri is a local and is still missing, he might." Aimee parked the Subaru Outback alongside the building housing the South Shore Carrier. The single-story, half-block-long structure served as the newspaper offices for South Lake Tahoe, California. Its name, proudly displayed on the building front, informed tourists who drove Highway 50, the city's busiest thoroughfare, that this place buzzed with news.

Aimee opened the car door and the sun's rays warmed her face, promising another beautiful day. "I hope he'll go for it."

Dolphine nodded. "Good luck."

Aimee followed Dolphine into the *Carrier's* tiny reception area. Dolphine went past the waist-high swinging doors and headed toward her desk. Aimee lingered behind. She glanced at Rich, who busied himself at the coffee table near the entry way. He removed Styrofoam cups from plastic bags and stacked them in two neat rows.

Aimee cleared her throat.

He turned and smiled. "Something on your mind?"

"I have an idea for an article."

"Tell me about it."

"A local teen is missing. The police are calling it a runaway."

"The girl?"

"Lauri Evans."

Rich refilled the bowl with packets of sugar. "And your story would be?"

"About runaways--the dangers they--"

"Been done before."

Aimee frowned. "I want to continue this discussion." She swept past him and felt his gaze follow her as she headed toward her cubicle, located near the large, open staff room. She opened her bottom drawer and tossed in her purse. Aimee looked up to see Rich still staring at her. Their eyes locked. She waved.

He waved.

She smiled.

He smiled.

Dolphine approached from behind and whispered in her ear. "I've been watching you and Rich interact. I see lots of flirting."

Aimee turned, giving Rich her back. "You're crazy, gal. There's no flirting going on here."

"Sure. Whatever you say." Dolphine wiggled her eyebrows.

Aimee rolled her eyes. "I'm just getting over John, and I don't have time to get involved. You know about my dream."

"Yeah, yeah." Dolphine dismissed the idea with a wave of her manicured hand. "Let me guess. You want to write for a big name newspaper and get lots of recognition and awards."

Aimee thrust her shoulders back, drawing herself upright, all five-two of her. "You're damn right, and I've set my mind to accomplish this before I turn thirty."

The front door opened and Louise Dietz hobbled in. Aimee, along with everyone else who knew her, called her Grandma Louise because she enjoyed taking care of others and hovered over people, much like grandparents do. Grabbing a small notebook and pen, Aimee worked her way toward the front counter. The pitch on writing about runaways would have to wait.

Rich offered Grandma Louise his hand and led her to a seat located in the reception area.

From a distance, Aimee noticed that the furrows across the older woman's forehead deepened.

"Is something wrong?" Rich asked.

"As a matter of fact there is, but now I'm not really sure if my coming here was such a good idea."

"Of course it's a good idea." Rich reached for the Styrofoam cups. "Let me get you a cup of coffee. Then we'll talk."

"Actually, I want to talk to the reporter who handles missing persons."

Rich handed her a steaming cup of coffee. "They all do, but the ones most likely to get such an assignment is either Aimee or Dolphine."

"Then I'll talk to both."

Rich nodded. "I'll get them."

"No need." Aimee and Dolphine stepped through the waist-high swinging doors. "We're right here." They pulled two chairs facing Grandma Louise.

Rich slid through the same waist-high

swinging door heading for an open workstation, keeping within earshot. He stopped at an empty desk, bent down, and busied himself studying the computer screen.

Grandma Louise blew into her coffee and took a sip. "I have a story for either of you. If you do it right, it might be your big break. You'll even be able to go work for a big name newspaper. How does that sound?"

Aimee glanced at Rich who still had his nose buried in his work.

"Funny you would mention that," Dolphine said. "You must be psychic. Aimee and I were just talking about her working for one of the big-time newspapers." Dolphine indicated Aimee. "That sounds more like a story for her."

Aimee cocked her head. "Go on."

"It's about Lauri Evans." Grandma Louise whispered as though saying the name would break some kind of rule.

"The runaway." Aimee's glance drifted toward Rich. He looked up. She glared at him. He shrugged.

"You've heard of her."

Aimee nodded. "Every day before showing up for work, Dolphine and I stop by the police department to see if they have any news leads for us. Today, they told us you had called them last night to report Lauri's disappearance."

"What did you learn?" Grandma Louise thrust her chin up, daring the police report to contradict her.

"They officially list her as a runaway," Aimee said.

"They're wrong." Grandma Louise pronounced each word carefully. "Last night I heard her scream--twice. Now she's gone. I swear that child did not run away."

Dolphine moved closer toward Grandma Louise. "We were told Lauri has a history of running away. Even her mother thinks she took off because they had a fight just before Mom left to do some typing."

Grandma Louise bit her lip. "But then Lauri must've come back and something made her scream."

"That's not likely." Dolphine shook her head. "From what I learned, when Lauri pulls one of her stunts, she's usually gone for two to three days."

"But Lauri--" Grandma Louise grew silent and rubbed her chin. Her eyes narrowed in deep concentration. "She was . . . maybe she--" Her voice faded away.

"Grandma Louise? What's wrong?" Aimee leaned toward her.

"I . . . I remember something. Something I didn't tell the police. Something I should've told them." Grandma Louise hugged herself.

"What is it?"

"I . . . I don't know. Something." She bolted upright, almost spilling her coffee. "I shouldn't have come." Slamming the cup on the counter, she spun and reached for the door handle.

Aimee took hold of Grandma Louise's arm. "You wanted to check on Lauri before calling the police. Maybe you stepped out and glanced at Lauri's apartment, or maybe you opened the door and stared down the hallway."

Grandma Louise stopped, turned, and stared at Aimee.

"When you did that, did you see something?" Aimee focused on Grandma Louise's eyes. The shallow gleam that appeared in them quickly disappeared.

Grandma Louise shifted her weight from side to side. She cast her eyes downward, as though the floor offered the best view of the room.

"Grandma Louise? What did you see?"

Startled, she looked up at Aimee. "What?" Grandma Louise's complexion turned pasty white and perspiration beaded on her forehead.

Aimee steered the elderly woman back to the chair. "Grandma Louise, are you okay? Do you want me to call someone?" Aimee's and Dolphine's eyes locked and Aimee recognized the concern in them.

Grandma Louise's gaze settled on Aimee. "What?" She blushed, her color returning. "I'm perfectly fine. It's just that I . . . it bothered me."

"What bothered you?"

"I . . . don't . . . know." She spoke slowly. "I

think I saw someone running down the hallway."

"Who?"

"All I saw was a shadow, but a young shadow."

A young shadow? What the heck was a young shadow? Aimee looked at Dolphine who shrugged. "A what?" Aimee asked.

Grandma Louise waved her hand, dismissing the question. "Oh, you know. It moved fast."

"Could it have been Lauri?"

"No, it wasn't Lauri. It was . . . it might've been . . . Gary."

"Gary Heely?" Dolphine asked, looking down at the police report that suggested maybe Lauri had left to be with him. "Her boyfriend?"

Grandma Louise nodded, tilted her head back against the wall, and closed her eyes.

"This is very important." Aimee paused for effect. "Are you absolutely sure?"

Again, Grandma Louise nodded. "That's why I came. I want both of you to look into this." She shivered as her gaze darted from a desk, down to the floor, up to a computer, and finally met first, Dolphine's and then Aimee's gaze. In a deep, low voice, Grandma Louise whispered, "He knows something." Slowly, her body sagged into the chair as her confidence evaporated.

"Grandma Louise, are you all right?"

"It's so strange. I've said too much. I like

Gary. He would never hurt Lauri. He really loved, uh, loves her. I certainly didn't mean to imply he--" She pursed her lips. "Please don't tell the police. I'm not even sure it was him. All I saw was a shadow."

She opened her purse. "I brought you a picture of Lauri and Gary." She handed it to Aimee and smiled, a curvature of the lips telling Aimee it was only a surface smile. "I'm afraid I made a terrible mistake in coming. The police don't suspect foul play--as they say on TV cop shows. Dolphine's absolutely right. Lauri is probably a runaway. I've made a terrible fool of myself. I'm so sorry."

Before Aimee could answer, Grandma Louise got to her feet and rushed out.

Chapter 2

Aimee stuffed the picture in her pocket, picked up Grandma Louise's unfinished coffee, and carried it to the back of the staff room.

"Well?" Rich said as Aimee went past him.

The musky scent of his cologne bombarded Aimee with unwelcome thoughts. "Well, what?"

"Are you going to probe into Lauri's disappearance?"

Aha! She knew it. "You were listening."

Rich shrugged. "I couldn't help it. We employ seven reporters and one photographer. That makes it a small business which means tiny offices. Besides, a good editor always--"

"I know. A good editor always listens to everything."

"Oops. I better be careful. You're learning the secrets of the trade."

"I can't help it. It's a tiny office."

Rich smiled. "So, are you?"

"Am I what? Learning the secrets of the trade?"

Rich cocked his head and looked at her. His deep-set blue eyes lured her in. "Are you going to follow up on Lauri's disappearance?"

She planned to, but it would be so much better if Rich thought the idea came from him.

"Should I?"

"It might be worth something--maybe a feature on runaways."

Bingo. She won the jackpot. If handled correctly, the story carried potential. Visions of awards danced in her head. "Okay, I'll look into it."

Behind Rich, Dolphine gave her the thumbs-up signal. Aimee ignored her friend and looked down at Grandma Louise's half-empty coffee cup. "Did you notice anything unusual about her?"

"I noticed she seemed almost senile."

That wasn't quite how she would describe Grandma Louise, but it would do. "She's normally strong and vibrant, not distracted and confused."

"That's not what I hear." Rich grabbed some papers out of the In Box.

"What do you mean?"

"Rumors say she has episodes where she forgets things or gets everything jumbled." Rich initialed the top paper and returned it to the Out Box. "Kind of like what happened today."

Aimee nodded an acknowledgment, stepped into the ladies room and dumped the remaining coffee in the sink. She tossed the cup into the trash and rejoined Rich by the assignment desk. She settled into a chair, resting her forearms on the edge of the desk. "Do you think that's why the police didn't put much stock in her story?"

"I'm sure that had something to do with it."

"Poor Grandma Louise."

Rich arranged and re-arranged the same papers into different piles. "Yeah, and right now she's probably under a lot of stress." He reached into a can filled with pens and scribbled something down.

"Because of Lauri's disappearance?"

"Exactly. She's worried to death about that kid. She's always concerned about others' welfare. For her sake, I hope Lauri comes home soon."

Aimee nodded, stood, and walked to her desk, thinking of the Donner Party feature she had to write. Important stories awaited her. Yeah, sure.

"Aimee?"

She looked back at Rich.

"Do you really plan to leave this job?"

Her eyes widened. She opened her mouth. Nothing came out. She closed it. A couple of seconds followed. "Oh, Rich, who knows what the future will bring? It's not as if I'm leaving tomorrow or anything like that."

Rich nodded only once.

Aimee bit her tongue. She planned on leaving sometime but didn't want to mislead him. "But I do have dreams."

"We all do." He looked away, his eyes squinting like a moose in pain.

"Hey," Dolphine said.

Aimee looked at her best friend. "Hey, yourself."

"I know you're anxious to get working on that runaway feature, but you've got a bunch of unfinished stories to complete."

"Yeah. Bummer, eh?"

"I'm caught up with all of my assignments. That means I can do some preliminary work on yours and report to you if I find anything."

Aimee cocked her head. "My story? Not our story?"

"Your story." Dolphine pointed at Aimee, emphasizing her point. "I'll help with the leg work and whatever else, but I want you to know upfront that this is your assignment."

Aimee held her breath. "Why?"

"Let's just say we have different goals."

"Meaning?"

"Your dream is the big newspaper office. My dream is here." She turned and walked away before Aimee could question her further.

Chapter 3

A single drop of blood plummeted to the ground, like a leaking tear.

Aimee Brent focused on that drop until nothing else mattered. Magically, the knife vanished and so did the hand holding it. Even the body faded from her view.

Nothing else remained.

Only that single drop of blood.

Falling . . . falling . . .

* * *

Aimee awoke, whimpering like a child.

Beloved Mother. Beloved Father.

If only she could reach out to them. Another nightmare had invaded her dreams. She placed her arms around herself, wishing it were Mom's or Dad's arms instead.

She lay still, sweat pouring out of every pore. She inhaled deeply, slowly. She swung her legs out of bed, planted them on the carpet, and quickly dressed.

Twenty-five minutes later, Aimee sat in her parked car, mindlessly tapping the steering wheel.

Over and over again.

Once in a while, her eyes would stray from

the road stretching ahead and to the cemetery beside her. From where she sat, she could see the two side-by-side graves. She glanced away, back to the road, a road filled with uncertainty.

"Oh Mom. Dad." The whisper escaped from Aimee's lips, like a cold breeze lurking in a graveyard.

Aimee grabbed the bouquet of flowers and headed for the graves. She plucked a single red rose out and laid the rest on top of her mom's grave.

Beloved Mother, Sister, Wife--the tombstone read.

Beloved Mother. Aimee would give anything if she could talk to her mom just once more. Time heals all, the saying goes. But it hadn't healed this wound.

Aimee laid the remaining single rose on her father's grave. She looked around. It seemed foolish, visiting her father here at this grave. True, her father was dead, but the dirt under her feet only held an empty casket.

Beloved Father, Husband, the marker read. She had loved him--still loved him--with all her heart. Oh, Dad, I miss you so much.

Aimee stared at both graves. She leaned down and stroked the parts that read *Beloved Mother, Beloved Father.* "Mom, Dad, I need your help. For more than fifteen years everything was fine. Then, for no reason at all, the nightmares returned, releasing a flood of memories and along with them, the raw pain. I have no idea what triggered it. It's like something is telling me it's all coming together. I'll finally get my answers, and that petrifies me." She cleared her throat, blew each of her parents a kiss, and headed back to the car.

When she reached her house, she spotted Dolphine's familiar car parked in her driveway. Aimee pulled up, and Dolphine stepped out of the car.

"I brought breakfast." Dolphine waved the McDonald's package she held in her hand.

"Thanks!" Aimee unlocked the front door, and Dolphine followed her in.

Ordinary people used their dining table for eating. Not Aimee. This one held her craft tools and materials, currently the thirty-odd origami animal figures she'd made. Most were swans, but she had some giraffes and a horse or maybe a zebra. Certainly, she couldn't tell when all the creatures were pink, blue, bright yellow, red, or orange.

"I'll clear a place in the dining room."

Dolphine pointed to the creations. "So you're into origami now." Dolphine studied her handy work. "Cute animals. What you gonna do with 'em?"

"Thought I'd take them to the children's ward at the hospital."

"Good idea."

Aimee finished clearing the space, and

Dolphine took out the two flat, yellow Styrofoam containers and opened them to reveal the pancakes.

Aimee went to the kitchen, poured two glasses of milk, and rejoined Dolphine.

"Bet you know why I'm here." Dolphine emptied a plastic cup of syrup on her pancakes.

"We're going to go over the runaway piece."

Dolphine set her fork down. "You're such a brain."

"And cute, too!" Aimee hadn't bothered to put on any make up or fix her hair properly before she left for the cemetery this morning. She probably looked like a scarecrow.

"You, cute?" Dolphine faked a cough.

Aimee smiled and cut her pancakes. "Where do you want to begin?"

"At the most logical place, at the beginning of the police report. It stated that at precisely 11:19 p.m., Louise Dietz--otherwise known as Grandma Louise--heard someone scream. At 11:29 p.m., she called 911."

Dolphine had quoted the report's introductory information verbatim. Aimee recalled reading the two seemingly innocent sentences, but what wasn't said in between had aroused her curiosity. Why had she waited ten minutes to call? "Do you really think it was Lauri's screams Grandma Louise heard?"

"That's my dilemma, too." Dolphine bit into her pancakes. "According to the police, one of

Grandma Louise's neighbors had the TV turned on to one of those horror shows that has lots of screaming. The police think that's what Grandma Louise heard."

"Do you agree?"

Dolphine flopped another pancake on her plate and buttered it. "I don't know what to think. Sometimes I say it was the TV. Other times, I think it could have been some rude teens out late at night carousing and shrieking."

"Or it could have been Lauri screaming like Grandma Louise claimed."

"Maybe, maybe not. Yesterday, I dropped by Grandma Louise's. She said Lauri and Gary had been at each other's throats lately. Seems he's a bit on the possessive side. Lauri told Grandma Louise that Gary suffocated her, not literally, of course, but you know what I mean."

Aimee nodded and swallowed hard. Many times, her ex had called Dolphine to check on Aimee's whereabouts--even after she had told him where she'd be. "When you're fifteen--or any age for that matter--it's not good to have a suffocating boyfriend." Not hungry, Aimee pushed her plate away.

Dolphine squeezed Aimee's arm. "You okay?"

Aimee flashed a weak smile.

"John was a jerk. I'm glad you got rid of him."

Aimee nodded. She didn't want to talk about

John. "I know Grandma Louise believes she heard Lauri scream. Even after the police left, Grandma Louise stayed up, watching Lauri's and her mother's apartment, and Lauri never came home. Grandma Louise called the police back at three."

"Yeah, I remember reading that in the report."

Aimee drank her milk. "What about her father? Where was he?"

Dolphine's eyes widened. "Stepfather, you mean. Don't you remember? He's that man who disappeared about six months ago. He got in his plane, took off, and was never heard from again. We ran the story."

Aimee gasped. Lauri's father missing, like her own. She closed her eyes and a picture of her father's empty grave flashed in her mind.

Beloved Father.

His body had never been found. The case remained open. "Have they found the body?"

"Are we talking about Lauri's father or yours?"

Aimee bit her lip and tasted the coppery sting on her tongue. She had to get past this point. Move on. Then maybe the nightmares would stop. "Lauri's, of course."

"You sure?"

Not really. If only she had gotten the chance to say goodbye. Then maybe the nightmares never would have started.

"Aimee?"

She cleared her throat. "You talked to Lauri's mom. Tell me about that."

"She claims she got home from work close to five in the morning."

Aimee's eyebrows arched. "Five? Where the heck does she work?"

"She works for a law firm, which, of course, was closed, but she often does freelance work. She uses the office's computer since she doesn't have one at home."

"She works until five in the morning?"

"I thought that was rather hokey until I found out why. Lauri's mom had a baby born with a defective heart. There's no money for the operation, so she freelances at night. That's what led to the fight. She wanted to leave for work and told Lauri to babysit, but Lauri told her mom she had other plans. They started a screaming match that ended by Lauri leaving. The mother had no choice but to pack the baby and take her to work. When they returned home, her mom checked on Lauri, but she was gone."

"So she's still missing?"

"Yeah, she obviously ran away. She's done it twice before. She leaves for two or three days, and then comes back like nothing happened."

Aimee perused the facts. Somewhere out there a desperate, lonely, confused, and frightened teen roamed the streets. She hoped the police would find the girl in time, but deep down she feared it wouldn't be that simple.

Chapter 4

One phone call to her police source told Aimee that Gary drove a black, four-year-old Jeep Wrangler. Armed with this knowledge and Gary's photo that Grandma Louise had given her, Aimee headed for Lake Tahoe High School, a ten-minute drive. But today, it took sixteen minutes due to extra-heavy traffic. Damn tourists.

Aimee drove slowly down each of the rows in the school's parking lot, looking at license plates. How could one place contain so many black Wranglers? She had counted fourteen so far. The lunch bell was about to ring and the area would be crawling with students. Best to forget looking for the car and concentrate on finding Gary.

She parked her Outback and got out. The morning sun beat down on her relentlessly, causing her blouse to stick to her. But that's one thing she loved about the area. It offered four seasons.

Standing in the parking lot, she considered her alternatives. Pine trees blocked the school's main entrance view. But if she stood at the edge of the teachers' parking lot, she had a partially obstructed view of the school's two main entrances, and at the same time, could look below into the students' parking lot. Hopefully, she'd get lucky and catch Gary coming out, provided she could recognize him.

When the bell rang, a handful of students rushed to their cars. Right behind them, a second wave streamed out. Then still more--and more, like ants scrambling out of their hole.

She approached a group of students to her right. "Excuse me, do any of you know Gary Heely?" She showed them his picture.

They glared at her. She considered telling them that she planned to revoke their lunch passes. That bunch of friendly, helpful folks walked away.

Okay, lesson learned. No more groups. Try individuals. The first two had no idea who Gary was. The third one, a stocky girl with dull, dangling hair clinging to her like ropes, seemed to have trouble remembering who she was, much less remembering someone named Gary Heely. The fourth student, a tall guy with buck teeth, knew him, but had no idea where he was.

She tried a fifth and a sixth student. No results. What a bummer.

"Hey, Miss," came a voice behind her.

Nothing else to do but try some more.

Someone tapped her shoulder. She turned and saw "Bucky," the student who claimed to know Gary.

"I've been calling you. Didn't you hear me?"

Oh, that Miss. "I was preoccupied. Sorry."

"Yeah? Well, there's Gary."

"Where?"

"Over there." He pointed to his right. "Coming out of the gym. Heading toward the parking lot."

Aimee thought she recognized Gary from the picture. "He's the one wearing the white polo shirt?"

"Yeah."

Aimee turned to thank Bucky, but the teen had already focused his attention on a group of friends. Aimee galloped toward Gary and did her best not to lose sight of him. She blocked his path, forcing him to go around her. "Excuse me. You're Gary Heely, aren't you?"

The longhaired youth eyed her. "Who wants to know?"

"I do. I'm Aimee Brent." That was stupid. Did she really expect him to know who she was?

Gary's eyebrows raised in an arch. "The reporter?"

Wow! He knew her. "That's me. I want to talk to you about Lauri."

By now they had reached his car. He leaned against it. "What about her?"

"Is she a runaway?"

He shrugged. "So the police say."

"What do you say?"

He opened the car door. "Do you really care what I think?"

Aimee nodded.

"Hell, no! She's no runaway." He plopped into the driver's seat and slammed the door shut.

"Gary, wait!" Aimee knocked on the tinted window. "I really want to hear what you have to say."

He rolled down the window. "It's lunch time, man. I've only got an hour."

"We can talk while we eat." No reaction. "My treat." Dammit, she scolded herself. There I go, depleting my already empty wallet.

"Hop in."

She silently patted herself on the back, and then realized she only had three dollars in her wallet. What kind of meal would that buy? No problem. Her dependable credit card would rescue her.

Even before she had completely settled into the passenger seat, Gary floored the gas pedal and sped away, leaving rubber on the pavement. Somehow Aimee felt no surprise when he drove past the South Lake Tahoe city limits and into the adjacent town of Stateline. She eyed the "You are leaving California" border sign followed by one that read "Welcome to Nevada." Soon as they crossed the state line, they were bombarded by a row of casinos lining both sides of the street.

Gary must have noticed Aimee clutching the arm rest and eyeing the border sign. "There's no law about transporting reporters across state lines, is there?"

Aimee smiled. "Don't worry. I won't turn you in."

Gary nodded and pulled into Harvey's parking lot. The casino sat across from Harrah's. One thing for sure, Nevada didn't waste an inch of land before building its casinos. Good news for Nevada, bad news for California.

Gary parked the Wrangler.

Before he had a chance to jump out, Aimee said, "We're eating here--at a casino?"

"You need to be twenty-one to gamble. You can be any age to eat. Besides, I may be seventeen, but I look twenty-one. Me and Lauri used to eat here all the time. We like their buffet." He got out and waited for Aimee to join him, but made no effort to help her out of the car. A real gentleman, this Gary Heely.

Aimee followed him through the casino. He obviously knew the layout. She threaded her way around the slot machines and caught up with him. They reached the buffet line and Aimee pulled out her VISA. Behind it, she found the twenty-dollar bill she had stashed away for emergencies.

That little trick had saved her more than once. She handed the cashier the twenty, asked for a receipt, waited for her change, and made a mental note to stash another twenty as soon as payday rolled around.

"So what is it you want to know about

Lauri?" Gary sat behind a mound of food, including pork chops, roast beef, mashed potatoes, corn, two types of bread, onion rings, mixed fruits, a slice of strawberry cheesecake, and a piece of chocolate cake.

Aimee looked at her own plate. She had a tossed salad, a wheat biscuit, and a slice of turkey. No gravy. If she ate like Gary, she'd look like a walking balloon. Life wasn't fair.

The waitress brought them their drinks, a Coke for Gary and a mixture of half-Coke and half-Diet Coke for Aimee.

Aimee thanked her. After she left, Aimee turned to Gary. "What makes you think she's not a runaway?" Aimee buttered her biscuit with real butter, dammit.

"Hell, I know her. That chick had problems, man, but not enough to split."

Had? Why the past tense? Aimee stared at Gary. "But she has run away before, hasn't she?"

"Yeah, sure. But not this time."

"Why not this time?"

Gary shrugged. "I just know, okay? Maybe it's the kind of problems she had."

"What kind of problems?"

"Oh, you know. The usual. Her and her mom fought like bitches. Then to top it all off, Lauri had problems at school." He fell silent and picked at his food.

The murmur of conversations close by surrounded them.

"What kind of problems did she have at school?"

Gary shrugged. "She didn't understand what the teachers wanted. She got bad grades. You know, that kind of thing." He frowned and pushed his food around with his fork. "Shit, man, why you wanna know all this garbage for?"

"Because I want to write a story about Lauri, but not just Lauri herself, but all the Lauris out there. I want to write a piece that touches and changes people's lives. Do you understand what I mean?"

Gary eyed her as though inspecting a strange species. "Why do you want to write that?" He shoved in a mouthful of food.

"To help people like Lauri."

"That's cool, man. She'd like that. Maybe you won't believe this, but Lauri always wanted to help people. Like she really cared, you know?"

"Then please help me. Tell me what you know about her."

Gary stopped eating but did not look up. The wrinkled frown on his forehead told Aimee he debated whether he could trust her. After a long pause he said, "Lauri knew you. Do you remember her?" Slowly he raised his gaze until it met hers.

Aimee held a surprised breath and searched her mind. Nothing clicked.

Gary's features tightened, and his eyes drew

into narrow slits. "Last year. Career Week, remember?"

Aimee recalled that sometime last year during Career Week, she had spoken to the tenth grade classes about job opportunities in the mass media field. A wide-eyed student sat at the very front and had seemed interested. After class, they briefly discussed the various journalism job opportunities. Thinking about it, that girl and the picture of the girl Aimee carried were one and the same. Now, more than ever, Aimee wanted to help Lauri. "I remember her."

"That's good because she really liked you."

"I didn't know that."

"Well, she did."

Did? Another Freudian slip? "Why do you talk about her in the past tense?"

Confusion and anguish temporarily covered Gary's face. "She's gone, man. She's gone." He looked down at his plate.

His voice carried a sadness that touched Aimee's heart. She found it hard to swallow her food. "What makes you think so?"

"She was into all this shit, man."

Were all teenagers this eloquent? "Like drugs, you mean?"

"No, no. Not Lauri. Me and Lauri, we know lots of people who use drugs or smoke pot. She used to call them *stupid.* Nah, Lauri wouldn't do drugs. That's not her style." Abruptly, he got up and served himself seconds even though his first

31

plate remained half full.

Aimee followed. She zoned in on the steak. It sizzled on the grill and its aroma attacked her stomach. She started to order it along with the huge baked potato next to the steaks. She looked down at her tummy and sighed. If she ate steak and potato, she'd have to go home and exercise.

She hated to exercise.

Empty-handed, she worked her way back to the table and gobbled down her turkey.

When Gary returned, his second plate contained chicken, some ribs, more mashed potatoes, and an apple. Aimee wondered if he really was going to eat it all. Serving himself such huge portions meant that either he wouldn't allow grief to interfere with his stomach, or he didn't care if he wasted food. Or maybe he handled grief by gorging. "Are you going to have enough time to eat all of that?"

"Yeah, sure," he said. "If I'm late, I'll just skip fourth period."

Great, add contributing to the delinquency of a minor to her list of accomplishments. She should make some brilliant statement about the importance of education. Yeah, sure. That would totally turn him off. "You mentioned that Lauri was into all of this stuff." *Shit* was what he actually said. She liked *stuff* better. "What did you mean by that?"

"All the problems she had--mostly at home, you know."

"You mean with her mother?"

"Yeah. I swear. That lady is weird."

Ah, again the eloquence. "Weird? How?"

Gary shrugged. "You know. She did all the junk moms do. She fed her and dressed her, but I don't think she ever loved Lauri." He focused on his plate as he continued to shove food in his mouth, an action that told Aimee he ate out of compulsion, and not for the joy of it. "If you ask me, she don't like being Lauri's mom."

Aimee twiddled her fork. *Beloved Mother.*

Gary's left eyebrow raised. "You look goofy."

"That's how it goes. You were saying?"

"That Lauri's mother don't care. She's got herself a baby with that new husband of hers. She's always fussing about that kid, and she don't pay no attention to Lauri." He pushed his plate away. "He's dead, you know."

"Who?"

"Lauri's stepfather. He died--or at least disappeared--before the ol' lady popped the new kid out. Maybe that's why she spends so much time with the baby. It's like maybe she's trying to be both father and mother. You know, kinda make up for the fact that the ol' man ain't there." He shrugged. "Or maybe not. Either way, she gives all her attention to that new brat."

Aimee took a small bite of her turkey and considered the idea that maybe Lauri suffered from strong feelings of sibling rivalry, after being an only child for fifteen years? "What about Lauri's biological father?"

"Who?"

"Her real father."

"Dunno."

The waitress set down another full glass in front of Aimee. "Here's your mixed drink," she said with a twinkle in her eye.

Aimee smiled. "It's the only kind to drink."

"That's a matter of opinion, honey." She turned and walked away.

"You were about to tell me about Lauri's real father." Aimee sipped her soda.

"Lauri tried to find out about him but her ol' lady was tight-lipped. One time when Lauri casually mentioned him, the ol' lady hit her so hard it sent her flying across the room."

Aimee's fork stopped halfway to her mouth. She stared at Gary. "Did her mom hit her often?"

"Even if it happened only once--and believe me, it happened a lot more than just once--wouldn't it have been once too often?"

Aimee nodded and ate in silence, digesting the information. "Gary, everything you've said so far gives me reason to believe Lauri ran away. I don't understand why you insist she didn't."

"I just know, man. If she was safe, she would've called." He looked away, temporarily closing his eyes. His Adam's apple bobbed.

Aimee placed the napkin on the table. "So, did Lauri ever find out who her father was?"

"Nope."

"Did she know his name?"

"Not that I know of, but she got along real good with her step-dad. Maybe he might've told her--if he hadn't walked out on 'em."

"Tell me about her step-dad."

"Not much to tell. Me and Lauri weren't an item then. I never met that dude. He just poof, disappeared one day. Maybe six, seven months ago. She hoped that he'd adopt her some day."

"Poor Lauri."

"Yeah. Nobody gave a shit about her--other than me and Grandma Louise. I guess that's why everyone likes Grandma Louise so much. She's always there for you, no matter who you are, how old you are."

"I'm sure her mother loves her, too."

"The hell she does. I know her, remember? You don't. And if sweet Mama loves her so much, can you explain why she took out a huge life insurance policy on Lauri last week?"

Oh, really? Aimee hadn't heard about that. "How do you know about the policy?"

"Lauri told me." He shrugged. "How else would I know?"

Aimee nodded. She finished eating and pushed her plate away. Gary had managed to empty one plate and began work on the second one. Aimee felt sure that Gary planned to miss fourth period, and at the rate he was going, maybe even fifth.

"Well, lady," Gary said between bites, "it

looks like the one you really need to talk to is Lauri's mother. When you do, you'll see what I mean."

Chapter 5

The La Mar Apartments stood at the intersection of Regal and Francis Streets. Considered to be on the seedy part of town, the once elegant, two-story art deco apartment complex had been beaten down by years of abuse and neglect. Aimee parked her car and stepped on grass tall enough to be cut for hay.

She found Lauri's and her mother's apartment almost immediately. Aimee reached for the doorbell, but couldn't find one. She knocked on the door.

The woman who greeted her wore a bright orange tank top and blue jean shorts. Her hair hung loose like the hippies of the seventies. "You the reporter?"

Aimee nodded, thankful she had called ahead. "Yes, I'm Aimee Brent."

"And I'm Karen Boyd, Lauri's mother." She stepped aside for Aimee to enter. Once inside, Karen pointed to the mustard-yellow sofa. "Make yourself comfortable. I'll be back in a minute." She disappeared down the hallway.

Aimee sat and busied herself by looking at the only knick-knacks decorating the room, a set of pictures. An inexpensive black plastic frame on the fireplace mantel held the first photograph that caught her eye. A radiant smile shone as Karen Boyd tenderly focused her attention on the baby in her arms, an ideal pose of a mother and her child.

A second photo on the wall seemed out of place. The fancy wooden frame contrasted sharply to the color of the walls, the same shade as tooth decay. Karen approached and Aimee shifted her attention to Karen, whose taut lips and deep, dark circles revealed turmoil. The picture showed her sparkling deep, soft brown eyes. Today, those same eyes bore a vacant, sickly look.

"I don't know what to tell you." Karen dropped onto the sofa and sat rigidly, as if refusing comfort. "At this point, I almost wish Lauri wouldn't come home. Things are quiet and peaceful when she isn't around." She glanced downward, refusing to meet Aimee's eyes. "That doesn't mean that I don't worry about her. I wish I knew which friend she's staying with this time."

Aimee leaned forward and squirmed into a comfortable position. "Have you tried to find her?"

Karen's face pinched in pain. "No, not really. I've been very busy, but I do plan to call some of her friends."

"That's where you think she is, with friends?"

Karen's forehead furrowed with confusion.

"Yes, of course I do. Where else would she be?"

"I don't know. Her boyfriend thinks she didn't run away."

Karen threw her arms up in the air. "Of course he doesn't. That would make him responsible."

"What do you mean?"

"He went out with Lauri that night. In fact, that's what our fight was about." She closed her eyes, pain etched in her face.

Aimee glanced around the living room, waiting for Karen to continue. Next to the mother/daughter portrait on the mantel was an unframed, eight by ten portrait of Lauri's baby sister. A pile of smaller photos of the baby rested on the bookcase. Scanning the rest of the room, Aimee spotted two more baby pictures, but none of Lauri. Talk about making someone feel unwanted.

"I don't know if you know this or not," Karen said, "but two months ago, I had a baby."

Oh, really? She would have never guessed.

Karen pointed with her head toward the hallway leading to the bedrooms. "She's asleep right now." Karen's voice cracked and she cleared her throat. "She, uh, was born with a defective heart. She needs surgery, but I don't have any insurance. So I took up typing at night. That's not going to make a dent in the bill, but it makes me feel like I'm doing something." She swept the air with her hand. "As you can see, I don't have a computer here at home, but there's one at the office. George and Marvin don't mind if I use it as long as I do it on my own time."

"George and Marvin? The lawyers?"

Karen nodded. "Yes. I work for them." She stood, paced, and folded her arms. "The night Lauri ran away, I asked her to babysit so I could go to work. She threw a temper tantrum and refused. She and that jerk boyfriend of hers already had plans, and she wouldn't change them. She stormed out, and I knew she wouldn't be back for several days."

"I'm assuming that means she's done this before?"

Karen nodded. "I stood by the window, watching, wanting to know which way she went." Karen walked toward the window, moved the faded curtain aside, and stared outside. She wrapped her arms around herself and sighed. "I never saw her."

"Why do you suppose that is?"

Karen turned to face Aimee. "I don't know. I waited by the window for what I thought was a long time, then Karen--that's also my baby's name. I named her after me." For a moment, she beamed. Then her lip quivered and her eyes misted. "Anyway, the baby woke up and I went to her, and that's probably when I missed Lauri."

"What happened then?"

Karen sank on the couch and remained quiet. She sighed and shook her head. "Nothing happened. I packed up the baby and took her with me to the office to do the typing. What else could I do?"

"What about Lauri?"

"What about her?"

"Weren't you worried about her? Didn't you check around as to where she might have gone?"

"What good would that do? When Lauri's ready, she'll come home. Don't take that wrong. I love Lauri, but, well, you know. Right now, I've got my baby to think about."

Aimee bit her tongue to prevent saying the obvious. If she spoke now, she'd regret it.

"Look, let me explain." Karen straightened. "The first time Lauri ran away, I immediately called the police. They rushed over and we talked. The second time, they took their time getting here." She looked down and shook her head. "When she left this time, I didn't want to waste their time. I packed and left. At least I did something productive. I made some money."

Surely a noble cause, Aimee thought, but shouldn't some of that concern be blanketed over Lauri? "Maybe I can help."

Karen cocked her head and studied Aimee through wide, unblinking eyes.

"Our paper can run a feature about Baby Karen's desperate need, and then ask that contributions be sent to such-and-such bank, where we'll open an account in her name."

Karen's eyebrows rose in an arch. "Th-that

would be so wonderful. I'll tell my hospital social worker what you said, so that both of you can do whatever needs to be done to set up an account. Oh, if only Charles could hear this."

"Charles? Your husband?"

Karen nodded. "I was three months pregnant when he disappeared. I heard the gossip. He walked out on us, but Charles wouldn't do that. I'm sure he's . . . dead. But since his body has never been found, there's all this talk."

Aimee drew a deep breath. Her father's body had never been found. *Beloved Father.*

"I know how you feel."

Karen squinted. "No, you couldn't possibly know." She spat out the words. "When there's no funeral, there's no ending. All you feel is this empty spot. It's the ritual of the funeral that forces us to let go. Without it--"

"You always wonder if maybe he's alive." How many times had Aimee prayed for that?

"Why, yes!" Karen's eyes narrowed as though reassessing Aimee. "You do understand."

"I was six when I lost my father in a boating accident." Aimee tensed, bracing for what would follow. The nightmare would play in her mind like an endless movie. It happened every time she spoke of the incident.

Within seconds, the expected image formed with an abruptness that lacked clarity or detail. If only she could understand, then maybe she could let go of the past. In quick succession, bits of memory flashed through her mind.

She saw the blinding fog, like a murderous cloud, envelop the day. She rubbed her eyes, wanting to see her father's boat. Then, like an answered prayer, the fog rose, and she could make out the shape of the boat.

Daddy steered and waved at her and Mom. He looked so handsome. So loving. Then, the explosion. The water burning. The boat, gone. And Daddy, Daddy. What of Daddy? He couldn't die. He simply couldn't die.

Beloved Father, Husband.

Karen's voice disrupted Aimee's thoughts. "Were you there in the boat with him?"

Aimee shook her head. "No, Mom and I were waiting on the shore while Dad went to get the boat. He was bringing it to us. There was this terrible explosion."

"I'm sorry. That must have been horrible."

Aimee flashed a weak smile. "It happened so long ago." By now, she should have accepted the tragedy. But to this day, she couldn't return to Emerald Bay.

Eager to change the subject, Aimee retrieved her spiral notebook and pen from her lap. "Let me get all the information I need about little Karen's condition."

When she finished, Aimee stood, making a mental note to contact both the baby's doctor to verify the information and Karen's social worker. She asked Karen to talk to her doctor and social worker to give them permission to speak to her. "Thank you for your time."

"I'm the one who should be thanking you," Karen said. "I really didn't know how I could raise the money for the operation. I know the social worker is there to help me. But still, there are so many bills. Paying them--helping my baby--that has always been my number one concern."

Yes, of course. We should always number our priorities. "What about Lauri?"

"Huh?" Karen's eyes widened. "Oh! Of course. I'm also concerned about Lauri. For a long time, before I met Charles, Lauri was all I had."

From beyond a closed door to her right, the baby cried. Karen shot to her feet. "Excuse me. My baby needs me. Is there anything else you'd like to know?"

"Yes. Just one quick question. I know my readers will want to know about insurance coverage."

"When Charles, uh, disappeared, we had nothing. No insurance, no savings. I vowed to rectify that. Just last week I took out a small policy on Lauri and me. All I could afford is the $25,000 one. Not much, I know, but it's something. There is, of course, no way to insure Karen, not with her condition."

By now the child's cries had become

desperate wails. Karen's sight jumped from Aimee toward the baby's room.

"I won't keep you any longer." Aimee made her way to the door. "I'll let myself out."

* * *

Back at the newspaper office, Aimee had just finished going over her notes when the phone rang. She picked it up on the second ring. "*South Shore Carrier*. Aimee Brent speaking."

"Aimee, this is Detective Tom O'Day. I normally don't make calls like this, but you've been around here asking questions about Lauri. On behalf of maintaining good relations between the press and the police, I thought I'd give you a call. We found Lauri Evans."

Aimee's heart jumped to her throat. "Hey! That's wonderful news." She reached for a pen and pad.

"Not so wonderful. She's dead."

Aimee felt her bottom lip drop and her heart rate increase. By the time she composed herself, her reporter instincts kicked in. "What happened?"

"It looks like homicide."

Chapter 6

Like all newspaper offices, the place buzzed with activity. Phones rang and nonstop jabbering infiltrated the air. The scent of coffee smells and day old pizza mixed together in the almost square room jammed with rows of desks. Each desk contained a bobble-head figure, a Christmas gift from Rich to each of his employees. They perched on the reporters' desks, like sentinels keeping watch.

"I'm sorry about Lauri."

Aimee looked up to see Dolphine standing on the other side of her desk.

A weak smile escaped Aimee's lips. Dolphine skirted the desk, hugged her, leaned closer, and whispered in her ear. "Let's go get a donut or some other fattening, forbidden, sinful delight."

"Why don't we go to the police station instead?" Aimee opened the bottom drawer and grabbed her purse. "I'd like to read the police report. Want to come?"

"Only if we get a donut afterwards."

Aimee smiled and wondered how her friend ate all kinds of junk food and maintained her figure.

* * *

46

Aimee and Dolphine were directed to a tall woman sitting behind a desk overflowing with paper. She had solid-black hair hanging shiny and soft to her shoulders. She looked up at them through deep brown eyes. "I'm Marie O'Day."

O'Day? Like in Tom and Marie O'Day? "I'm Aimee Brent and she's Dolphine Birescik. We're reporters for the *South Shore Carrier*."

"Yes, Tom told me. He's in charge of the investigation, but he's not here now. You can wait for him, or you can talk to me. I should be able to answer all of your questions. I am sort of his partner." Detective Marie O'Day glanced at the stack of paperwork piling up on her desk.

Sort of his partner? Aimee looked at Dolphine. She shrugged.

Marie pointed to the metal chairs by her desk. Aimee and Dolphine sat.

"What details can you give us about Lauri's murder?" Aimee flipped her notebook to a blank page.

"Lauri was stabbed in the back two times." Marie recited the facts with the enthusiasm of a high school student reading a term paper. "The shock and pain must have caused her to turn to face her killer. The third stab to her abdomen probably killed her. There were no defensive wounds, leading us to believe that she knew her attacker. She traveled less than seventy feet before collapsing."

"Where did this happen?" Dolphine asked.

"In the woods above Emerald Bay."

The woods. Emerald Bay, where Aimee had watched her father's boat explode. She squirmed and sat straighter. "When will the autopsy report be ready?"

"Soon as it's available, I'll make sure you get a copy."

"What about suspects? Do you have anyone in particular?"

The detective's eyebrows came together. "You know this is an ongoing investigation. I'm not at liberty to reveal such information."

Dolphine leaned forward and eyed Marie, daring her not to answer. "Is Gary a suspect?"

Marie straightened up. "We're looking at several persons of interest, Gary being one of them." Marie's cell rang. She glanced at the caller I.D. "Excuse me, I have to take this." She swiveled her chair and gave Aimee and Dolphine her back.

For a moment she was quiet as she listened. When she spoke her voice came out an octave higher. "Blackmail? But--" She stood and walked away from the reporters.

"Wonder if that conversation had anything to do with Lauri's case." Dolphine eyed the detective. "Wish I could read lips."

"Me, too. Maybe that's something we need to learn."

"Not a bad idea."

Marie closed her cell and headed back to her

desk. "Sorry about that. Got a new lead on another case I'm working on." She sat down.

"Anything the press would be interested in?" Aimee had her pen ready to jot the information.

Marie half-smiled. "No, just an old case. Nothing of interest."

Aimee nodded. "Okay." She wrote in her notebook *blackmail*, followed by a question mark. "Anything else you can tell us?"

"Not really. Details are still sketchy, but I'll keep you informed as new developments occur."

Yeah, sure. Aimee stood. "Thank you for your time."

"My pleasure, ladies. I'll tell my husband you were here."

"You do that." Aimee headed out, and Dolphine hurried to catch up. "We're still going to the Donut Hole, right?"

Aimee smiled. "Sure. Why not?"

Half an hour later, they were back at the *South Shore Carrier*.

Chapter 7

Aimee ran through the woods, dodging the objects in her way. The gnarled tree branches slapped out and grabbed at her. She screamed and pushed on harder.

No, she'd been wrong. The branches hadn't reached for her. Something else had reached and grabbed.

Gasping for breath, she pivoted to look behind her.

He was there, ready to spring. In her haste to get away, she jammed her foot into a rock and fell, diving headlong into the dirt and tall grass, pain shooting up her leg. Skin ripped from her hands and elbows. Horror gripped her and she remained frozen, giving him a chance to catch her.

The huge devil eyes hypnotized her and drew her in.

* * *

Aimee jumped out of her chair, raking her hair with her fingers. The chair shot out from behind her, crashing to the floor. Her coworkers stopped and stared.

Rich set down his coffee cup and rushed to Aimee's desk. "What's wrong?"

She stared at him, her mind still in the

woods, still with the man with the devil eyes.

"You're shaking all over. Are you all right?" He reached out to touch her but she recoiled. He smiled, half-embarrassed, and straightened the chair.

Aimee collapsed into it, attempting to rationalize what had happened. She hadn't fallen asleep. At least she didn't think she had. Yet, the dream had come. A dream or a memory? Of what? If only she could talk to her parents.

Beloved Father. Beloved Mother.

She took a deep breath and slowly let it out though her mouth. Her shoulders relaxed.

Dolphine squatted beside her. "You okay?"

Air fled out of Aimee's lungs in harsh gasps. She nodded.

Dolphine handed her a glass of water. "If you need me, I'm here." She returned to her desk.

Aimee slouched in the chair. If she could disappear, she would. Why did the entire newspaper office have to be one huge room? Although her co-workers no longer stared at her, she knew they listened. If it'd been the other way around, she would've paid attention to something so bizarre. Why didn't the phone ring when you wanted it to? Why was the place so quiet?

Rich pulled up a chair and sat beside her. "What's bothering you? Lauri's murder?"

Better to blame her quirky behavior on the

murder rather than her nightmares. "Yes."

"In that case, I've got some information I think will interest you."

"What's that?"

"Earlier today I got a call."

"From?"

"Jose."

Aimee recalled his round face, brown skin, high cheek bones, and long, black hair pulled tight against his face. "Our infamous Navajo source."

Rich nodded. "He called with a lead about a man from Truckee." His glance traveled toward his office, the only enclosed area outside of the darkroom. Even so, little privacy existed in the glass-enclosed room. Rich had spent money to install Venetian blinds, but mostly, he kept them open.

"What's so important about a man from a town located toward the top of Lake Tahoe?"

"Let's go to my office." He stood and Aimee followed him. He closed the door behind them. Aimee sat on the cushioned office chair facing Rich's desk. He grabbed his yellow notepad. "Here are my notes, but before telling you about what I'm calling the Truckee Mystery, let's get to the part that will really interest you."

Aimee cocked her head.

"My research on the Truckee Mystery came to an abrupt end, and seeing how I had plenty of time left over, I decided to check out Lauri's old neighborhood. Did you know she was born in Truckee and spent her early childhood there?"

Aimee sat up and shook her head.

"I was lucky enough to find an old lady who remembers the family quite well. She used to live next door to them and kept in touch with Lauri's mom even after she moved away."

Aimee automatically reached across Rich's desk for paper and pen.

Rich waited until she was ready and then continued, "Mrs. Dority, the neighbor, told me about Charles Boyd, Lauri's stepfather who vanished. The police suspected foul play but were never able to prove anything." He stood up and walked over to his computer. "Our paper ran a small story about his disappearance. Would you care to see his picture?"

The one thing Aimee had learned in this business was you never knew when you were going to need something. "Sure, why not?"

Rich retrieved some files, found the picture, printed it, and handed it to Aimee. She studied it carefully. On his right cheek he had a one-inch scar, which, instead of detracting from his looks, enhanced his ruggedness. "Do you mind if I keep this for a while?"

"I printed it for you. If I need one, I'll make a copy."

Aimee nodded and slid the picture under her notes. "You said Lauri was eight when her mother married."

"Yep."

"So who is Lauri's biological father?"

"Mrs. Dority delighted in talking about that. She's quite a gossip, believe me. When Karen was sixteen, she was raped. Lauri was the result of that rape."

"Oh, God."

"Apparently Karen's parents demanded that she have an abortion, but she refused. She swore she would love that baby, but apparently Karen's parents--Lauri's own grandparents--had other ideas."

"What do you mean?"

"They constantly picked on Lauri, making her feel like she had been--and I'm quoting this-- ill conceived, and according to them, the baby was, of course, evil. Karen, a mere teenager, was influenced by her parents. Eventually Karen moved out, taking Lauri with her, but according to Mrs. Dority, things never really worked out between Lauri and her mother."

Aimee remembered seeing only Karen's second child's picture on display at her house. She also recalled Karen's words, "My number one priority is getting the money for my baby's operation." Under the circumstances, an understandable remark, but shouldn't she have also been more concerned about Lauri's disappearance?

"Maybe Karen tried to love Lauri, and in a way, I suppose she did." Aimee imagined the hurt Lauri must have felt. "But for Lauri, I don't think that was enough."

"I don't follow you."

"I'm assuming Lauri's main problem stemmed from the fact that she felt unloved. In her mind, she was just what her grandmother had said--ill conceived." Aimee rubbed the bridge of her nose. "Poor Lauri. Only fifteen. What a miserable life she lived." Aimee glanced at her notes. "That's why I'm committed to bring Lauri justice." Aimee closed her notes. "What else?"

"That's about it, but there's something else I want to talk to you about."

Aimee glanced down at her closed notebook. "Oh?"

"I want to hear your opinion about another dilemma I'm facing. It involves the Truckee Mystery."

"You mentioned that before. What's that?"

Aimee looked through the glass enclosure at her co-workers, who were paying rapt attention. Caught in Aimee's gaze, they quickly resumed their work.

Rich walked around his desk, pulled a chair closer to Aimee, and pointed to his notes. "Let me see if I can explain this without messing it up. The setting is Albany, Georgia. The characters are a husband and a wife. The wife dies of apparently natural causes. But her family--some distant nieces the husband didn't know existed--started asking questions about her money and their inheritance. They keep probing until the police took an interest in the case." He set his notepad down. "They are looking for the husband, who's originally from Truckee, and, according to reliable sources, left Georgia to return to Truckee." Rich pointed to his yellow pad.

On top he had written Truckee Mystery. Underneath were the handwritten notes. "Sounds like maybe a good story, no?"

"I guess."

"I'm glad you share my enthusiasm."

"That's me all over, Ms. Enthusiasm." Aimee looked up and saw Rich smiling. "I'm sorry. My mind is still with Lauri." *And the man with the devil eyes.* "It seems like the story has possibilities. Did you want me to pursue it?"

"No, this is something I want to work on."

"You? But you're the editor."

"Right, but this is a much smaller story than the murder investigation. I can put this one on the back burner and it won't make a difference. I miss the writing part of this job so I thought I'd challenge myself and take this story on."

Aimee nodded.

The front door to the office building opened. "Duty calls." Rich stood up.

Aimee followed him out of his office and watched him walk away. "Rich."

He stopped and turned.

"I know I'm supposed to be doing a feature on runaways, but under the circumstances, since Lauri was my main angle, I'd like to drop the runaway angle and concentrate on the murder. After all, I've already interviewed Gary and Lauri's mother. Grandma Louise is more likely to talk to me than anyone else. What do you think?"

"I think that's a great idea. You can be the lead reporter. Dolphine is interviewing Lauri's friends and classmates. Carl is hounding the police for details. I'll tell them both to report to you."

Aimee smiled. "Thanks!"

"You're welcome, but there's one more thing."

Aimee held her breath.

"Promise me you'll be very careful. You're very valuable."

"As a reporter?"

Rich hesitated and whispered, "Yes, as a reporter, but also as a person." He leaned over and with his index finger touched the tip of her nose. He winked, turned, and left.

Aimee stroked her nose and smiled, ear-to-ear.

Chapter 8

Aimee watched Rich greet the two identical looking men at the door.

"I'm Richard Cole. How may I help you?" He extended his hand to the one on the left.

The man responded with a curvature of the lips that could hardly be called a smile. "I'm Earl Dietz." They shook hands. "This is my brother, Burley."

Rich's forehead furrowed. "Dietz . . . Dietz."

Earl nodded. "Yeah, Louise Dietz's sons."

"Ah . . . Grandma Louise's sons? I wasn't aware she had any children."

"When we graduated from high school, we both left. Burley moved back just a couple of months ago. I came to visit so that Burley and I could check on Mother."

"Correction," Burley took a small step forward. "He's here to check on Mother. I'm here because he dragged me along."

Earl looked down and shook his head.

Rich waited for a few seconds to pass. "I should have known you're both Grandma Louise's sons. The resemblance is undeniable." Rich focused on Earl. "If you don't mind saying so, I would have thought you'd be a lot older."

"Looks are deceiving--or at least in my case. I'm pushing forty. My brother is two years younger."

Rich's eyebrows shot up. "You're not twins?"

Earl flashed a side grin. "Hardly. We're as different as two brothers can be."

Burley rolled his eyes.

"That's remarkable. I could have sworn you're twins." Rich pointed to the coffeepot. "Why don't we sit down and have a cup of coffee?"

Burley looked at his watch.

Earl shook his head. "No, thanks. We really can't stay. My brother has an appointment he can't miss. We just came to snoop a bit."

Rich's face lit up. "If there's any snooping to be done, I suppose a newspaper office is a good place to do it."

Earl smiled. "It's about my mom. I--we--don't know what to do for her. We thought maybe, if you could, you'd tell us what you talked about. Then we'd know how to help her."

"Actually, she spoke to me." Aimee stood by the waist-high swinging door separating the reception area from the main working room. Earl turned toward her, and she studied him. He was, by far, the best looking man she'd ever seen. His strong, firm body and his deep green, hypnotic eyes had probably broken many hearts. She glanced at Burley and saw a mirror image of Earl.

"You're either Aimee Brent or Dolphine Birescik." Earl's eyes smiled at her. He shook her hand with a firm grip.

She nodded a hello. "What can I do for you, Mr. Dietz?"

"You can begin by calling me Earl."

Aimee stood taller. "Earl."

Earl pointed to himself and his brother. "The reason we came here was to talk to you about Gary and Lauri, and to find out what Mom told you."

"So you know Gary and Lauri."

Burley shook his head. "He does. I don't. You see, I don't try to meddle in my mother's affairs." He glanced at his brother. "Unlike other people."

Earl cast his gaze downward and shook his head. "I'm not meddling. I'm just concerned." He looked at Aimee. "But to answer your question, I met Lauri and Gary briefly. Mom all but adopted Lauri and most everything I know about Lauri and Gary is through Mom. I wouldn't be a good source of information concerning them. All I'm interested in is what Mom told you about them."

Aimee's gaze riveted on Rich, seeking his support, but he had busied himself with the layouts. How convenient.

"Let me help," Earl's gaze traveled from Aimee to Rich, then back to Aimee. "You're wondering if what you have to say falls under the reporter/source confidentiality--or whatever the heck you journalists call it. Believe me, I'm not trying to start any problems or anything. All I want to do is help. Frankly, I'm very concerned about Mom."

Aimee studied the brothers. Earl stood with his chin slightly raised. Burley's gaze shifted around the room. "Is she ill?"

"Not ill, but maybe a little crazy," Burley said.

Earl bit his lips. "She's neither ill nor crazy, but at her age, her mental health is as important as her physical health. She insists that she made a terrible mistake by coming here. She says she made a complete fool of herself. She's not eating or sleeping well, and frankly, we're worried."

"You're worried. I'm not," Burley mumbled.

Earl shook his head, frowning.

"She didn't make a fool of herself," Aimee said. "She was concerned about Lauri, and as it turned out, rightly so."

Earl crossed his arms. "What do you mean?"

Aimee paused. "It's all over the news. The radio. The TV. Haven't you heard?"

"Sorry. I haven't had a chance to watch the news. What's going on?"

Aimee searched for the right words. "Lauri's body was found in the Tahoe Basin. She was murdered."

"Jesus! Poor kid." Burley's eyes opened wide.

Earl paled. "That's terrible! How did it

happen? Do the police have any leads?"

"None that I know of. That's why Grandma Louise's report about the screams she heard is so important."

Earl sighed. "Please don't take this wrong. I love my mother, but lately she's gotten very forgetful, and she tries to compensate by making up stories."

"Are you telling me there were no screams?"

"If there were, could you tell me why Mom was the only one who heard them? Surely, in a large apartment complex like hers, someone else should have reported them, too."

No debate on that one. Still, there were other things to consider. "What about Gary?"

"Lauri's boyfriend? What about him?"

"Grandma Louise told me she saw him going down the hallway, away from Lauri's apartment."

"She might have--then again it could have been a different night, and Mom got confused. It's possible he was there. He loved Lauri and probably hated the idea of having to break up."

"Whoa, back up. Are you saying Lauri and Gary were breaking up?" Strange, Gary hadn't mentioned this.

"Yeah. The night before Lauri disappeared, she came over to see us--well, actually she came to see Mom. I just happened to be there. Lauri was very upset because she found out that Gary was doing drugs--"

"Pot, you mean."

"No, real drugs. The hard stuff, and he was selling, too. Lauri wanted the strength and the courage to tell that creep to buzz off. Apparently she found it, and Gary got rather abusive--threatened to kill her if she ever talked like that again."

"Was that information given to the police?"

Earl nodded. "I'm sure Mom mentioned it. In fact, I know she did."

"Do you think Gary was capable of hurting Lauri?"

"My brother isn't a policeman. How could he possibly answer that?" Burley looked at his watch again. "I'm going to be late. Let's get rolling." He grabbed Earl's arm and pulled him along.

Earl shrugged him off. "It's not going to hurt your friends to wait for a few minutes. Besides, I'm almost finished."

"Hurry up."

Earl shot his brother an angry look. He turned to Aimee. "Sorry for the interruption, but no, Mom doesn't think Gary could hurt Lauri. But she remembers the early, drug-free Gary--the guy who loved Lauri when nobody else seemed to want her."

"What about you? Do you think he could have hurt Lauri?" she asked, looking at Burley.

"Drugs do strange things to people," Burley answered.

Chapter 9

As Gary walked out of school, heat waves rose from the pavement. Great, it promised to be another warm day, the kind that caused his head to ache and give birth to a stone-like laziness. On days like these, he and Lauri would ditch school and spend the afternoon at the lake. He dropped his shoulders and hung his head. When he neared his car, he got his car keys out of his pocket and glanced up. "Shit," he said under his breath.

Three creeps sat on the hood of his Jeep. Had Gary not known them, he would have assumed they were derelict winos, complete with sloppy clothes and long, wild hair. But, unlike the winos, these hoods wore an air of meanness.

Gary pivoted one-hundred and eighty degrees and headed in the opposite direction, only to stop again.

Moving toward him were two more wanna-be gangsters. They were both beefy and stupid-looking, like thugs in prison. Gary watched as they advanced, their chins thrust out as if stalking prey. Gary looked to his right, his left. He could run, but what would be the use? They would eventually catch up, if not today, then tomorrow. Or the day after that.

Gary swiveled slowly to look behind him. Two of the three scumbags slid off the Jeep's hood, stood, balled their left hands into fists, and pounded them into their right palm.

Gary involuntarily trembled but held his head higher.

The asshole in the middle remained sitting on the car's hood. Beneath his wiry eyebrows, his green eyes glowed like cool emeralds. Even though Gary had gone out of his way to avoid him, he knew it was only a matter of time before Blade caught up with him. That time had arrived. His legs felt like Jell-O as he headed toward Blade. He bit his tongue, cleared his throat, and pretended he didn't see the two toughs behind him.

The green-eyed dirt-bag studied him. "Are you cool, man?"

In spite of Blade's smile, Gary noticed the unmistakable toughness in his eye.

Blade took out a knife with a six-inch blade. He wiped it against his jeans. "I'm waiting for an answer, and you know how I hate to wait."

Gary focused on Blade's knife. Whenever Blade had a point he wanted to emphasize, he took out a knife and played with the blade, thus earning him his nickname.

Blade cupped his ear. "I didn't hear you."

"Yeah, Blade, I'm cool."

Blade put the knife away. "You heard they found her body."

Gary stared into his eyes, but found only green ice. "Yeah."

"So it's over, and you're cool."

Gary looked away.

Blade jumped off the hood. His long, Afro hairstyle made him look taller than his six-foot frame. "Again, I didn't hear an answer. I sure would hate to go to the cops."

"You wouldn't do that. It wouldn't be long before the police would tie you in."

Blade shrugged. "There's ways. I got friends. The bottom line is the idiot cops would know what you did." He swept past Gary, hitting him on the shoulder. The rest of his gang followed close behind him. "So are you cool?"

"Yeah, I'm cool."

"Good. Stay that way."

Gary watched them walk away. As he climbed inside his car, his hands shook and his eyes danced with tears. He banged the steering wheel with his palm.

"God-dammit, Lauri." The tears ran down his cheek, and he did nothing to wipe them away. "I'm so sorry."

Chapter 10

Aimee walked past the banks of quarter slot machines and retrieved a quarter. She put the coin into the slot and pulled the handle. The machine whirred, buzzed, and dropped three quarters. Hey, she could get used to this.

She picked up the money from the bin and fed another quarter into the machine, pulled the handle, and lost it. She couldn't get used to that.

She opened her hand to reveal the other two quarters. The slot machine demanded to be fed. She wouldn't be ruled by a machine. She dropped the coins in her purse. At this rate, she'd never make it into the high rollers' league. Tough luck.

She threaded her way to the underground walkway that connected the two casinos, Harvey's and Harrah's. She found Gary there, playing video games.

Aimee stood behind Gary and watched him maneuver a rough-looking hero as it punched and kicked an oversized goon. "Hello," she said.

"Got a couple of quarters?" Gary's eyes never left the video display.

"Depends. You got some answers?"

"For a couple of quarters? You're crazy, lady."

"No, not for the quarters. For Lauri."

Gary pivoted toward Aimee. His ever-so-strong hero died. "Damn." He frowned. "There's a Hard Rock Café upstairs."

She swept the air with her opened hand. "Lead the way."

Once there, she ordered her usual mix, Coke and Diet Coke. Gary asked for a Sprite, and a chicken sandwich with lots of fries. She was sure he would have dessert, too. Aimee would get the bill, of course, or maybe not. The paper should pick up the tab.

"Gary, I hope you know that I'm really sorry for your loss."

Gary shrugged. "Well, yeah."

Well, yeah? What kind of a response was that?

Gary briefly met Aimee's gaze, then looked away. "So what do you want to know?" The waitress brought the drinks and Gary drank a large swig of his soda.

"You didn't tell me you had a date with Lauri on the day she disappeared."

"Shit, wish we had. Maybe she wouldn't have died." He stood up and walked away. Aimee wondered if he planned to return. They had ordered, but their meal hadn't yet arrived. Yep--as Rich would say--he'll be back.

Minutes later, Gary headed back and sat down just in time for the waitress to serve his food. He dipped a French fry in ketchup, set it down, and looked at Aimee. He threw her a grin, as insincere as it was ugly.

"If Lauri wasn't with you, then where was she?"

Gary shrugged. "I guess there is no harm in telling now."

"Telling what?"

"Lauri used me a lot as an excuse to get out of the house. True, man, at the beginning we were always together. Then she got that job with those fancy-ass jerks and things started changing."

"Why didn't you tell me before that she had a job?"

"Well, you know, man." He shrugged. "I didn't want to get her in trouble because she's underage. But since she's . . . she's . . ." He shrugged once more.

Aimee retrieved her notebook and jotted the information down. "Where did she work?"

"With those dudes Lauri's mother works for. You know who I mean?" Gary opened his sandwich, removed the tomato, and gulped it down.

"Stockton and Teague?"

"Yeah, that's them. They hired Lauri."

Aimee looked up from her note taking. "To do what?"

Again, Gary shrugged. "Beats me. Lauri was very tight-lipped about the job."

"Why was that?"

Again, Gary shrugged. He salted his fries.

Aimee leaned forward. "Are you sure they hired her? She was underage."

"Yeah, I'm sure and on top of that, I got the feeling that whatever she was doing wasn't quite legal."

"What do you mean?"

He took a big bite of his sandwich and swallowed down the soda. "Just the way she carried on--afraid of what she was doing, afraid of how it was going to turn out."

"If she was so afraid, why was she doing it?"

He bit into his sandwich once again and wrinkled his face. He set the sandwich down, and took out the pickles. "That's nasty stuff." He pushed the pickles away and looked up at Aimee. "Can't you answer that yourself? Sweet Mama was forcing her to do it."

"Why?"

"For the money. Lauri told me she got one thousand dollars--and every single penny Sweet Mama kept for her baby's operation."

Aimee paused and studied Gary. He looked her straight in the eye. "This job, was it a onetime deal?"

"I don't think so. Lauri said they might call on her again if something came up." He stuffed the last of his meal into his mouth. A few minutes later he added, "Whatever Lauri was doing, it had to be big."

"What do you mean?"

Gary balled his napkin and threw it on the table. "Hell, I should have seen it coming. I could have helped her." He banged his fist against the chair. "The last thing she told me was that she had this deal going that would land her a lot of money."

"Tell me about it."

"She figured her mother didn't really love her--that she cared more for her baby sister. Lauri hoped to get enough money from this deal to pay for the baby's operation, then her mother would be proud of her and would start loving her, too." He pushed the rest of his fries away. "It's not fair. Nobody should have to do shit like that just to make their own mother like her."

That's not exactly how Aimee would phrase it, but she definitely agreed. "How much money was Lauri talking about?" She reached for her soda and gulped some down.

"Fifty K--maybe more--is what she said."

Aimee choked and began to cough. The word *prostitute* popped into her head. She cleared her throat. "How's that possible? She was only fifteen." Her eyes watered from coughing, and she wiped them.

Gary shrugged indifferently. "She wouldn't tell me, but I'll bet you a million-to-one those fancy-ass lawyers would know." Gary drank the last of his soda. "Either that or the guy I've seen with Lauri."

"What guy?"

"Beats me. He's old--like you."

Old? She glared at him.

"Oh, sorry. I didn't mean it like that. He's just older--like in his thirty's or forty's."

"I'm twenty-five." Did she really look that much older? Last time she looked, her light brown hair hid no gray.

Gary shrugged. "So he's older."

So I'm still only twenty-five. "You don't know who he is?"

"Nah."

"Tell me about him." She sipped her soda, more carefully this time.

"He's just a guy." He shrugged.

Oh boy, this was going to take a while. "Is he short or tall?"

"About my height, maybe a little taller, I guess."

"What about his eyes? His hair?"

"Yeah, he's got some."

Aimee looked at him. Was this guy serious?

"I mean, he's got brown, wavy hair. Dunno what color eyes. Never really looked, I guess." Gary stirred his ice with his straw. "Oh, yeah, he's got a scar on his cheek."

Aimee's hand froze halfway to her drink. "When did you last see them together?"

Gary shrugged. "Couple of days, I guess, before Lauri . . . before she, uh, disappeared."

Aimee retrieved the picture of Lauiri's missing step-father from her purse. Her hand shook as she held it out. "Is this him?" Her voice was barely above a whisper.

She saw genuine surprise in Gary's face. He nodded. "Yeah. I'm really impressed. You're on the ball. So who is he?"

"A ghost from the past."

Chapter 11

If she hurried, Aimee could drop in on the Stockton and Teague Law Firm. As she ran to her car, she dug into her purse, fished out the keys, looked up, and stopped. A mini-van parked next to her car had its side door open, and a man bent halfway inside helped a child off the car seat.

Aimee watched as the man, his back to her, locked the van. He bent down, picked up a little girl and turned toward Aimee. She couldn't help but stare. Something about him, perhaps the way he carried the child, made the scene look familiar. Aimee strained to focus on his eyes.

The memories flooded her mind, like a breach in a dam. The thoughts came in fast, flashing rushes. She was seven years old. Daddy had been dead for three months, or at least that's what Mommy had said. It seemed more like years and years, yet the pain wouldn't go away. Mommy, wanting to help, had taken her to Disneyland, the place where dreams come true. Aimee knew exactly what to dream.

She was already forgetting what Daddy looked like. She closed her eyes and tried to remember, but each time the image became dimmer. She fought the tears welling in her eyes.

She couldn't forget Daddy. She loved him with all her heart, and she wouldn't forget him.

"Come, let's go on the Peter Pan ride. You've always liked Peter Pan." Mommy wrapped her arms around her, steering her toward the ride. Aimee relaxed in the comfort of Mommy's arms.

The ride was great. They flew out the window and rode way up high in the sky. The city looked so tiny below them. She was up in the sky, close to Heaven. Close to Daddy.

The ride ended and she wanted to do it again. She was about to ask when a figure caught her eye. His movements and his mannerisms reminded her of someone she knew . . . Daddy!

Reality hit. Daddy had come back. Dreams do come true in Disneyland.

She pulled away from Mommy's hand and ran toward him. She didn't care that he carried another little girl in his arms. All she wanted was for him to hold her that way, too. Just one more time. "Daddy!" she screamed.

He turned and his eyes widened.

She stopped. Something was wrong. He wasn't smiling. He wasn't happy to see her. This man wasn't Daddy. This man was evil. His eyes burned with hate and anger. She stood, unable to move, waiting to be consumed by the eyes. She squeezed her own eyes shut and waited.

Someone yanked her away. Aimee gasped and her eyes popped open as Mommy pulled her along. Mommy held onto Aimee so tightly that her arm hurt. But Mommy didn't seem to care. Her entire attention focused on getting away from this evil man.

"Mommy, stop. Slow down. I can't keep up."

Mommy continued to hurry, dragging Aimee along. They didn't stop until they left Disneyland and were inside the car. Mommy shoved her in and locked the doors.

Then Mommy cried.

Aimee had never felt so alone, so helpless.

Years later, late at night, the memory still tormented her, and now Aimee wondered if that man had been her father. Rationalizing it, the idea seemed ridiculous. But why had her mother reacted the way she had?

* * *

The man in the casino parking lot glared at Aimee through narrow, suspicious eyes. He held his arms closer around his daughter and walked faster, as far from Aimee as possible.

Aimee stepped back, giving him as much room as possible. Once he was out of sight, Aimee opened the driver's seat and got in.

Beloved Father.

Aimee tightened her features and closed her eyes. "Twenty years," she whispered. "You've been dead for almost twenty years." Why couldn't she let it go?

Chapter 12

A plain, beige, two-story building housed the law offices of Stockton and Teague. Aimee pulled into the parking area around back and approached the building from the rear door.

She went past a real estate agency and a loan company and headed directly toward the spiral staircase. While the first floor businesses made no visible claims to appeal to the wealthy, the second beamed elegance. Aimee opened the beveled glass doors. Her feet sank into the deep piled, soft-brown carpet that covered the reception room. An immaculate blend of oak furniture and richly upholstered couches greeted the visitors.

A small bronze-on-wood nameplate claimed that the desk facing Aimee belonged to Karen. The antique, French provincial desk was small and delicate. The solid oak file cabinets behind her desk gave off an aura of sophistication.

The room's richness contrasted sharply with the temporary secretary who filled in for Karen. The elderly lady with short, gray hair and a round face wore a simple white blouse with black pants and no makeup. She looked up at Aimee and smiled. "May I help you?"

"I'm Aimee Brent from the *North Shore*

Carrier, and I'd like to speak to either Stockton or Teague."

The temporary receptionist thumbed through the pages of the desk calendar. "I'm sorry, Miss Brent, but Mr. Teague and Mr. Stockton are booked, and the earliest they can see you is next Thursday. I could set you up with Mr. Teague at ten-thirty. How does that sound?" She reached for her pencil and was about to write Aimee's name.

"No good." Aimee read the secretary's nametag. "Margaret." Then she leaned over and whispered, "You do know Karen Boyd?"

"No, not personally, but I know who she is. She's Mr. Teague and Mr. Stockton's permanent secretary. I'm filling in until she gets back."

"Right." Aimee raised her index finger and waved it up and down to emphasize the word. "You know, it's really a shame what happened to her daughter."

"I agree." Margaret shook her head. "Like I said, I don't know Karen personally, but I feel bad for her."

"I'm sure she'll appreciate that. When I see her, I'll tell her."

Margaret's face lit up as though she had done her good deed for the day.

Aimee moved closer to Margaret and whispered even though no one else was there. "Karen is already familiar with the office procedures, but with all she has to deal with, she probably forgot to tell you about me."

Margaret shot her a quizzical look. "What about you?"

"About the little arrangement we have." Aimee leaned over closer to Margaret. "I want you to know I understand and I'm not upset or anything. It's not your fault." Aimee smiled reassuringly. "It's just that every time I come, Karen would know that I'm supposed to go right in. All she'd do was check to see which one was the least busy." She sneaked a peek at the closed doors behind Margaret. Each was inscribed with the occupant's name. Thank God for small miracles. "It's good for public relations, you know."

"Ah, yes, of course." Immediately Margaret rechecked the calendar. "Mr. Teague. Mr. Stockton's got a--"

"Thank you, Margaret. I'll go see Mr. Teague." Aimee headed for his office, curving around Margaret's desk.

"Maybe I should let him know you're here." Margaret eyed the intercom button.

"Don't bother." Aimee reached for the doorknob and pushed through.

* * *

George Teague, a large, powerful-looking man with high cheekbones, aquiline nose, and bushy eyebrows, looked up from his stack of papers. A frown formed across his forehead.

"You are?"

"I'm Aimee Brent." She moved toward him with her arm extended.

"The reporter?" He stood up and shook her hand.

Wow! He was the second person who had recognized her by name. The fact that it was a small town definitely helped, but why worry about such details? Aimee nodded.

"I'm always receptive to the press." He pointed to the chair in front of his desk. Aimee sat down and so did he. "I'm rather curious as to how you got past my secretary."

"I lied to her--told her I always do this."

Teague puckered his lips as he slowly nodded. "Thank God she'll be here only two more days. I'll talk to her."

"Please don't. This is my fault, not hers."

Teague smiled, but the smile didn't reach his eyes. He intertwined his fingers across his chest. "So what can I do for the press?"

"I'm here about Lauri Evans." Aimee watched for the slightest reaction.

"Lauri . . . Evans." His features tightened for just a second.

"Yes, Lauri Evans. You know, Karen Boyd's daughter."

"I know who Lauri is, uh, was. It's hard to believe that someone could have done that to a child."

"Yes, it's a real tragedy. And that's why I'm

here."

"Oh?"

"I was hoping you'd be able to tell me something about Lauri. Our paper is doing a follow up on her murder, and I'd appreciate anything you can tell me."

Teague looked up at the ceiling as though searching for an answer. Slowly, he shook his head. "I'm sorry. I didn't know Lauri very well. All I can say is that I feel sorry for her mother, but I suppose that's what happens when someone runs with the wrong crowd."

"That's true." Aimee nodded. "But what amazes me is how teenagers manage to find time for everything."

He reached for a Mont Blanc fountain pen, made a notation on a yellow legal pad, returned the pen to its holder, and looked back up at Aimee. "They're young and full of energy. It's a shame teenagers don't channel this energy in the right direction."

Aimee first glanced at the fine paintings adorning the walls, and then slowly focused on him, hoping to make him squirm. "At least we've got to give Lauri credit for trying to channel some of that energy in the right direction."

"What do you mean?"

"I'm talking about her job, of course."

Teague stared at her, and except for the slightest twitch of his cheek muscle, there had been no reaction. Aimee made a mental note.

Teague leaned back in his chair and placed his hands behind his head. Aimee got the message. He had nothing to hide. He was as pure and innocent as the devil himself.

"So Lauri had a job? Karen never mentioned it, but then, of course, we seldom discussed family matters." His smooth tone betrayed no hint of hidden secrets.

"I can understand that. People like to keep their personal and their work lives separate. Even so, I want to talk about the job. I know this is a very far-fetched idea, but as a reporter, I must follow all leads. Anyway, I was told that she worked for you and Mr. Stockton."

A vein in Teague's temple pulsed slightly. "What can you tell me about the job?" she asked.

Teague's fingers formed elegant steeples in front of his face. His eyes narrowed as they focused on Aimee. He nodded once. "You must be talking about a babysitting job Lauri did for Marvin once, which, incidentally, turned into a disaster. Lauri invited her boyfriend and the kids went unattended. Marvin was sorry he hired her, but he was trying to help Karen." Teague shook his head. "My partner said he'd never hire her again, and, as far as I know, that's the only job Lauri's done for Marvin."

"I wasn't talking about babysitting. Rumor has it that she worked for both you and Mr. Stockton."

Aimee noted the lack of reaction. He must

have learned how to control his twitches and pulses. This man had talent.

"I don't think you could even call this a rumor." Teague picked up the pen and tapped the desk with it. "It's more like misinformation. Karen works for us, Lauri is underage, and your source probably got confused."

"I'm sure that's what happened." Yeah, sure. Aimee stood up.

Teague also stood and walked Aimee to the door. He reached for the doorknob. "Is there anything else you'd like to know?"

"As a matter of fact, there is." She retrieved Lauri's father's picture from her purse and showed it to him.

Teague stared at it, perhaps a bit too long. He shrugged. "I'm sure I've seen him before, but I can't, for the life of me, place him. Care to fill me in?"

"Apparently, he's someone connected with Lauri's death. I'm showing everyone the picture, hoping to identify him." She put it away.

Teague glanced toward his desk.

"I'm sorry to have wasted your time." She took a step toward the door.

"Don't mention it. It's always my pleasure to talk to beautiful, young ladies. Thank you for coming to confirm gossip instead of just printing it."

Wouldn't think of publishing gossip. It's so unprofessional. She smiled. "By the way, this is an absolutely gorgeous office."

"Thank you. My wife will be pleased to hear that. She did all of the interior decorating. It's sort of a hobby with her."

Chapter 13

As Aimee walked by the secretary's desk, she noticed the intercom line lit up. More than likely, that was Teague, contacting his partner. She'd give her right arm if she could hear that conversation.

She headed toward Margaret's desk. "George wants a cup of coffee."

Margaret looked around the room. "Coffee? Mr. Teague has never asked for coffee."

"Well, you know bosses. Some of them are still living in the dark ages. They think coffee and immediately the word *secretary* pops up. At least he was nice enough to give me a five-dollar bill. He told me to tell you to get him a cup of coffee with lots of cream and sugar. He said you could get a cup too, if you wanted one. He also said that his favorite brew comes from the café two doors down."

Margaret's eyebrows arched in surprise. She started to reach for the money but hesitated. "I'm alone. I can't possibly leave the office."

"Don't worry. I'll wait here. If anyone comes or calls, I'll tell them you'll be back in a few minutes. Now you better go get that cup of coffee before George gets impatient."

Margaret hesitated, but then tucked the

money in her pocket, and hurried out.

Aimee waited until she was out of sight before picking up the phone. She covered the mouthpiece and listened.

"Now, George, I think you're overreacting."

"No, Marvin. You didn't talk to her. That reporter knows. We better destroy the evidence before she comes snooping around."

"That's not such a good idea. We can still use it."

"I realize that, but he doesn't have to know it's gone. Listen to me. We have to destroy it."

Carefully, Aimee returned the handle to its cradle. She stepped outside and waited for Margaret. When she saw her, Aimee approached her. "He changed his mind." Aimee reached for the cup. "But I'd like that."

As Aimee returned to her car, she wondered what it was that George Teague was so desperate to destroy. He had mentioned that someone wouldn't know it was destroyed. Who was *he* and what was *it*? She set the cup in its holder, started the car, and drove off.

* * *

As Aimee turned into her driveway, she glanced at her next door neighbor's picturesque flowerbed, then at her own. Not a single bud peeked out. Fine. If she couldn't grow flowers, she could make them. Eager to start on her new project, she let herself in and called the cat. "Hi,

Fluffs. I'm home." As usual, the gray and white cat was nowhere in sight.

Aimee opened a can of tuna and Fluffs magically appeared. "I knew I could make you come." As she set the food down, the phone rang. Aimee read the caller I.D.: Dolphine.

"Just curious," Dolphine said. "I wanted to know how it went at the lawyer's."

Aimee told her and Dolphine listened without interrupting. When Aimee finished, she said, "I swear, they're scheming something. I sure would like to find out what it is."

"How do you plan to do that?"

Aimee cleared the table to make space for her new project. "I'm not sure. Maybe I could follow them."

"Don't think that'll work. They probably spend the majority of time at their offices or the courtrooms."

"You're right. What I really need to do is visit their offices, go through their files." She might as well be wishing for a fairy godmother to make her invisible.

"Good luck with that."

"It's not that impossible. Men have walked on the moon, you know." She wondered if she would have enough courage to break into Teague and Stockton's office. The words *illegal* and *morally wrong* popped into her mind. She forced the idea away.

"Honest to goodness, Aimee, I'm rooting for

you. Finding out what those lawyers are up to may be the only way you can bring Lauri justice. Stay determined."

That, she could do--especially if Rich helped her. "I'll do my best." Aimee disconnected and tossed the idea around as her hands quickly worked, creating her first paper flower.

Tomorrow would be Saturday, the ideal day to pay the lawyers an unscheduled visit. Chances were that they wouldn't in their offices.

But Rich would be. That man breathed and lived the newspaper business. His grandfather had started the enterprise and passed it to his son who by now took little or no interest in it.

Rich sweated for years trying to prove to his dad that even though he was young, he was more than capable of being the editor.

First thing tomorrow, Aimee would confront Rich about her idea.

Fluffs meowed and Aimee looked up. The cat sat on the window sill, looking out. She better close the window. As she approached it, she noticed a white Pontiac parked diagonally from her house. She had never seen it before. Probably it belonged to a neighbor's friend. Or someone got a different car. Not that it mattered.

She slammed the window shut and focused on her project.

Chapter 14

"No! Absolutely not! I will not help you break into the Stockton and Teague Law Firm."

Aimee took a small step back. She had never heard Rich speak in such a loud tone.

He turned his attention to the computer monitor that he had been working on when Aimee entered the office. In a much calmer voice he asked, "Think this layout will work?"

Unbelievable. She was talking about paying Stockton and Teague an unofficial visit, and he's talking about how the paper will look. Men! "They're going to destroy whatever it is they don't want us to see."

"In that case, why don't we tell the police?" His attention remained focused on the computer monitor. He clicked on the toolbox, then on the picture corner and increased the picture size.

"And tell them what? That there's something that Mr. Teague and Mr. Stockton are going to destroy? We don't know what it is, and it may or may not have anything to do with Lauri's death. And I got the information by listening in on their phone. Do you really believe the police are going to find a judge who is willing to issue a search warrant?"

Rich threw up his arms. "You're right. You're

absolutely right, but I still don't like the idea." He walked around his desk and sat on the edge of it, facing Aimee. "Listening on their phones is illegal. It's unprofessional, and the break-in is even worse--a felony. What are you thinking? Get a grip, Aimee."

Caught in his gaze, Aimee stammered, "I . . . I don't like it either."

Rich's features softened and Aimee regained her composure. "My mom taught me to always respect other people's property. I feel like I'm violating her trust, but I don't see any other way around it. Please help me." Adrenaline pumped through her body as she waited for Rich to answer.

Rich opened his mouth to speak and then closed it. He rubbed the edge of his eyes. An uncomfortable pause followed. He shrugged and walked back around his desk. "I would like to run that story on Baby Karen's heart operation as soon as possible."

Aimee's heart sank. He wasn't going to help her. She knew when she was licked. Besides, it really was a bad idea. "I thought I had already turned that in."

"You did, but it reads like a statistics report. It needs more personal interest stuff, more heart-felt facts. Actually, I'm surprised you'd turn in something like that. You can do better."

Aimee felt like a high school girl who flunked a major exam. "I know. I really did mean to polish it." She shifted her weight. God! She was even acting like a high school girl.

"Good." Rich seemed oblivious to Aimee's embarrassment. "I knew you would want to interview Karen a bit more, so I took it upon myself to set up an appointment. I hope you don't mind."

She frowned, but quickly wiped it off her face. "No, not at all. When is it?"

Rich looked at his watch. "Half an hour from now. I called your cell and left several messages. Didn't you get them?"

Aimee looked at her phone. The display on the front of the phone showed a little envelope informing her that she had at least one message. "My phone never rang. It must have gone directly to voice mail."

"That happens. Glad I was able to tell you about the interview."

Aimee nodded. "I'll get ready." She stood. "Before I go, last chance. You sure you don't want to come with me?"

Rich frowned. "Like I said, it's unprofessional. Unethical. I don't want to know anything about this. You're on your own. This is not official paper business."

"I know. But I feel I owe it to Lauri. Even if you don't come with me, I'm doing it."

Rich squinted. The lines between the eyes pulled into a little frown. "While you're interviewing Karen, why don't you find out what kind of job Lauri was doing for Mr. Teague and Mr. Stockton? Then we'll discuss it during dinner, and afterwards, when it's dark, we'll check out those lawyers' offices."

First came shock, then relief. Her heart fluttered. "It's a date."

"It may be, but I still don't like the idea."

Neither did Aimee.

Chapter 15

Across the street from the *South Shore Carrier*, the driver of a white Pontiac came to a stop and stared at the newspaper office window. He watched Aimee and Rich talk.

He reached beneath the carpet under the car seat and produced a trophy book. He opened it to the page that contained five small clippings. They were plain, insignificant obituaries packed with all the relevant information: name of deceased, surviving relatives, the deceased's profession and age at the time of death. But there was one very important thing they didn't contain.

They never mentioned the fact that he had killed them all. Up until now, he'd gotten away. Then Aimee came along. Her snooping was bound to lead to him. He reread the articles and slammed the book shut.

His gaze darted toward the newspaper window where he saw Aimee engrossed in conversation with her editor. His right hand stroked the book's cover. He looked at it and back at Aimee. "Damn it!" he said. Time and time again, he had enjoyed looking at his trophy book, but this had become a luxury he could no longer afford. If Aimee ever got hold of this treasure, he'd be a dead man.

He flipped the book open, grabbed the first page, prepared to shred it, and hesitated. It held so many wonderful memories. Maybe later, he'd get rid of it. In the meantime, he'd look for a better hiding place. He pulled up the carpet under the car seat and replaced his precious volume.

He straightened up, his hand trembling and sweat oozing from every pore of his body. He took three deep breaths. Several seconds later he felt calm. He had to take care of Aimee before she created any ripples. He reached for the door handle.

At that moment, Aimee stepped out of the newspaper office and turned toward her car. She seemed surprised to see him. She smiled and waved. "Hi." As she eyed the white Pontiac, she stood perfectly still.

"Something wrong?"

"No, for a moment, I thought the car . . . I saw it parked across the street by my house."

He laughed. "Do you think I own the only white Pontiac in this town?"

"No, of course not." She flashed him a reassuring smile. "Did you come see me?"

"No, I came to see Rich." He took several steps toward her. "I didn't realize you worked on weekends too."

"Occasionally I have to come in, but I try not to. I have a small office at home where do my writing, but that doesn't always work out." Aimee looked at her watch. "Oops. I'd better run or I'll be late for my interview." She waved goodbye, got in her car, and drove off.

He stood staring after her with an unmistakable toughness in his calculating eyes.

Chapter 16

Aimee analyzed the picture of the little girl, sitting on a swing, smiling shyly at the camera. With the exception of a few bangs, her honey-blond hair was pulled away from her face. Her warm, brown eyes spoke of mischief and dreams of things yet to come.

Karen looked away from the picture and toward the living room ceiling. "This is the last picture I have of Lauri," Karen said. "My God, I don't even remember how old she was when this picture was taken." Karen turned to look at Aimee, who sat across from her in a tattered recliner. "The last time you were here," Karen continued, "I saw you staring at all of the baby's pictures. Did you notice I had none of Lauri?"

Without replying, Aimee looked up from the worn-out carpet to Karen's face which was a mask of sheer, hopeless misery.

"Yes, of course you noticed." Karen seemed to search Aimee's face for an answer. "Do you think Lauri did too?"

Aimee shrugged. "I can't answer for Lauri."

Karen's face tightened, as though she might cry. "You don't have to answer for her. I'm sure Lauri noticed it too." Karen stroked Lauri's picture, perhaps reliving a happier time. "She never mentioned it to me, and now it's too late. I've been doing some thinking. I really did love Lauri, but now she'll never know." Karen hung her head, and a sob, stemming from deep within, shook her body.

Aimee sat beside her on the couch and wrapped her hands around Karen's. "I'm sure she knows that now."

Karen's eyes filled with hope. "Do you really think so?"

God, Aimee certainly hoped that was the way things went. She nodded.

"Thank you." Karen's voice sounded rough and dry. "Thank you for telling me that. I don't want people to think I was horrible to Lauri. That's why I took her picture out. I should have taken it out before, but it never dawned on me."

"You can do more than that."

Karen cocked her head. "Oh?"

"You can help me find her killer."

"Of course, I'll do anything to help."

"I need some questions answered."

"Such as?" Her guarded voice betrayed her suspicions.

Aimee remembered Detective Marie O'Day mentioning a possible blackmail angle. Aimee decided to try her luck. "How did Lauri plan to get hold of all that money?"

Karen's eyebrows knit. "What money?"

Aimee glued her gaze on Karen's face. "The fifty thousand dollars."

Karen gasped as though stabbed by a thousand needles. "I . . . have no idea. I didn't even know she was--what was she doing?"

"I can't say for sure. All I know is that she had a plan that involved getting hold of some big money."

Karen shook her head in disbelief. "Do you have any ideas?"

"I think so."

Karen's wide eyes met Aimee's, and her mouth opened in anticipation.

Aimee leaned forward so she could watch Karen's reaction more carefully. "I think she tried to blackmail someone, and that someone killed her."

A soft moan escaped from Karen. She bowed her head. "Blackmail? Why would she do something so stupid?"

Interesting. Karen asked why--not who--Lauri was blackmailing. "I suppose she wanted to help pay for her sister's operation."

Like peeled-away layers, Karen's strength seemed to crumble. First she stared at Aimee through unblinking eyes, then like the heroine of the silent movies, she placed her open hands to her throat. "I didn't think she cared."

"She did."

"I know that now." Karen plastered her hands to her face in a kind of terrible, hopeless sorrow that made Aimee feel her heart catch in her throat.

When Karen removed her hands, her face had paled. "There's so much I didn't know about my own daughter. How could this have happened?"

A group of questions, like lava erupting from a volcano, popped into Aimee's mind. Did you ever sit down and talk to her? Did you let her know you were there for her? Did you tell her you loved her? Did you make an effort to be a real mom? Questions she wanted to ask but didn't.

Aimee pushed the questions aside. She cleared her throat. "I don't know how it could've happened. It just did. Maybe it had something to do with that job Lauri did for your lawyer friends."

Karen's body stiffened and her face looked like it belonged in a coffin. Aimee would love to play poker with her.

"Job? What job?" Karen's voice sounded unusually high. "Lauri was barely fifteen, too young to work. I simply wouldn't allow it. Besides, it's against the law." Karen's fingertips constantly rubbed back and forth along the seam of her jeans.

"Look, it's all right if you gave Lauri permission to work. It probably did her good. I'm not here to judge you. All I want is what might lead to her killer."

"Are you saying that you think George and Marvin killed Lauri?" While Karen's eyes beaded in mistrust, her voice dripped with contempt. "Do you know how ridiculous that sounds? Why, they're two of the most respected lawyers in the entire area."

That, they were, but what difference did that make? History had shown that some serial killers were well regarded in society. "I'm aware that they're respected, and no, I don't think they personally killed Lauri. But they do have something to hide, and maybe--just maybe--through this job of hers, Lauri met someone."

Karen closed her eyes, and her face twitched. Abruptly, she stood. "You must excuse me. I believe I heard the baby stir." She walked out and stopped. "When I come back, I'll fill you in on my baby's heart operation."

Ten minutes later, Aimee was in her car. She glanced down at the notes lying on the front passenger seat. They were mostly about Baby Karen, with very little about Lauri.

Brilliant, Aimee. You bungled that interview. She needed this story. She owed this much to Lauri.

Aimee slammed her open hand against the steering wheel and accidentally honked. Startled, she jumped.

She glanced at her watch. She had a little over an hour before Rich picked her up, giving her just enough time to rework the Baby Karen story.

Chapter 17

He drove the piece of crap, otherwise known as the white Pontiac by Aimee's house and slowed down. Entering would pose no problems. He'd have to remove a screen, raise the window, climb in, replace the screen, close the window, and make sure no one saw him. For that, the bushes in front of the house provided protection from any nosy neighbors.

However, anyone looking out of the side windows of the house on the right could easily spot movement in Aimee's yard. He eyed that house, but no one seemed to be at home. He'd better hurry and take advantage of this opportunity.

He sped up, drove two blocks, turned the corner, parked the car, and hurried back on foot. Through dark sunglasses, he scanned the neighborhood. A breeze blew and the pines swayed. No other movements caught his eye. He strolled up the walkway and rang the doorbell.

He listened, glanced around, and waited. He rang the bell again and let the seconds tick away. Maybe he was being overly cautious, but this trait had often kept him from going to prison. He'd killed all those women, and he remained a free man to do as he pleased. To kill again.

He drifted to the side window where he popped the screen, tried to slide the window open, and found it locked. "Damn!" he whispered. If he had to break a window, that would complicate matters.

He replaced the screen in its frame, glanced in all directions, then moved on to the second window, which was also locked.

"Dammit!" Why weren't people more trusting? Now he'd have to check the windows facing the backyard. He hated going into a place he hadn't surveyed. He looked around, saw the area deserted, headed for the chain link fence and found the gate padlocked. He yanked it, but it didn't open. "Shit!" he mumbled under his breath.

Aimee was more cautious than he expected. He took another quick look around. When he saw that he was still alone, he climbed the fence.

The first window to his right led to a bedroom. He didn't bother to check it. The one attracting his attention was the serve-through kitchen window. People often forgot to lock this type of window.

He tried it but found it locked.

He held his breath. Through the glass' reflection of the glass, he saw that the latch was only half closed. After shaking the window several times, the latch slipped open. He let himself in.

His foot landed on something soft. He gasped and almost lost his balance as it squirmed under him. A gray and white cat hissed and ran away. "Stupid cat," he mumbled to himself. "You scared the shit out of me."

He scanned the living room, but found nothing of interest. He glanced into the dining room. The table, filled with scraps of paper, ribbons, bows, scissors, glue, and boxes holding all sorts of miscellaneous items, indicated that either Aimee was a pack rat, or she was heavy into arts and crafts. Either way, that didn't concern him.

Directly across from him, he saw the study. He'd begin there.

Two large filing cabinets stood off to the left and beside them, a bookcase followed by an extra-wide door with a transom over it. He opened the door and found a wall furnace. He got in and closed the door behind him. He felt cramped, but he could stand up and through the louvers, he had an unobstructed view of the study area. He stepped out, smiling.

He glanced at the bookcase that held a handful of books. Stacks of paper filled the rest of the space. He ignored those and turned to the desk located in front of the file cabinets. Like the shelves, papers cluttered the desk. He reached for the first stack and heard a familiar sound, a car approaching. He tilted his head like a dog at attention. Outside, a car door slammed.

He hurried toward the front window. Aimee, with keys in hand, quickly approached. Panic gripped him. Automatically, his right hand reached into his jacket pocket. The cool, metallic touch calmed him. He had come prepared.

He bolted to the furnace closet and opened the door. He heard the front door open and footsteps cross the threshold. He stepped in and closed the door behind him.

Chapter 18

Hot days like today absorbed all of Aimee's energy. She felt as though she had walked a thousand miles. No, she felt as though she had run the thousand miles--uphill. She looked longingly toward the bedroom. She threw her purse on the couch and gently set the petals down on the crafts table.

"Hi, Fluffs. I'm home." She looked around, but once again the cat made itself invisible. Next time, she would volunteer to pet sit a dog. She had never met one that didn't run to the door when someone entered. "Fluffs?" The cat still hadn't materialized. "I hereby christen you Houdini." She opened a can of tuna, knowing the cat would immediately come to her. Except that he didn't.

Aimee worried her lip, set the food down, and headed back to the living room. "Fluffs?"

No answer.

Her gaze searched the room. The house seemed icy. Empty.

No, not empty. Someone--she waved the thought away.

She had been told that sometimes Fluffs liked to hide and when he was ready, he'd come to her. She would give him fifteen minutes, and if he didn't show up by then, she'd go looking for him. In the meantime, she'd work on her story.

She glanced around once again, wishing the coldness would leave her. She sat at her desk, her pen in her hand. Even though a computer occupied the space at the other end of her desk, she preferred to do her rough drafts and proof readings by hand. One of these days, she promised herself, she would become Modern Aimee and do everything on the computer. In the meantime, her world of modern technology revolved around her blue pen.

Aimee focused on the far corner of the room and tried to concentrate, but her mind whispered a warning. An unexpected feeling of being watched overwhelmed her. She wasn't alone.

She set the pen down and stretched, slowly rotating her chair. She studied every item in the room: the curtain, the bookcase, the file cabinets, the furnace closet. She found nothing out of place. Her mind must be playing tricks on her. Again.

Scolding herself, she forced her attention back to the article she was revising. As soon as she started to write, the feeling that someone was watching her returned. She looked back up.

Nothing.

No one.

She had been so sure, he'd be there. Waiting

for her. The man with the devil eyes.

She rubbed the bridge of her nose. *Go away,* her mind whispered. *Please don't come back again.*

She tried to push the images away, but they remained. The woods. The knife dripping blood. The devil eyes. The man chasing her. Always chasing her.

The images existed only in her mind, she knew. No one stalked her. Not anymore.

Concentrate. Think of Lauri, uh, Baby Karen. What would she say if she could talk? The answer would open a world of ideas on how to revise the article.

A hushed sound, like the shifting of weight, came from behind her. Someone was there. This time it wasn't in her mind. She stood up so swiftly that her right leg struck the chair. She caught it before it fell.

She stood paralyzed, listening. She heard breathing. Her own?

She stared at the area where the curtains met the floor. No shoes. Had she really expected to find any? She looked to her left, first at the file cabinet and bookcase, then at the furnace closet. She took a step toward the closet.

Then another.

She couldn't continue living in fear. If she ran now, if she didn't confront her past, she'd remain defeated. She had to prove that she was alone.

If she wasn't . . .

If she wasn't . . . Why would anyone be here?

He doesn't exist. Not anymore. Reach out for the door handle. Open the door. Prove that you're alone. Do it.

Something from above jumped out and grabbed at her hand.

Aimee let out a scream. Fluffs had been perched on top of the bookcase. A nervous giggle followed. She picked up the cat and scratched the top of its head. "You're a bad boy. My heart is thumping a mile a minute because of you. You were the one watching me, weren't you?" She set the cat down and stared at the closet.

She started to shake. It had just been the cat.

No one else.

Then prove it.

She reached for the doorknob and began to turn it.

The doorbell rang.

Aimee flinched.

The doorbell rang again.

She looked first at the front door, then at the closet.

It figures. Murphy's Law. She released the doorknob. Why shouldn't she? It had just been the cat. Only the cat.

Her mind was still on Fluffs and the closet when she swung the front door open. She was surprised to see Rich wearing a baby-blue dress shirt and tight jeans that fit ever so nicely. His provocative smile did nothing to calm the wild loops her heart made. She hoped he hadn't noticed. "You're early." She stepped aside to let him in.

"It's okay?"

"Yeah, sure, but I'm not ready."

He looked at her from top to bottom, and then back up again. "You look perfectly fine-as always." Again, he flashed her that crooked little smile that tugged at Aimee's heart.

"Thanks." She pointed with her head toward the study. "I've been trying to work on the story."

"Any luck?"

Someone's eyes had followed her, and for a moment she became an alert bird, ready to take flight. She listened to the normal house noises.

Rich studied her.

Aimee cleared her throat and stepped away from him. "I'm not quite satisfied with the story yet, but it'll be ready tomorrow." She led him to the door. "So where are we going?"

"How about Rojo's?"

Rojo's, originally built in the 1920's or 30's, had served as a gas station, then a grocery store, a bar and restaurant, and a hotel with rooms upstairs. Now, once again a restaurant, it offered a variety of foods that attracted the locals.

Aimee's spirits brightened. "I love that place."

"Me, too."

"Then what're we waiting for?" She grabbed her purse. "Oh, hold on." She opened the top desk drawer, retrieved a small, neatly tied bundle and stuffed it in her purse.

Rich looked at the bundle, then up at Aimee. "My tools," she said.

He nodded, raising an eyebrow.

She ignored him and they walked out.

* * *

His entire body ached from not being able to move for so long. He opened the furnace door but didn't step out. He rubbed his back.

For a while he'd been sure he'd have to kill Aimee. His leg had cramped and shook involuntarily. She had heard him. He knew because he watched her. Even now, he could remember her sitting ramrod straight, like a rabbit sensing danger, not moving.

But now she was gone and the tension eased. It had been several minutes since the front door closed, but he didn't venture out. He would wait until he felt sure Aimee wouldn't return.

Later, much later, he crept out, feeling confident with the thought that Aimee wouldn't be back for several hours.

He could search at his leisure. He began by opening Aimee's computer. It had been set to remember her password. He skimmed every file and when his search turned fruitless, he closed the program and turned off the computer. Next, he moved to Aimee's desk and continued to search the stack of papers on the bookcase. He even thumbed through the books. Finally, he tackled the file cabinets.

Gradually, his mind began to relax. He had found nothing incriminating. No clues indicating she even suspected.

The confidence he felt soon faded like a withering flower. Maybe the information he sought lay on top of her desk at work. Or maybe even in her purse.

He needed to know for sure. He sat on her chair, facing her work. His thoughts flowed like a river, curving, dropping, before finally reaching its destination.

He knew exactly what to do.

Chapter 19

"It's a bit dark, but that's part of the atmosphere that I find so attractive." Aimee looked around Rojo's. She sat next to Rich in a circular booth with leather seats and hardwood tables.

Rich set the menu down. "I read somewhere that they used granite rock from the local mine and weather-aged pinion pine from the lumber industries to create this unique look."

"Yeah? I read that, too. It's on the menu."

"Dang! And I was hoping to impress you with my vast knowledge of trivia."

Aimee laughed and realized how refreshing it felt to be with Rich. Unlike John, Rich was an uncomplicated man, at ease with the world. Something tender nipped softly at the tips of her nerves.

The waiter arrived. Aimee ordered the barbecued ribs, and Rich decided to try the lobster and shrimp plate. They sipped their beers and talked shop while waiting for their meals.

The waiter set a warm, fresh loaf of bread on their table, its aroma causing Aimee's mouth to water. Both Rich and Aimee simultaneously reached for the knife. They looked at each other. Their eyes met, and his hand lingered on top of hers. He smiled his crooked little smile that sent Aimee's heart fluttering. Being with Rich was like awakening on that first morning of a summer vacation. The expectation of the good times to come made it all that more exciting.

"I'm starting on a new project."

"What are you making this time?"

Aimee told him about Ms. Marriott's multi-colored garden, and how she had tried to imitate it. She wanted to surround herself with color, just as Ms. Marriott had. "So if I can't grow any flowers, I'm going to make them."

Rich laughed. Aimee found it contagious, and she, too, laughed.

The couple across from them frowned. The woman let out a loud "Hmm." That only caused them to laugh harder.

Their meals arrived and they got down to the serious business of eating. "Do you have any ideas about tonight?" Rich scooped some meat from the lobster tail and dipped it in drawn butter.

"I think we should wait until dark."

Rich nodded. "And we'll drive by the place a couple of times just to make sure it's empty."

"Good idea." They fell into a comfortable silence while both ate.

When Rich finished, he pushed his plate away. "You've got a bit of barbeque sauce." He pointed to the right side of his own mouth.

Aimee wiped. "Is it better?"

"Still there."

Aimee wiped again. "Gone?"

Rich shook his head and reached out with his finger and wiped the corner of her mouth. His finger traveled up and made little circles around her cheek, then back toward her mouth. He traced the outline of her lips and Aimee parted them slightly.

The tingling sensation ran up one side of Aimee's body and down the other. His tender touch both startled her and frightened her. She thought of her career, her dreams of working for a "real" newspaper. Her logic told her she shouldn't allow this to go any further. Her heart told her otherwise. Aimee licked her lips. "You taste like seafood."

"I've been told worse." He laughed and leaned toward her.

Aimee knew he was going to kiss her. She wanted to feel his lips on hers although the logical part of her shouted to pull away.

"Ready for your check?" the waiter asked.

Rich scooted back and handed the waiter his VISA.

Disappointment mixed with relief flowed through Aimee's veins.

Chapter 20

An unexplained nervousness gripped Aimee as Rich drove by the Stockton and Teague Law building. The two stories loomed before her, and its darkened windows beckoned her. She rubbed her arms, forcing the chill away.

"Are you all right?" Rich asked.

"I'm at my very best," she answered and wondered what her very best was. Or even if she had a very best. What they were about to do was not only illegal but morally wrong, and it bothered the hell out of her. But she felt she had no choice. She had to do it for Lauri's sake. Too late, she wished she hadn't dragged Rich into this.

Aimee's attention returned to Rich when he spoke. "We'll drive by it again. You can never be too careful."

Aimee nodded and waited until the law firm once again came within sight. "It looks like no one's there."

"I'll park the car a block away, just in case." He stepped on the gas, and Aimee watched the speedometer needle climb to thirty.

"Tell me about their offices," Rich said.

"They occupy the entire second floor."

Rich slowed down and looked at Aimee.

"What's on the first floor?"

"A loan company and a real estate office. Nothing that would be open now."

Rich let out a sigh of relief.

"Once you reach the second floor, a set of double doors leads to the firm. Soon as you walk in, you'll see a reception area with a desk. Off to the right is the library. To the left there's a records room and public restrooms. Behind the reception desk are two sets of double doors. The one on the right leads to Teague's office, the other one, to Stockton's. I didn't go into Stockton's office, but I guess it's about the same as Teague's."

"Tell me about Teague's office."

"It's plush. Big desk, lots of books on the shelves. Very expensively decorated. Maybe the door to his left leads to a bathroom, which probably also connects to Stockton's office."

"What about the file cabinets? Where are they?" Rich pulled to the curb and brought the car to a stop.

Aimee closed her eyes, trying to remember. She shook her head. "I'm not sure."

"Yes, you are. Force yourself to remember." He turned off the ignition and put the keys in his pocket.

Again, Aimee closed her eyes, and in her mind she saw the reception area. "Behind the secretary's desk, between the office doors, there's three--no, four--cabinets."

"We'll do them last." Rich adjusted the rear-view mirror so he could see the sidewalk behind him.

Aimee turned to see what drew his attention, but all she found was a deserted street. "I agree. I think we should start with their offices, provided we're able to get in."

Rich briefly took his eyes off the road and stole a glance at Aimee. "I've been meaning to ask you. Just how do we plan to get in?"

Aimee opened her purse and retrieved the small bundle she had grabbed as they left her house. She opened it, revealing a set of picks. "With these."

Rich blinked twice on rapid succession. "Where in the world did you get hold of those?"

"Remember Elaine?"

Rich glanced up as though searching his mind. "Oh yeah. She's the one we called the Cat Lady, right?"

Aimee nodded.

"Yep, she could pick almost any lock in existence. I also remember that you wrote a good feature about her."

Aimee almost smiled. Rich had sent her a bouquet of yellow carnations, a tradition he reserved for when one of his reporters did an exceptionally good job. That had been her first bouquet. Rich's voice interrupted her thoughts.

"Tell me about the tools," Rich said.

"Elaine said that I wrote a wonderful article,

and to show me her appreciation, she gave me this set of tools."

"How thoughtful of her. Weren't those supposed to be confiscated?"

"She had an extra set. She said she'd rather I have them than the police." She retrieved a small flashlight from her purse and put it with the tools. "I then went online and learned how to use them."

"Isn't the Internet wonderful?"

Aimee chose to ignore Rich's sarcasm. "You can find an answer for everything. You just need to know how to ask."

"Why would you want to learn something like that?"

"At the time, it helped me to write the story. You know, know-my-character-better type of thing. I never thought I'd actually be using them." She reached down and touched the thinnest pick. It felt as cold as a snake. "Doesn't change a thing. I still feel like a criminal."

Rich patted her hand. "That's because what we're doing is criminal. You know, it's not too late. We don't have to do this."

"You're right. We don't have to do this. I do. I can't explain it, but I feel I have to help Lauri. Somebody's got to, and I'm it. I can't let her down." She remained quiet for a moment. "It's not too late for you to walk out."

"I'm not doing that. If I walk away, I know you'll still do this on your own. That, I can't allow. You have to help Lauri. I have to help you."

Aimee thought about asking him why he felt he had to help her, but she knew the answer. If any of his reporters were in danger or needed help, he'd do anything for them. She stuffed the picks in her pocket along with the flashlight.

Rich frowned. "Life's ironic, isn't it?"

"What do you mean?"

"In order to do the right thing, we must first do the wrong thing." He reached for the door handle. "Ready?"

She pushed her purse under the seat and nodded.

The feeling that something would go wrong gnawed at her jittery nerves.

Chapter 21

Rich and Aimee strolled down the street. Anyone driving by would assume they were lovers enjoying the night breeze that blew soft and warm. Just a man and a woman.

Taking a last glance around, they stopped in front of the building. "Looks like the coast is clear," Rich said.

Aimee scanned the area and reached into her pocket. She retrieved the set of picks and a small metal flashlight.

"Aimee, wait!"

"What?"

"Have you thought about an alarm?"

Of course she had. When she left the lawyers' offices, she hadn't noticed any wires or any kind of a box. There could be a silent alarm, though. She hoped not. "There won't be one."

"You've checked?" He let out a sigh of relief. "Thank God."

She hated to mislead him. "Not thoroughly."

"Not thoroughly?"

"It's a small building. Chances are they wouldn't have one. None of the businesses around here have one. Why should they?" When she saw Rich frown, she quickly added, "We've gone this far. We might as well go the rest of the way."

"But what if--"

"Stop worrying." She handed him some surgical gloves. He looked at them, then back up at Aimee.

"We don't want to leave any fingerprints, do we?"

Rich continued to stare.

"Just in case." She pulled on her own gloves and handed him the flashlight. "Here, keep the light focused right there." She pointed to the doorknob and knelt down so she could see.

"Must you do that?" Rich put on his gloves.

"Do what?"

"Kneel down like that. It's so obvious what you're doing."

"I'm only doing what I was taught." She took out a pick that resembled the ones a dentist uses to clean teeth and a thin, flat one. She inserted them in the keyhole and hit the tumblers inside the lock. Nothing happened. Aimee tried again. This time the latch slipped back. "I did it!" she beamed. "I actually did it!"

Rich looked away and surveyed the area. "Good grief, keep your voice down." He pushed the door open. Both he and Aimee held their breath. The alarm, if one existed, was silent.

Rich relaxed and scooted in. Aimee followed close behind and shut the door. He swept the area with the flashlight, keeping its beam low so that it wouldn't be seen through the closed curtains. Heading for the stairs, Rich whispered, "Let's get this over with."

Aimee liked that idea. Now that they were here, she was anxious to leave. It took Aimee even less time to open the law firm's door than it did the front door. "I'm getting better, huh?"

Rich smirked and shook his head. "If I ever need a lock picker, you'll be the first one I call."

"I bet." She took out a flashlight for herself. "Where do we begin?" She snapped her fingers as she remembered. "The desks." She led him into Stockman's office.

Like the receptionist's room, Stockman's office was simple but elegantly decorated. A large wooden desk dominated most of the area. The built-in bookshelves held books and expensive-looking knickknacks. An eight-by-ten framed family portrait, framed diplomas and awards for community services decorated the walls.

Aimee took all of these in with a quick glance, ignored them, and headed directly to Stockman's desk. She and Rich eyed the computer, both wondering about the password. Rich shrugged and turned it on.

Aimee bit her lip while she waited for the machine to boot.

The screen demanded a password in order to continue. They tried *lawyers*. When that didn't work, they tried its singular form. Nothing. They keyed each of the lawyer's names, the company's name, the words *criminals, burglar, defense, judge, court, bailiff,* among others. "The password is probably something more personal, like a favorite pet's name. We're not privy to that information. We're wasting time," Rich turned off the computer.

Aimee hated to admit defeat, but nodded anyway. "Maybe whatever secrets are locked inside that computer are also out here in their desk drawers or files."

"Let's hope so," Rich said as he pulled out the top drawer. "It's unlocked. That's bad news."

Damn. "We'll still look. Maybe we'll get lucky anyway."

They didn't.

Next, they concentrated on the bookshelf. They thumbed through the books, just on the off chance that someone had slipped a note in there. They found no notes, not even handwritten ones in the margins of the text. Some of the texts did have stickers, but all concerned specific cases, mostly dealing with casino lawsuits.

The stack of papers that rested on the shelves promised to be of interest. They weren't. Rich wiped his gloved hands on his pants. "Nothing here either, except for a lot of dust."

Aimee shone her beam of light on the thick, soft-brown carpet. No torn places existed, indicating that nothing could be hidden underneath it. "Maybe we'll have better luck in Mr. Teague's office."

"Let's hope so."

Aimee moved toward the side door, and Rich opened it. Just as Aimee had suspected, the door led to a bathroom. Directly in front of her was another door. Rich scooted in front of Aimee and swung it open. She had been right. It led into Teague's office.

Once there, she turned to look at Rich. They both said simultaneously, "The desk."

As before, their efforts proved fruitless. Aimee worried her lip and raised her head higher. "Let's check the reception area."

"Do you really think that'll do any good?"

No, but it would make her feel better. "It's Karen's office, and if she's part of the conspiracy, we might hit gold."

Rich nodded. "Sure. Why not? We're here anyway."

Their rushed search lacked the enthusiasm of discovery that had marked their earlier adventure. Still, they opened every drawer, went through every file, but to no avail. They checked the computer. No surprise there. It too required a password.

Aimee frowned in defeat.

Rich grasped Aimee's arm, leading her out.

Aimee shrugged him off as she studied the room one last time. Something screamed out at her. But what? They had gone through every nook and cranny.

"Ice cream has always helped me to release

tension. Let's grab some on the way home," Rich said.

As much as Aimee hated to admit it, their search had come to an end. "Ice cream sounds good."

"Atta girl," Rich walked to the window and glanced through the shades. "We've got a major problem. Two men pointed our way. They might be coming here. They have a dog."

Aimee grabbed Rich's hand and jerked him toward Teague's office. "Maybe we shouldn't go for ice cream just yet," she whispered.

"Girl, you have a talent for understatement." Rich closed the door to Teague's office behind him. "Let's hide in the bathroom."

Aimee shook her head. "If he needs to go, that would be a nice convenient one." She pointed to the desk. "We'll hide under the desk."

"I can't believe I'm doing this." But even though Rich complained, he followed Aimee to the desk. Silently, Rich folded himself under the desk beside Aimee.

"Rich, your flashlight!"

Rich turned it off just as they heard the men climb the stairs.

Chapter 22

Marvin Stockton opened the front door, reached for the switch, and flooded the waiting area with light. Behind him stood a small, muscular man with short, curly, brown hair. He wore faded blue jeans and a red polo shirt that read Basil's Guard Dog Services. In his hands he clutched a leash hooked to a Doberman pinscher sitting beside him.

"How do I know he isn't going to mess in the office?" Stockton stood several feet away from the animal's reach.

"Look, Mr. Stockton," Basil said, "I can't give you a written guarantee, but I will promise that I'll come in fifteen minutes before the office opens, get him, and if there's a mess, I'll clean it up. Haven't had to clean a mess yet, but I can't guarantee it. Best I can do is promise to clean it, and if I can't clean it, I'll replace the carpet."

Stockton considered this for a moment. "Look, I'll be straight with you. I tried to have an alarm system installed, but the earliest they can get to it is the middle of next week. I also tried hiring a security guard, but no one's applied that I'm happy with. That leaves you and your dog. I'm willing to give you a try, but you'll have to guarantee me that dog will do his job."

"He's a trained guard dog."

As though on cue, the dog jerked his head, stood up, and growled menacingly. He alerted on the closed door leading into Teague's office.

Stockton took a step backwards. "What's the matter with him?"

"Just anxious, I suppose."

The dog barked and tugged at its leash.

Stockton's eyes riveted toward the closed door, then toward the dog, then back at the door. "Let's see what it is about Teague's office that's worrying this dog." He grabbed the door handle. "Keep hold of him. I don't want him accidentally ripping into me."

He threw the door open and turned on the light. His eyes swept the room. Off to his right, he saw the bookcases. Next to them stood a long table that held several documents, then the desk, a couch, and the chairs. Everything appeared normal.

Satisfied, he turned off the light, closed the door, and went to his office. Once again, he followed the same procedure. Just as he was about to close the door, his gaze rested on the bathroom door. He took two long strides toward the bathroom and swung its door open. No one there. "Stupid dog," he mumbled as he closed the door.

He returned to the reception area. "If things go smoothly tonight, your dog's got a job for the next few days, or at least until I can have a permanent security system installed."

"Believe me, Mr. Stockton, with my dog here, you won't need to install any of those fancy and expensive security systems. If anybody plans to break in, Butch here isn't going to let 'em get far." His voice rang with pride as he patted the dog in an attempt to keep him quiet. He opened his hand and moved it down, as though pushing down some air.

Following his owner's command, Butch sat down quietly. His eyes focused on the closed door.

Stockton followed the dog's gaze and shook his head. "See that he does his job properly." He pointed his finger at Basil for emphasis. "I'll wait for you in my car." He turned and left.

Basil bent down so he was eye to eye with the dog. He released him from his leash. "Kill!" he hissed.

As Basil closed the front door behind him, the Doberman pinscher turned his nose toward Teague's office, sniffed, and stiffened.

Chapter 23

For three full minutes, Rich and Aimee remained in the dark, crammed against one another under Teague's desk. When she thought it was safe, Aimee felt for her flashlight and reluctantly turned it on. "I think it's safe to crawl out now."

"Yeah, I guess so." Rich's voice came out weak and shaky.

Aimee crawled out from under Teague's desk. "Come on. I don't think they're coming back."

Rich turned on his flashlight before crawling out. "This is a fine mess you got us into." He straightened himself out.

"Me? Who's the one who wanted me to take on this story?"

Rich's forehead furrowed. "You did."

Aimee shrugged. "So I did. See what I mean?" Before Rich could respond to her illogical answer, she reached for the door handle leading into the reception area.

"Aimee, wait!" A note of urgency rang in Rich's voice. "The guard dog, remember?"

"Yeah, but it's so quiet out there. They must have taken it with them."

Rich looked at her.

"Okay," she agreed. "Not likely, but maybe he's downstairs or something. We can use the time to get out of here." She studied the closed door. She wished she had x-ray vision.

Rich cocked his head as though straining to listen. "I don't hear anything either. I guess you're right."

His words did little to calm Aimee's heart. The idea of a ferocious dog waiting to pounce on them left her feeling numb. She opened the door just a crack. "Here, doggie-doggie. Nice doggie." She held her breath.

Nothing happened.

Aimee breathed. False alarm, thank God. "He's gone. Come on, let's get this finished." She swung the door wide open.

The Doberman lunged toward her, teeth bared, barking ferociously. Its eyes, a bright yellow, shone like angry stars on a dark night.

Aimee gasped and froze.

Rich kicked the dog as hard as he could and shoved the door shut. The dog whimpered but came back growling. Even before Rich could completely close the door, the dog banged against it.

Rich put his weight against the door until he heard it click closed. On the other side, the dog scratched and thumped against the door. "Are you all right?"

Aimee nodded. "And you?"

"I'm shaking like leaves in a hurricane." He

waited until he caught his breath. "So how are we going to get out of here?"

"I'm thinking."

"Now, that's a scary thought."

Aimee sighed. Rich was right. How had she managed to get them into this mess? She glanced around the room and an idea began to formulate. "I think I have a plan. Let's perfect it."

"Great. I just love your plans."

"Good, 'cuz you'll love this one."

"Let's hear it."

"We open the door to the bathroom and one of us stands by its entry way. The other one opens the front office door."

"Oh, oh. Sounds dangerous."

"Whoever is by the bathroom starts making all kinds of noise to attract the dog. When the dog is halfway in, the person by the bathroom closes the door, locking himself--or herself--safely in."

"In the meantime, the other person is fair game for the dog."

Aimee smiled faintly. "In the meantime, the other person waits until the dog is halfway in, then jumps out and slams the door. Now, instead of us being locked in here, the dog will be."

"Won't Mr. Teague have a nice surprise waiting for him tomorrow morning?"

"So what do you think?" She turned to look at him. Their eyes locked for one long second.

"Think it'll work?"

"I think so."

Outside, the dog growled, and Aimee felt like a caged animal in a burning room. "Who's going to stand by the bathroom and who's going to open the door?"

"You stand by the bathroom, and I'll open the door."

"No way. The person by the bathroom will be relatively safe. I'll open the door."

"Hey, I'm the boss here. I'll open the door." He pushed her away from him. "Now go."

Aimee scooted toward the bathroom. She turned and glanced at Rich.

"You know that by locking the dog in the office, Teague and Stockton will know that someone has been here," Rich said.

"Maybe not."

"How you figure that?"

"I'd imagine that most dog owners pick up their dogs early in the morning before the business opens. In this case, he'll find the dog locked in the office. He'll look around and see that everything looks normal. He'll think maybe the dog was sniffing behind the door, and it got closed on him."

"Or maybe he'll suspect that someone was here."

"True, but either way, he's not going to mention it to Teague or Stockton. He knows he'll lose his job if he does. I'm willing to bet he'll keep it to himself."

"Let's hope you're right." He grimaced at her. "Let's get this done so we can get out of here."

Aimee's flesh crawled. Her knees creaked. Her throat felt dry. She wasn't meant to live the life of a burglar. She should have listened to her mother.

At least, she should never have talked Rich into coming with her.

When she got out of this, she would never do anything illegal again.

If she got out.

Chapter 24

When Rich and Aimee heard the dog slam against the door, they exchanged looks from across the room. Aimee gave him thumbs-up even though she felt like jelly inside.

Rich wrapped his hand around the doorknob. "Ready?"

No, not really. But this had been her idea. She nodded.

"Here we go."

By now the attack dog's growling had become a defiant bark. Aimee's heart caught in her throat.

Rich position himself, stood behind the door, and turned the knob.

The door had been opened but an inch when the beast pounced on it, opening it wider.

Rich tumbled.

Aimee yelled and waved her arms. The dog turned toward her. Aimee drew in a deep breath at the sight of the monster dog. She froze, grasping the bathroom doorknob.

The dog bared its teeth and gathered its rippling muscles to leap.

"Aimee!" Rich screamed. He grabbed the nameplate resting on top of the desk and hurled it toward the dog. It hit the animal on its rump.

The dog turned on Rich.

That moment was all Aimee needed. She dashed into the bathroom.

Rich stepped around the door, heading toward the reception office. His foot caught on something, and his face met the floor.

Aimee threw the door open and growled, barked, and stared the dog in the eyes. The dog crouched, ready to spring for Aimee's throat.

She waited long enough to give Rich a chance to get up and get out of the room. She whispered a silent prayer that he had had enough time, for hers had run out. She slammed the door shut a half-second before the dog crashed against the wood.

She leaned against the closed door and waited for her breath to return to normal. Behind her, the dog growled and scratched at the door.

Her victory lasted no more than a minute.

The dog had stopped its attack.

Oh, God, he's going after Rich, Aimee thought.

Chapter 25

The dog growled.

Rich's screamed.

Aimee threw the door open. She focused the beam of light on them.

Rich, wrestling the dog, lay on the floor.

Aimee bolted toward Teague's desk. She grabbed the stapler and hurled it in the direction of the dog. Her aim fell several inches short of her target. "Heel! Stop!"

The dog ignored her, intent on its attack.

She threw the Scotch tape dispenser. Again, she missed. "Settle!" she screamed. She threw Teague's solid-gold Mont Blanc set of pens. This time, she hit the dog on the head.

The dog yelped and turned toward Aimee.

Rich kicked the dog, knocking it against the desk, stunning it. He scrambled through the doorway and slammed the door shut.

Aimee darted into the bathroom. Lungs bursting, she smacked the light switch, charged through Stockton's office, and out into the reception area.

Rich sagged against Teague's door, his shirt ripped and his right arm bleeding.

"How bad is it?"

Rich flexed his fingers. He breathed hard,

through his mouth. "It's not as bad as it could have been. Thank God I had the flashlight with me. I was able to ram it into its mouth. Mostly, I got some scratches. They sting, but that's all. A little rubbing alcohol and some very big Band-aids will take care of them."

"Rich, God, I'm so sorry. It's my fault." She cast her gaze downward. "When I saw that dog coming toward me, something happened. I snapped and couldn't move. If you hadn't had to waste your time throwing that nameplate, you could have gotten out safely. Instead . . . I'm so sorry."

Using the index finger of his left hand, Rich raised her chin. "It's not your fault. You did good in there. Besides, I'm okay."

She smiled gratefully and nodded. "We didn't find anything."

"Maybe you didn't, but I certainly did."

"What?"

Rich smiled. "What I'm trying to say is that I've had one heck of a night."

Boy, was that an understatement. "Me, too." Aimee glanced at his still bleeding arm. "Let's patch you up."

Rich took out his handkerchief and dabbed at his wounds. "Shouldn't we get out of here, then patch me up?"

"We should at least clean it. We don't want it to get infected."

"Okay, you've got a point." He glanced

toward the closed door. Behind it, the dog growled and barked ferociously.

"Let's go see what we can salvage from the bathroom."

They found a bottle of peroxide. Rich washed his arm and nodded at Aimee. She poured the peroxide over his wounds, and Rich bit his tongue and tightened his face. "I think we'd better clean up our mess. We don't want to leave any evidence behind."

Aimee nodded, finished applying First Aid, and returned the peroxide to its place. She opened the doors to the cabinet under the sink. She saw a stack of plastic bags and confiscated one. She placed the trash in it and handed the bag to Rich.

He waved his hand, indicating Aimee should follow him out of the room. Rich flipped off the light switch and stuffed the trash bag into his pant pocket. Aimee focused the light beam downward to guide them. They returned to the reception area and continued their search.

Inside Teague's office, the dog continued to throw itself against the door. "We better hurry." Aimee looked at the door and suspected it might disintegrate at any minute. "That dog is making enough racket to attract the attention of anybody walking by. Thank God this is a quiet street."

"Hope you're right." Rich glanced around the room. "As far as I can tell, all we have left are the file cabinets. Let's get them done." Reaching for the handle, he whispered, "Hey, we might get lucky." He pulled the drawer handle. "Rats, they're locked."

That was her cue. She opened the roll of tools, chose a pick, and the locks opened in less than a minute.

"You're getting to be a real pro at this."

Aimee pointed to the file cabinets. "I am, aren't I?"

Rich rolled his eyes.

Aimee smiled. "Which cabinet do you want?"

"You start on the right, and I'll start on the left."

"Right." Aimee opened the top drawer and stared at the files. "How will we know if any files are missing--or even which file to look under?"

Rich shook his head. "I'm not sure, but maybe we'll get lucky and find something which isn't quite right."

"Let's hope so." Aimee thumbed through the first folder, then moved on to the next one. Less than ten minutes later, she knew it was no use. She slammed the last drawer shut and looked up at Rich. "Now what?"

He shrugged. "Hey, we gave it our best. We came out empty-handed, but did you really expect to find anything?"

Silly question, wasn't it? Why would she have gone through so much trouble if she hadn't expected to find something? "I was hoping for at least a tiny little clue." She shrugged and sighed. "There has to be something we're missing. Otherwise, he wouldn't have brought that dog." Her gaze landed on the calendar resting on the secretary's desk. "I have an idea."

"Oh, no. Not another idea." Rich placed his open hands on his cheeks.

Aimee smiled. She sat on the desk and focused her flashlight on the calendar. She flipped through its pages. "This is about the time Lauri was supposed to be working for Mr. Teague and Mr. Stockton. I'll read you the names of the people who had appointments during those months. You tell me if you can find a file for them."

"Good thinking." Rich nodded. "Shoot."

Aimee waited for Rich to open the file cabinet before she read the first name. Rich found the file.

Three minutes later, they had found all but one file: that of Nevada State Senator Ashton E. Nye.

Chapter 26

"Do you think Senator Nye really ties in with Lauri?" Rich asked once they were both in the car and safely driving away. "Oh, by the way, still want some ice cream?"

Aimee shook her head. "No way. My stomach is still in turmoil." She paused for a moment. "Not quite sure about Nye, but it's something worth digging into."

"I agree." Rich made a right turn and shook his head, a small smile forming on his lips.

Aimee watched him. She too felt her muscles beginning to relax. She liked seeing Rich smile. "What?"

"I was just thinking about our adventure."

Aimee leaned back in the seat. "Yeah. That was a rush."

Rich stole a quick glance at her.

Aimee sat up straight. "But it's a once-in-a-life time thing. I'll never do that again."

"Glad to hear that. If we kept this up, we'd both age beyond our years." He slowed down for a traffic light. "By the way, what do you plan to do with the set of tools?"

Aimee looked at the small bundle that had gotten them into so much trouble. "Stash them someplace safe, I guess, until I need them again."

Rich faced Aimee. "What? Did I hear you correctly . . . need them again?"

Aimee giggled.

"I get it. You were joking."

Aimee nodded and they settled into the first comfortable silence since their ordeal began. Aimee's thoughts drifted to the significance of the missing file.

Seven minutes later, Rich pulled into Aimee's driveway and let the engine idle. "To be one-hundred percent truthful, I'm thirsty, and I'd love to go in with you and get a drink." Rich pointed toward Aimee's house. "But if that makes you feel uncomfortable, then I'll just say goodnight here and head home. It's your call."

Whoever said chivalry was dead knew nothing. She glanced at Rich and realized he still waited for an answer. Yes, she wanted him to come in. Yes, she would feel very uncomfortable. Yes, it would be wiser for him to head home now. "Yes," she said aloud and surprised herself.

"Yes?"

"Uh, yes. Like yes, turn off the engine and come in for a few minutes."

Rich's eyebrows arched and his eyes were as huge as saucers. His smile couldn't be bigger.

Aimee opened the door. "I have tea, beer, or Coke. What would you like?"

"You."

Aimee pivoted to stare at him. "What?"

"You." His voice came out so husky, he had to clear his throat.

Passion consumed Aimee, but she forced herself to think of her dream of one day working for a big time newspaper. "Silly, I'm not a drink." She bit her tongue. What a stupid thing to say.

Rich half-smiled. "An ice-cold beer sounds great." He sat down on the couch, and Aimee headed for the kitchen.

She opened a bottle of Amber Bock for Rich and mixed her regular drink: Coke and Diet Coke on the rocks. She carried them to the living room and set them on the coffee table.

Fluffs jumped to the couch and curled up next to Rich. The cat glared at Aimee, daring her to move him. "Don't you have to go outside or something?" Aimee shooed the cat.

In response, he snuggled closer to Rich and purred.

Aimee returned to the kitchen and opened a can of tuna. Within seconds, Fluffs was there, rubbing against her leg. "Now how did I know you'd do that?"

She set the food down, scratched Fluffs on the back of his head, and rejoined Rich in the den. She sat next to him where Fluffs had been.

As he reached for his drink, his leg rubbed against hers.

Aimee didn't move her leg, but if she had, it would have been toward Rich. She sipped her soda and silently repeated, Think career.

Remember your dream. Aloud, she said, "Someday I'd like to go to work for one of the big-time newspapers." Aimee felt, more than saw, Rich's body tense slightly. "You knew that, didn't you?"

Rich nodded. "Only a moron wouldn't know that." He set his beer down and as he did, he scooted over so that now their thighs were next to each other.

A tingling sensation ran through Aimee's body. She should have let the cat sit there. What had made her sit next to Rich?

Rich's gaze sought Aimee's eyes. She felt as though he were swallowing her whole.

"It seems to me that you've gone to great lengths to make me aware of that. Why did you choose this time to do so?" He leaned back and put his arm behind the couch.

"Why?" Her voice broke and she cleared her throat. Because I'm losing control. "I want to be honest with you. That's all."

His arm dropped to her shoulder. "That's all?"

She didn't trust herself to speak. She nodded.

With his opened palm, he caressed her upper arm. "I hate the thought of losing you."

Aimee held her breath.

"You're the best reporter I have."

Aimee's heart sank. Was that all she meant to him? Why was he holding her? Why did his eyes speak of tenderness? "I don't have any plans to leave just yet."

"I know." Rich's voice revealed a deep sadness. "But the time will come when you will want to go." He lowered his face toward Aimee's. He gently kissed her lips. "And I promise you that when your big break comes, I won't hold you back. In the meantime . . . " He cupped her head in his hands and looked at her with an intensity that both thrilled her and petrified her.

Aimee sucked in some air. When he kissed her it was like inhaling the aroma of a rain forest. She wanted this moment to never end.

Rich broke the embrace and stood up. "And now I must go before . . . before . . ."

Before what? Say it, Rich.

"Do you have an extra key to your apartment?"

Aimee gasped. That's not what she expected him to say. "I . . . why . . . what . . ."

"I make a real mean breakfast."

She considered saying all sorts of brilliant things, but all that came out was "What?"

"I'd like to make you breakfast tomorrow morning. What time do you normally get up?"

"At seven."

"By seven-fifteen, I'll have breakfast ready. Of course, if you'd rather not give me a key, I can wait until you're up so you can let me in. But then we won't be eating until close to eight and we'll both be late to work."

"Dolphine lives a block from here. She always stops by and we drop by the police department on our way to work."

"Think maybe she can go by herself tomorrow?"

Aimee nodded. "I'll call her." She retrieved the extra key from the desk drawer and handed it to Rich.

"I promise that after I leave tomorrow, I'll return the key and I won't make any duplicates."

Aimee smiled and nodded.

"See you tomorrow at seven-fifteen." Rich kissed his finger and touched her lips. "Good night. 'Parting is such sweet sorrow.'" He shrugged. "That's the extent of my Shakespearean knowledge. Lock up behind me." Shakespeare turned and left.

The touch of Rich's lips on hers lingered in Aimee's mind. She would make those seconds last an eternity.

Chapter 27

The aroma of freshly brewing coffee tickled Aimee's nostrils. She smiled, thought how wonderful it was to be alive, and rolled over in bed.

And wished she hadn't.

A carving knife, dripping with blood, hovered a mere two inches from her face. The tangible horror engulfed her, smothered her.

She forced her eyes to travel past the blade and to the hand clutching the knife. The hairy arm bulged with muscles. Her gaze travelled past the arm, to the neck, and finally, the face. Where the mouth should have been, there was nothing. No nose, no lips. Only the eyes--houses of evil--dwelled there, fierce and angry, hungering for blood.

Aimee screamed.

She sprang up in bed, perspiration pouring down her forehead.

Her bedroom door slammed open, and Rich came running in, a spatula in his hand, his eyes wide and alert. "What's wrong?"

Aimee sat ramrod straight, trying to dispel the horror of the Evil Eyes. She looked up at Rich and felt foolish. "It was just a dream--a nightmare." She tried to calm herself, but the reality of the dream left her trembling. "I'm sorry I scared you." Rich nodded as he appraised her body. Aimee realized she was wearing nothing but a flimsy nightgown. She reached for the bed sheet and covered herself. "Have you been here long?"

He seemed oblivious to Aimee's discomfort and sat at the edge of the bed. "I've been here about half an hour. Breakfast is almost ready." He reached for Aimee's hand. "Do you have nightmares often?"

She opened her mouth and quickly closed it. The last person she had told was her ex-fiancé, John. She had trusted that bum and confided in him. He listened attentively and stroked her cheek. "Aimee, sweetheart, I will always love you. But you know I want to go into politics. I can't afford to get involved with someone whose life might bring on a scandal." He kissed her forehead, walked out, and never returned.

Aimee cleared her throat. "I have a recurring nightmare. It has something to do with a knife and blood and some demon eyes." She closed her eyes and saw the knife dripping blood. A chill formed along her neck and traveled down her spine. "You know how dreams are." She looked away. "They don't really make much sense."

Rich held her. His warmth reassured her, and gradually she felt the horror evaporating like steam escaping from a hot pot-a very hot pot.

"Do you know--" His voice was husky and he cleared his throat. "--what your dreams mean?"

She pulled away from him. "Yeah. It means I'm eating too much spicy food."

Rich's gaze strayed to her body. "You, you look . . . all right. More than all right. Downright sexy, I'd say. Are you okay?"

She reached for her silk dressing gown resting at the foot of the bed and put it on. "It was just a dream. It doesn't mean anything." She bit her lip and looked downward. Slowly, she raised her eyes to meet Rich's. She sprang out of bed and sniffed the air. "What's that I smell?"

"My specialty---omelets. I didn't ask. Do you like omelets? If not, I can make--"

"Omelets are perfect. Do you need any help?"

"No, not really. I've got it under control. Why don't you stay here and get dressed--not that what you're wearing isn't perfect. In fact, if you'd ask me, I'd rather you would come to breakfast wearing that sweet little nothing." He grinned, and his eyes twinkled.

Aimee smiled a bit self-consciously. Her hair was probably a mess, but Rich wasn't looking at her hair. She ran her fingers through it anyway. "How are your dog bites doing this morning?"

"Not bites, scratches. They're fine." He looked at her. "On second thought, they really bother me. But a kiss from you will make it all go away."

Her heart skipped a beat as he approached. His kiss was warm and tender.

"I'll leave you now so you can get dressed."

"How long have I got?"

"As long as you need. The only deadline I'll ever give you is one for the newspaper stories." He turned and closed the door behind him.

Chapter 28

Aimee took a quick shower and changed into denim shorts and a shocking pink pullover blouse. Still barefoot, she joined Rich in the kitchen. "What can I do?"

Rich stopped cracking an egg and stared at Aimee. "You can stand there and just let me look at you all day long. But if you do that, we'll never have breakfast. So I'd advise you to work on your article or your project. When I finish here, I'll call you."

"I really don't mind helping."

"I know, but I'd like to do this for you." He turned and continued breaking the eggs.

Aimee walked over to the study. There were a couple of articles that needed polishing, but Rich was in the kitchen--her kitchen. She would never be able to concentrate. *Get your hands moving, gal.* The sooner, the better.

She sat at the dining table and hummed a nameless tune as she folded the tissue paper and traced different sized patterns.

Rich stepped out of the kitchen. "Breakfast is ready."

Aimee looked up. Breakfast with Rich. Was she ready for this?

"It's really not that difficult." Rich placed his

hand on her shoulder. "You get up, join me at the dinette in your kitchen, and we eat. If you don't like what I made, you don't have to eat it. I'll take you to McDonald's. I'll even pay."

Aimee's cheeks felt warm. "Oh, no. It isn't that. It's just that my mind was far away, uh, with my project." She pointed to the materials on the dining table.

"Tell me all about your project." He waited for her to join him. "Paper flowers, right?"

She nodded.

"Hmm, I'll have to see those when you're finished. If I like them, you'll just have to make some for my apartment, too."

* * *

After breakfast, while Rich washed the dishes and Aimee put the plates up, she turned to Rich. "Are you going to Lauri's funeral? It's today, in case you didn't know."

Rich drained the sink. "Yep, I know, and yep, I'm going. I'll have to go home and change first. I'll pick you up around ten-thirty."

"Do you think he'll be there?"

"Who?" He rinsed the sink.

"Lauri's killer."

"He'll probably be there, looking sad, his face blending in with the crowd. We may be standing next to him."

Aimee wiped the crumbs off the dinette table while Rich cleaned the stovetop. "How will we recognize him?"

"Use the same procedure that we use for our stories. We follow leads until they blossom or die." He dried his hands and looked at Aimee. "That reminds me. I want you to follow up on Lauri's stepfather."

Images flashed across Aimee's mind. A knife dripping blood, a little girl's fear as she scrambled through the woods, the devil eyes following, always getting closer.

The silverware slipped out of her hand. Spoons and forks twanged when they hit the floor. She didn't want to have anything to do with finding Lauri's stepfather. "I was thinking of following up on Senator Nye first." Her voice was barely above a whisper. She bent down to pick up the fallen silverware.

Rich helped her. "I need to do some library research on that Truckee story. I can check on Senator Nye at the same time. You look up her stepfather and see if he's magically reappeared."

A shiver spread through Aimee's body. She got busy sorting out the silverware before Rich could notice it.

Chapter 29

Because Karen wasn't a believer, there would be no chapel service, only a graveside ceremony for Lauri. That wasn't right, Aimee thought. She wanted to call Karen and tell her that everyone--especially Lauri-deserved a chapel service. "At least it will be a closed casket." Aimee's stomach tightened as she and Rich neared the cemetery.

Rich didn't look at Aimee. He kept his eyes on the road and on the cars around him. Traffic was unusually heavy, partly due to the unseasonably warm day. "Would you have preferred an open casket?"

Aimee glanced at the cloudless sky and wondered if Lauri had a clear view of Earth. "Good heavens, no. A lot of times the mortician makes the deceased look 'lifelike'--a term and concept I despise." Her vision remained focused on the sky. A darkness descended, coating the sky with a dull gray tint. "I know this is completely stupid and illogical, but if I see a dead person look like he's only sleeping, then I feel that maybe he'll get up. He'll have a second chance to do everything over again, and do it right this time." She must sound like a fool. "What I think I'm trying to say is that I wish

Lauri had that second chance. I feel so bad for her." Aimee found no hope in the metallic dusty sky.

"Are you all right?"

Aimee nodded. Rich stole a quick glimpse at her, his frown telling her that he knew she had lied. "Okay, maybe I'm feeling . . . funky. I just want to make sure that whoever did this is caught."

Rich turned into the cemetery. "Me, too." He parked the car, walked around, and opened Aimee's door. She got out, and they made their way toward the crowd of mourners who had already gathered around Lauri's gravesite.

The number of people who had shown up stunned Aimee. There must be several hundred people here, Aimee thought. Most of them were teenagers, school peers who probably never spoke to Lauri when she was alive. The drama of the moment had lured them here, but even among this sea of unfamiliar faces, Aimee spotted several she recognized.

Directly in front of her stood George Teague, looking as large, powerful, and as intimidating as he must look in the courtroom. Beside him was a slightly chunky woman wearing a two-piece navy-blue outfit with a white blouse and thin high heels. She held onto Marvin Stockton, probably as added support for her shoes.

Aimee studied the lawyers. If they were involved in Lauri's death, they wore no mask of guilt, nor showed any sign of concern for their ransacked offices.

Off to her far right, a very dejected looking Gary Heely tried to mingle with a group of teens. He only succeeded in betraying his loneliness. He stood a little apart from everyone, avoiding eye contact. None of the teenagers were dressed in proper funeral attire, but somehow Aimee knew Lauri would have preferred this.

Aimee searched for anyone who might be Gary's parents, but nobody seemed to fit the bill. Their obvious absence made a strong statement about their relationship with Lauri.

Up ahead, Karen sat on a chair under a green canopy. The baby, wearing a bright yellow outfit, was asleep in her infant seat next to her mother's feet. Karen stared at the casket with hard and dry eyes.

"Here comes Grandma Louise and her son," someone whispered in Aimee's ear.

Aimee turned to see Dolphine and Robert, the newspaper's photographer. "Where?" Aimee nodded at Robert.

He returned the nod.

Dolphine pointed to the parking lot. "They're pulling in now."

Aimee's attention switched to the parking lot. Earl--or was it Burley?--drove up. He moved with reassuring steps as he walked around to the passenger's side of the car, opened the door, and helped his mother out. That had to be Earl. She wondered where Burley was. Earl could use some help with Grandma Louise who seemed much older and more exhausted than on the day she had come to see Aimee and Dolphine at the newspaper office. No wonder Earl had been so concerned about his mother's health.

Aimee and Rich worked their way toward Grandma Louise and Earl. "How're you doing?" Aimee directed the question toward Grandma Louise and smiled at Earl.

"I've been feeling very tired lately, but I'll make it. I just wish we could say that much for Lauri." Grandma Louise moved toward the grave, and Aimee followed her. Earl flashed Aimee a smile.

Grandma Louise stopped. "There he is."

Her harsh tone brought Aimee back to reality. "Who?"

"That good for nothing boyfriend of Lauri's. He looks so sad. Yet, not more than a week ago, I heard him with my own ears say that he'd kill Lauri if she ever threatened to leave him again. He probably made that threat good, and now he has the nerve to show up looking all sad."

Aimee first glanced at Gary, then at the lawyers, and wondered if Grandma Louise was right.

* * *

Aimee half-listened as the preacher droned on. Mainly, she studied the people's faces.

Halfway through the service, a movement caught Aimee's attention. Someone stood a bit behind the funeral crowd. When she turned to see who it was, he dodged behind the ponderosa pines. She glued her gaze on that general area, but she didn't see him again.

Dolphine leaned closer to Aimee. "Don't look now but a man to your right seems unusually interested in us." With a nod of her head, she singled out a husky looking man with dirty blond hair and a high forehead. When the man noticed that both Dolphine and Aimee had spotted him, he focused on the speaker.

"You and Robert keep an eye on him," Aimee said. "I think there's someone hiding behind the trees. Rich and I will focus on him." From the corner of her eye a movement once again attracted her attention. This time, the shadow glided between the trees.

She glanced at Rich, and he indicated with a slight movement of his eyes that they should make their way toward the trees. She inched to her left, and Rich followed her.

Aimee's gaze traveled to the man who peeked from behind the trees to observe the funeral proceeding. Next time he peeked, she would concentrate on his features.

Aimee never got the chance. He bolted from his vantage point and ran in the opposite direction of the funeral crowd. Without hesitating, Rich pursued him like a hungry lion after an antelope.

Rich chased the mysterious figure, and Aimee scanned the crowd, searching for the husky stranger. Without hesitating, he broke into a run, heading toward the mysterious man.

Dolphine stared at Robert, who took off after the runners. Dolphine followed him.

Great! What was Aimee supposed to do? Join in on the great marathon? She knew she should have taken up jogging. She inhaled deeply and joined the chase.

Rich, who was several yards ahead of her, reached the crest of a hill and disappeared. So did Robert and Dolphine.

The stranger from the crowd did likewise. Aimee pushed harder to catch up. Huffing and puffing, she reached the area she had last seen Rich. About ten feet directly in front of her, Rich wrapped one arm around a tree. His other hand clutched his side.

Robert trotted toward Rich, Dolphine close behind him. The husky stranger continued after the man.

Aimee approached Rich. "Are you all right?" she asked.

"I lost him." He panted. "He's somewhere in there." He moved his head slightly, pointing to his left.

Robert and Dolphine joined them.

"You see where he went?" Rich asked.

Robert pointed to a crowd of people who

had gathered for another funeral. "He's one of those over there. The other guy is in there too, but which ones they are, I couldn't tell. Can you?"

Rich shook his head. "Ladies?"

Aimee and Dolphine simultaneously said, "No."

"That's too bad. Whoever they are, I bet they have an interesting story to tell."

They worked their way back to the service which by now had ended. They offered Karen their condolences and left. On their way back to the newspaper office, Aimee's thoughts meandered like a river. Who were those two men?

Chapter 30

Rich stared at the monitor and shook his head. "Aimee, come over here. I need some help on this layout."

"Well, that's a first." Aimee headed toward him. "Normally you don't want anyone butting in on layout decisions."

"This is different. It concerns your article."

"Which one?"

"The one on Baby Karen."

Aimee glanced at the monitor. Her story along with her article featuring the murder investigation, and another one about the funeral were prominently displayed on the front page. "I like it. What's the problem?"

"Do you think the murder articles dwarf your Baby Karen story?"

Maybe just a little, but under the circumstances, that was inevitable. "It'll do." She glanced at the layout. "What it dwarfs is your Truckee story."

Rich shrugged. "I'm still working on that."

"Tell me about it."

Rich settled into his chair. "Seems like in Albany, Georgia, a seventy-year-old woman named Daniela died of an apparent heart attack. The police in Albany are looking for her husband, an Ernie Loom, originally from Truckee."

"Why are the police looking for him? Did he disappear?" Aimee leaned against Rich's desk.

"My questions precisely, but no one is talking. And here's where it gets interesting." He stabbed the air to accentuate his point. "There was another case, this time in Fargo, North Dakota, involving the Marcil family. Apparently Barbara, a sixty-one-year old lady, died in a car accident. At the time of the accident, her husband and several other people were doing some volunteer work for their church. Even though he was nowhere near the accident, the Fargo police are still looking for him." He looked at Aimee as though expecting her to fill in the gaps.

Okay, maybe she missed the point. Other than the fact that the two elderly women died and left their husbands behind and the police were searching for them, she couldn't see the connection. Surely, there had to be more than that. "I give up. What ties the two incidents together?"

"The fact that both Mr. Loom and Mr. Marcil are from Truckee. Plus in both cases, the husbands were much younger than their wives and both involved big estates."

Aimee raised her eyebrows and looked closer at Rich's notes. "I can see why you're so intrigued with this story." Rich's enthusiasm lured her.

Rich's eyes brightened. "Maybe we can work on it together."

She'd like that. Then again, it meant working closer than normal. As it was, every day her attraction for him grew. Even now, as they held a perfectly innocent conversation, a charged electrical line connected them. She didn't want to yield to the impulse, mostly because she had her career, her dream, to think of. But, at the same time, it would be so nice. So very nice. "I wouldn't mind, but let me wrap up a few loose ends on Lauri's story first."

Rich looked deflated, like a balloon that had lost most of its air. "Of course. That's the newspaper's biggest story. I thought maybe . . ." He shrugged. "Never mind. Best to use your energy on the murder investigation." He set his notes down and pointed to the monitor. "So what do you think of the layout?"

Aimee nodded with approval. "I think--"

The front door opened, and much to Aimee's surprise, the same husky stranger she had spotted yesterday at Lauri's funeral walked through the door. Detective Marie O'Day accompanied him.

Chapter 31

"Morning," the man said. "I assume you are Rich Cole and Aimee Brent." He carried a manila envelope.

"It seems you have us at a disadvantage." Rich stepped in front of Aimee.

"I've talked to you several times on the phone, but I've never had the chance to meet you. I'm Tom O'Day--Detective Tom O'Day, and I believe you already met my partner, Marie O'Day." He showed them his I.D.

Rich and Tom shook hands.

Aimee blinked. "O'Day? Are you two-- "

"Married?" Marie finished for her. "Yes, we are--much to the department's discontent. That's why we left the Los Angeles Police Department and came here. We don't really team up too much, but this being such a small force, it's almost impossible not to work together. It's something we both enjoy."

"Interesting." Rich's eyes wandered off, as though considering a story idea. He looked at Tom. "I remember you. You and I chased a man at Lauri's funeral."

Tom nodded.

"What can we do for you?" Rich asked.

"I'm here to talk about Lauri."

"Oh?" Rich's face brightened. "Do you have something we can print?"

"Maybe. Maybe not. I thought we could compare notes."

Rich pointed to the coffeepot. "Care for a cup?"

"Don't mind if I do." Tom set the envelope down next to the coffeepot. "I take mine black."

"And I'll take decaf," Marie said.

"I have both." Rich poured two cups and handed one to each. "You said you transferred from Los Angeles. How long have you been here?"

Tom accepted the cup of coffee. "Less than two months."

"Brand new and you're already working homicide. That doesn't speak very well of our town, does it?" Rich sighed. Even though beauty surrounded Lake Tahoe, it did have a high crime rate.

"All towns, regardless of size, have problems." Marie poured cream in her decaf.

Rich waited until she had finished fixing it. "Why don't we go to my office so we can talk in private?"

Tom grabbed the envelope, nodded, and followed Marie, Aimee, and Rich into the office. Rich closed the door and settled behind his desk.

Aimee remained standing. "Dolphine has been working very closely with me on this story. Should I call her in?"

Tom nodded. "Yes, please."

Aimee opened the door, made eye contact with Dolphine, and signaled for her to join them.

Once everyone had gotten comfortable, Rich introduced Dolphine to the detectives. "What can we do for you?"

Tom answered. "You can fill us in on what you know about the kid."

"By the 'kid,' you mean Lauri's boyfriend," Aimee said.

"That's the one." Tom set the envelope on Rich's desk.

"Does this mean he's your main suspect?" Rich eyed the large envelope.

"At this point, everyone's a suspect." Tom retrieved a notebook and pen. "Tell me about the kid."

Rich pointed to Aimee and Dolphine. "It's their story."

That was Aimee's clue. Time to test her theories. "I personally feel he's innocent, but sometimes he does or says something that makes me wonder."

Marie's eyebrows arched. "Oh? Care to explain?"

"First time I talked to him--and that's before Lauri's body was found--he referred to her in the past tense. Then there's that bit about Grandma Louise maybe seeing him the night Lauri disappeared."

Tom took a sip of coffee. "What else?"

Dolphine spoke up. "I have some information about Lauri wanting to break up with Gary, and him threatening to kill her if she ever did."

"Do you think he loved her?" Tom gulped his coffee and set the cup down.

Aimee nodded. "I think he still does."

Tom looked up from his notes. "What do you think, Dolphine?"

"I've talked to several of Gary's friends, and they claim the only reason he started dating Lauri was to spite his parents."

"'Spite his parents?'" Tom repeated.

"The Heelys are rather well off, and Lauri was not exactly high society material. They resented her."

Aimee nodded. She had gathered that from the conversations she'd had with Gary. "I have that bit of information filed away, too. Do you take this to mean that maybe Gary didn't really love Lauri?"

Tom and Marie looked at each other and remained quiet.

Aimee frowned.

"Micah, one of Gary's friends, told me that at the beginning of Lauri's and Gary's relationship, he often bragged about Lauri being his trophy." Dolphine opened her notebook and glanced at her notes. "Maybe it was easy sex--he wasn't sure--but he said that later, Gary fell head over heels in love with her."

"Maybe that's what made Gary so possessive," Aimee added.

"Which means that if anybody was going to do any breaking up," Dolphine said, "Gary should be the one. So when Lauri threatened to leave him--"

"--he went wild," Tom finished for her.

Aimee thumbed through her notes. "Are you pressuring him for a confession?"

Marie emptied her cup of coffee. "We would love it if the murderer walked in and gave us a confession, but we're not counting on it." She crumpled the cup and threw it away. "What else can you tell us?"

"We may be climbing up the wrong tree, but we have reason to believe Lauri's stepfather has come out of hiding." Marie took a deep breath and swallowed hard.

Tom's head jerked to the right. "Hiding? I thought your paper reported his death. Airplane accident, wasn't it?"

"That's correct," Rich answered. "But according to Gary, Lauri had been talking to a man who fits the stepfather's description. However, we don't know if that's really him, and even if he is, we know of no reason why he'd kill Lauri."

"Do you suppose that man at the funeral was possibly him?" Tom made a few notations in his notebook.

"You mean the one we all chased?" Rich

asked.

Tom nodded.

Rich shrugged. "I didn't get a good look at him."

"But do you think it was him?" Marie jabbed the air to emphasize the question.

"Could have been, but then that's only my opinion, not worth much."

"I'd say it's all speculation anyway, but at least it's a place to begin." Tom stood up. "We've got a couple of snitches--you do too, I'm sure. Let's talk to them and see if we can figure out if it was him, and if it wasn't, let's try to find out who he is. Is there anything else any of you can tell us? Something that will help us solve this case?"

"Gary seems to blame Karen's employers, Stockton and Teague," Aimee said.

Tom and Marie looked at each other. Tom nodded, and Aimee wasn't sure if the nod meant he knew, or if he was acknowledging the statement.

"I understand that they were out of town on the night Lauri died," Dolphine said.

Tom looked at her, then down at his notes. "Anything else?"

"Unfortunately, nothing at the moment," Aimee said.

Marie stood up and followed Tom out the door.

"Detectives," Aimee said.

They stopped and turned around.

"Was Lauri raped?"

"Oh, that reminds me." Tom picked up the envelope he had set down on Rich's desk. "Freddy at the Medical Examiner's Office gave me a copy of the coroner's report. He said he promised he'd give you a copy as soon as it was available. Seeing how it's a public document anyway, I have no problem with being the delivery boy." He handed Aimee the report. "But to answer your question, no, she wasn't raped-- at least not at any time close to her death. The report will tell you, though, that she wasn't a virgin. There was evidence of what may have been rough sex several days prior to her death."

"Evidence?"

"Old bruise marks, partly healed scratches-- that kind of thing." Marie looked away as though the thought bothered her.

Aimee closed her eyes. "Oh."

"*Oh* is right. Please, let's work together on this. Help us catch the bastard who did this to a child." Tom cleared his throat. "And one more thing, I want to remind you not to use our names as a source."

Marie nodded. "We like our jobs and we'd like to keep them."

"You have our word," Rich said.

"That's good enough for us." Wearing a grim look, Tom and Marie followed Dolphine out.

Aimee picked up the cups and threw them

away.

Rich rubbed his chin, a far-away look in his eyes.

"A penny for your thoughts," Aimee said.

Rich's gaze met Aimee's. "Something Tom mentioned just clicked. He said Lauri had rough sex several days ago--that would correspond to the time Lauri was supposedly working for the lawyers."

"You're right. Should we call the O'Days?"

"Nah." Rich shook his head. "They've got enough work to do. This is something we can check. Besides, I've got the feeling they think pursuing the lawyer angle will lead to a dead end. Let's wait until we get something concrete, then we'll give the O'Days a buzz."

"If it's a dead end, do you think we should spend our time pursuing it?"

"Of course. Basic Journalism 101: always follow every lead."

"And speaking of leads, let's look at this report." Aimee undid the clasp and skimmed through it. When she finished, she looked up at Rich. "Nothing we didn't know before. It lists a stab wound to the abdomen as the cause of death although she was also stabbed twice in the back. There were no defensive cuts or other signs of trauma. Nothing--no hair, skin, or fibers--were found under her fingernails. Toxicological results are pending." She set the report down. "I'll look at it more carefully when I have an hour or so."

"Let me know if you find anything."

"I will."

"Good. Then let's get back to work."

She turned away from Rich.

"Hey! Where are you going?"

"To my desk."

"Why? I thought you were going to verify whether Lauri's stepfather has returned. We've got to find out if that was him at the cemetery."

As Rich spoke, Aimee's mind, like a television set, played several frames. She saw a shadow. The woods. A knife dripping blood. A trail. Someone reaching for her. Darkness. Death. She stifled a scream as her hand groped for something--anything—to help steady herself. She found that the desk gave her a sense of balance. "Rich, I . . ."

"Yes?"

She would never succeed as a reporter if she let her fears rule her. "I'll get my purse and be on my way."

Rich took a step forward. "Aimee, are you okay?"

"Of course. Why wouldn't I be?" Had she spoken too soon, too fast? She flashed him a weak smile, headed for her desk, grabbed her purse, and opened the door. Rich's eyes followed her, a frown on his face. She turned and gave him the thumbs up signal.

He returned the gesture.

Dolphine and Robert did it as well.

Aimee sighed and closed the door behind her. Her hands trembled and she drew several deep breaths.

There's nothing to fear but fear itself.

She opened the car door and adjusted the rearview mirror. She closed her eyes.

There's nothing to fear.

She opened her eyes, started the engine, and drove away.

Nothing to fear.

Chapter 32

Aimee arrived at the high school before the first bell rang. She had no idea where Gary hung out, but surely some of the students could help her. She spotted a large group and made her way toward them. "Excuse me, do any of you know Gary Heely?"

"Sure! Who doesn't?" a rather plain-looking girl with a long, oval face said.

"That's Lauri's guy," another girl beamed. She said it as if Gary had won the lottery.

"Yes, that's him. Can you tell me where he is?" Aimee smiled, hoping to make them feel at ease.

"He usu--"

"Who wants to know?" The plain-looking girl interrupted her friend and stepped in front of her.

"I do." Aimee introduced herself. "I'm working on Lauri's story."

"Oh!" The girl seemed impressed. "I don't know exactly where he is, but do you see those two guys by the gym door?" She pointed to her right so fast that Aimee wasn't sure if she pointed at all.

Aimee nodded.

"They always hang out with Gary. They'd

know."

"Thanks, I'll go talk to them." She turned to leave, but stopped and faced the girls. "Did any of you know Lauri very well?"

The plain girl scrunched her face as though regretting something that only she knew. "I don't think she had any real close girlfriends. Mostly, she hung around Gary."

"What about Anyah Platt?" another girl said as she sidestepped from behind her plain girlfriend.

"She don't count."

Tell that to Anyah. "Why not?" Aimee filed the name in the Names-to-Remember compartment of her brain.

"'Cuz she moved away. She moved to South Dakota. I remember because that's right by the ocean."

"You're full of it. She moved to North Carolina." Her friend stressed the word north.

"It was neither," a third girl said who up to now had remained in the background. "I distinctly remember. She moved to one of the Virginias."

"That's right!" the plain girl said. "It was South Virginia."

Aimee tried not to smile. She knew a geography lesson would be wasted on these girls. She thanked them once again, headed toward the boys, and introduced herself.

"He's not comin' to school today," said the

first of the two boys, a youth with scraggly shoulder-length hair. "He was feeling kinda down. You know, about Lauri. So he said, 'Shit, I don't wanna go to school,' and he's not here."

"Do you have any idea where he went?"

"Probably to Emerald Bay."

Aimee took a step backward. *Emerald Bay.* She hadn't gone there since dad's accident.

Beloved Father.

"Hey, Miss, you okay? Is something wrong?"

Aimee stood still, a forced smile etched on her face. "I'm fine." Good thing she wasn't Catholic. She was getting too good at telling lies, and she would hate having to go to confession. She cleared her throat. "You were saying about Gary?"

"That him and Lauri used to go there all the time."

Aimee thanked them and headed for her car. Even before she reached it, the voices began. *Emerald Bay. Remember Emerald Bay?*

Aimee increased her pace and soon reached the Subaru. She started the engine, drove off, and turned on the radio. She changed stations. Then again. With an abrupt jerky movement, she turned it off.

She thought of the three miles that encompassed Emerald Bay, the lake's most photographed spot. Its peaceful, picturesque vistas captivated tourists from all over the world. Its emerald-colored water, which often

176

looked more like a dark turquoise color, attracted a flock of tourists each year. They found peace and comfort. The fools.

She rolled down the window and concentrated on the sweet vanilla fragrance of the area's most common tree, the Jeffrey pine. She had smelled the same scent the day her father died. She rolled the window back up.

Stark, eerie silhouettes projected in the dark corners of her mind. She saw the fiery explosion as red as an angry sun. She jerked the steering wheel to avoid the explosion before realizing it existed only in her mind. She swerved to correct her earlier mistake. A horn blasted to her right.

"Watch it, bitch!" The driver shouted as his car swept past her. He flipped her the finger. It could have been worse. He could have flipped her a rock.

Aimee pulled over, her hands trembling. She took a deep breath, followed by another. She swallowed. *Beloved Father.* She blinked away tears, took a deep breath, and felt calmer. She eased her car back into traffic.

By now she had reached Camp Richardson Resort. From here on, the road consisted of switchbacks and hairpin curves that would require her full attention.

She could do this. She would do this. She'd go to Emerald Bay and prove that it no longer harbored yesterday's ghosts.

She took each curve with care. Would the

next one lead to the horseshoe of cliffs encircling Emerald Bay? Best not to think of that. What had Mark Twain said about camp life on Lake Tahoe? That it would restore an Egyptian mummy to its pristine vigor? Yes, that was it.

She smiled at the image. Mark Twain could always do that to her.

Her smile faded.

She reached Emerald Bay and spotted Gary's car pulled off to the side of the road. She pulled in behind and momentarily stared at the turquoise water. Her hand lingered on the ignition key. Swallowing hard, she turned off the engine and stepped out.

Chapter 33

Aimee found Gary huddled in the protective shade of an incense-cedar. Its thick, shaggy red bark made him look small and insignificant.

Aimee placed her hand on his shoulder. "Gary?"

He shrugged, forcing her hand off. "Leave me alone. I didn't ask you to come."

By the way he slurred his words and by the tone in his voice, Aimee could tell that Gary had been crying or was perhaps a bit high, either on booze or drugs or both. She sat down beside him and avoided looking out toward the lake.

"Go 'way."

"Why don't you want to talk to me?"

"What for?" For the first time he looked up. His eyes, narrow slits in his face, were red. "The police think I killed Lauri."

"Did you?"

"Hell no!" He jumped up and walked away from the shore. Aimee followed him. "I loved her. Hell, you oughta know that. Why can't people believe I wouldn't hurt her?"

"You threatened to kill her."

Gary's features expanded in alarm, then relaxed. "We had a fight. Okay? That's all."

"I used to date this guy and sometimes we

179

had some very ugly fights. But he never threatened to kill me."

"Look, it was wrong. I know." He raked his hair with his fingertips. "I went out with the guys and got drunk, so Lauri got pissed off. She started yelling at me. I yelled back and one thing led to another and--" He gazed toward the lake. "I didn't mean it and she knew it."

"Was the fight about drinking?"

"It started out that way, but that wasn't the main issue."

"Then what was?"

He rubbed his lower lip as he focused on the water. "It was over her damn job."

"You didn't like her working for the lawyers?"

"It wasn't so much that." He looked straight ahead, then down at his shoes. "It's what she did for them."

"And what was that?"

"Hell if I know. She was so damn secretive-- and that's what pissed me off!"

Aimee turned, giving the water her back. "I need to ask you a personal question, and it's very important that you answer truthfully." She paused for effect. "Can you do that?"

Gary momentarily studied her. "What do you want to know?"

"When you and Lauri had sex, did--"

"We never had sex. Man, I would have loved to, but Lauri wouldn't do it. She was a virgin."

Aimee's eyes narrowed. "Are you sure? You never had sex with her?"

"Of course, I'm . . . sure." A startled, wild look came to his eyes. "Are you telling me she was raped before she was killed?"

"No, not at all. According to the medical report, she wasn't raped, but she wasn't a virgin either."

Gary's jaw stiffened, and his eyes glowed like hot coals as he examined Aimee, as though hoping she had told him a very bad joke. His face contorted spasmodically. He took off running.

Aimee ran after him but gave up the chase after a few strides. He was definitely a young shadow, as Grandma Louise had described him. She waited until he stopped before approaching him.

Breathing heavily, he leaned against a ponderosa pine, his head hanging low.

"Are you all right?" she asked.

"Do you know what I find kinda funny right now? For the first time, I agree with my parents." He wiped an angry tear away. "They hated Lauri. They said she wasn't good enough for me." He slammed the tree with his palm. "That little--"

Before he could finish the phrase, Aimee interrupted, "Why didn't your parents like her?"

"She was born poor and without the right breeding--whatever that means. So I dated Lauri just to piss them off. That was at the beginning. Then I realized that she really was a nice broad."

He waited for a few heartbeats to pass then added, "No, my parents are still full of it. She was a good girl." He seemed on the verge of tears. "If she wasn't a virgin, then I'm sure she must have been raped. I don't care what your reports say. She was raped, don't you think so?"

Maybe, maybe not. Aimee recalled that the medical report had mentioned evidence of rough sex. Had that been rape? "I don't know."

Gary's fist shook by his side. "I do 'cuz I knew Lauri better than anyone else. That guy who killed her must have raped her."

"Maybe so."

"I told you, Lauri wasn't like that. I wish I could get hold of that--" He looked up at Aimee and frowned. "--creep."

Aimee half-smiled. "I'd like to see him captured, too, so please tell me everything and don't hold anything back."

Gary flopped down on the sand, his finger forming the letter *L*. "A few days before that night--"

"The night she disappeared?"

"Yeah. Lauri came to see me. She'd been crying, and she wasn't making much sense. She said--" He stopped and blew some air through his mouth, trying to control the tears which threatened to erupt. "She said that someone was going to die, but she couldn't help her. She needed the money for her sister's operation. Then her mama would love her. She kept repeating that over and over again."

Gary formed a tight fist and shook it. "How the hell was I supposed to know she was the one who was going to die? She came to me for help, and I let her down." Tears streamed down his face, but he didn't bother to wipe them off.

"She said she couldn't help her. Are you sure those were her exact words?"

Gary nodded.

That meant the other victim was also a female. Was Aimee looking for a serial killer? She crossed her arms in front of her. "I don't think Lauri was the intended victim. I don't think she expected to die. I think she found something out, something that put her life in danger."

Gary's eyes widened. "You mean he killed her to keep her quiet?"

Aimee nodded. "Her mistake was going to him instead of the police."

"Why would she do that?"

"The money. How else could she get hold of fifty thousand dollars?"

"Blackmail?" Gary gasped. "Lauri attempted to blackmail a killer?"

"That thought crossed my mind. I need to find out who else died."

"How are you going to do that?"

"By asking questions. Let's begin with the

man with a scar on his face. Where can I find him?"

"You know that small mall in Stateline--the one with the waterfall fountain?"

"Yeah."

"Me and Lauri, we went there. Lauri went inside the bookstore. Me, I don't like books, so I went somewhere else. When I came back to join her, she was at that Mexican cafe inside the mall talking to the guy with a scar on his face. I could tell she was upset, but she didn't introduce me. She just walked away and never said nothing to me about him. She was funny that way."

"Do you know if she ever saw him after that?"

"Oh, yeah. Me and Lauri, we went back two, three, maybe four more times. She always met Scar Face at the same place."

Chapter 34

Gary leaned against a sugar pine and slowly slid down. He wrapped his arms around his knees and buried his head. He heard Aimee's car drive away.

"Lauri," he whispered, and the wind carried the sound away to the darkest corner of the lake. His entire body ached with the sense of loss and longing. Why did it have to end like this?

Someone tapped his shoulder. That damn reporter. Why couldn't she leave him alone? "I thought you left."

"Not until I get a couple of things clear," a male voice answered.

Startled, Gary looked up.

Blade put a cigarette in his mouth and wrapped his arm around a brunette with shoulder length hair. Gary recalled seeing her in the school's hallways. "Meet Jinny. Her real name is Jinetta, but I like to call her Jinny."

"Hey." Gary nodded.

She smiled.

Blade lit his cigarette, took a deep puff, and let the smoke drift out. "So what were you telling that nosy reporter?"

Gary felt a burning sensation. He stood up. "Don't sweat it, man. She's way off base."

"Meaning?"

"She's chasing this dude with a scar on his face. Lauri was with him a couple of times."

Blade fixed his eyes on Gary. "Are you shitting me?"

"No, man. That reporter is after him, and she's got Lauri's ol' lady's bosses mixed in too."

"Nothin' about us?"

Gary shook his head.

Blade's neck veins stood out and seemed to pulsate. When he spoke, his voice sounded harsh. He took out his switchblade and flipped it open. He rubbed the six inch blade on his jeans."I swear, if you're lying--"

Gary thought of walking away, but couldn't find the nerve. "Think what you want, I told you what was said."

"Okay, cool." Blade closed the knife and put it away. "We shouldn't be seen together."

"Last two times I've seen ya, you came to me."

Blade flipped the cigarette to the ground, wrapped his arm around Gary's shoulder, and started walking with him. "True, but I'm all through taking chances. That's why I brought Jinny here. That reporter starts getting wise and she figures what you did, you get word to Jinny. She knows what to do." He tightened his grasp on her. "Huh, Jinny?"

She nodded.

Blade stepped back and released both Jinny

and Gary. "Great. So all's cool?"

"Yeah," Gary mumbled.

Blade left but Jinny lagged behind.

For the first time Gary noticed the other two hoods who always followed Blade. They had been waiting for him by the shade of a large, quaking aspen.

"Gary," Jinny said after Blade had rejoined his friends. "I'm sorry about Lauri."

"Me, too."

Gary started to leave but Jinny caught up with him. "I don't want you to get the wrong idea. I'm not Blade's girl. My brother and him are tight and he knows he can trust me. I'm still footloose and free."

"That's cool." He continued to head toward his car.

Jinny walked with him. Her voice sounded small and timid. "Do me a favor?"

"What's that?"

"Call me Jinetta. I hate being called Jinny."

"Sure." Then after a slight pause, he added, "Jinetta."

She had a nice smile. They continued to walk in silence for a while. They had almost reached Gary's car when Jinetta stopped and grabbed Gary's arm. "There's something I have to know. I hope you don't mind me asking, but before I get too involved I have to know. Did you kill Lauri?"

He looked at her and walked away.

Chapter 35

Even though the café was inside the mall, the open-style seating arrangement in the atrium gave the diner the feeling of eating outside. That appealed to Aimee. She relaxed and sipped her Coke mix.

She glanced at her watch, sighed, and munched on the ice. She had spent the last two hours showing Lauri's stepfather's picture to all of the mall's employees. No one had recognized him. She pushed her drink away and reached for her purse.

Just then, someone pulled up a chair beside her. "Hi! Mind if I join you?"

Aimee looked up and saw one of Grandma Louise's sons. Burley or Earl? What was he doing here? "Earl, right?"

He nodded.

"Good to see you, but I have to go."

"I'm really thirsty, and I hate to drink alone." He tilted his head to the right and said, "Please."

Oh, for Pete's sake. "Sure, why not?" She leaned back in her chair. "What brings you here?"

Earl sat down. "Their nachos. I love them. Ever had them?"

Aimee nodded. "I've had them a couple of

times and I've always enjoyed them."

Someone's arrival interrupted them. At first Aimee thought it was the waiter, but when she looked up, she saw Burley.

"Mom said you'd be here." He nodded a hello to Aimee, then turned his attention to his brother. "Have you been to the post office yet?"

Earl shook his head. "Nope, why? Do you want me to mail something for you?"

Burley bit his lower lip. "Can we talk in private?"

"No need for secrets. What do you want from the post office?"

Burley hesitated. "Those letters you're returning to the post office, I want them. They're mine."

"Yours?" Earl retrieved the three letters from his jacket pocket. "They came to Mom's addressed to different people." He shuffled the letters in order to read the recipients' names. "They're not yours."

"Just let me have them." Burley extended his hand.

Earl's eyebrows came together.

"Give them to me." Burley ran his fingers through his hair. "They're mine."

Earl handed them to his brother.

Burley stuffed them in his pocket. "Thank you." He turned to Aimee. "It's good seeing you again." He forced a smile and left.

Earl's gaze followed him out. "I could've

sworn that yesterday he received a letter addressed to Allan something-or-the-other. Now it's Phillip and Jacob and who knows who else. What's going on?"

Aimee cocked her head. "I don't know, but I sure would like to find out."

"Yeah, me too, but I don't have time to worry about him. I've got to think of Mom."

"How's she doing?"

"Mom's fine, or as fine as she'll ever be." He placed his elbows on the table and leaned his head on his hand. "One minute she's perfectly normal. The next, she's raving about things which don't make one bit of sense."

The waitress came, and Earl asked for two Cokes and a large order of nachos with no jalapenos.

She looked at Aimee. "Just a Coke? Not a mix?"

Aimee smiled. "Make it a mix."

She wrote the order and left. Earl's eyebrows pinched together. "What was all that about?"

"Nothing important--just my choice of drinks."

Earl nodded. "I see," but it was obvious he didn't.

"How's your Mom?"

Earl frowned and the lines that formed on the side of his eyes gave him an air of sophistication. He continued, "I'm beginning to think that for her own safety, I might have to put her in a nursing home."

"I'm sorry to hear that. I didn't know it was that bad."

Earl released a breath with an audible sigh. "Well, it is."

"Are you considering any particular nursing home?"

Earl shook his head. "Not really. I can't bring myself to do it. If I did put her in one of those, it'll kill her. I'm thinking maybe I should move back into the area. I could hire a full-time nurse to take care of her, and I'll be able to be near her."

"I didn't know you weren't a local."

"My brother and I were born and raised in Truckee."

A little bell rang inside Aimee's head. Burley had aliases and he was from Truckee. She would follow up on this. Rich would like that. She could tell Rich that she had finally started working on the Truckee Mystery. "Truckee?"

"Yeah, Truckee. Burley's got some kind of business over there and he visits Truckee quite often."

"What about you? Where do you live?"

"In El Paso, Texas, but not for long." The waitress brought them their drinks. After she left, Earl continued, "But enough about me. Tell me all about you."

"What do you want to know?"

"I want to know what makes Aimee Brent

tick."

"Writing makes me tick," she told him without hesitating, and then she proceeded to talk about her dream and how she wished to work for a big-time newspaper. Their nachos arrived and they ate as they made small talk.

Aimee glanced at her watch. It read 12:33. Startled, she jumped out of her chair. "I've got to go. I didn't realize it was so late. I'm supposed to be working."

Earl also stood. "It's almost lunch time. How about joining me?"

"Oh, no, I think I've already used more than my lunch hour."

"Dinner, then?"

Aimee hesitated. She would like to talk to him about Burley's Truckee connection, but she didn't want to raise Burley's or Earl's suspicions. A nice, leisurely meal would be just what she needed.

"I'll wait until whatever time you get off." Earl's tone begged her to accept. "Please, Aimee, I need to talk to you about Mom. You seem to understand. I need to hear your advice. What do you say?"

"Sure. It sounds nice."

"May I pick you up at six?"

Aimee shook her head. "Too early. I need to get some work done at the office. Make it seven, at home. I'm in the phone book."

"Seven it is. At your house." He smiled and

walked away.

"Yeah, seven," Aimee said. That meant she had less than seven hours to find Lauri's stepfather. The restaurant's cook for the next shift should be in by now. She'd begin with him.

She bypassed the waitress and headed toward the kitchen. The aroma of cooking oil attacked her nostrils. She found the cook frying tortillas. "Hi," she said. "I'm Aimee Brent, a reporter for the *South Shore Carrier*. Do you know this man?" She shoved a picture of Lauri's stepfather in front of the cook.

He glanced at the picture. "Should I?"

"I would hope you do. I'm trying to find him."

"Then keep trying. I've never seen him before." Some of the grease splattered and landed on his hand. He jerked it back, mumbled something, covered the burns with butter, and gently blew on the burns.

"Are you okay?"

He shrugged. "Happens all the time. I'm used to it."

Aimee put the picture away. "Thanks anyway," she said, but by now the cook had turned his attention to the tortillas.

What now? She could spend the rest of the day talking to people and passing the picture around, but so far, that tactic had only produced one dinner date--if it could be called a date. What she needed--

She stopped. Mother Luck arrived. Not ten feet away from her, she recognized the old, gnarled man with earth-brown skin. The Navajo headed up the stairs. "Jose," she called out. Just the person she needed to see.

For a second he hesitated, and then continued the climb. Aimee ran to catch up with him. He wore a checkered shirt and faded blue jeans. His predominantly white hair was pulled back over his ears in the traditional bun. As always, he wore his Navajo hat.

"Where are you going in such a hurry?" Aimee didn't offer to shake his hand because she knew that like many Navajos, he felt uncomfortable with this white man's tradition.

He turned and looked at her. The faintest of smiles formed on his lips. "Upstairs."

Aimee glanced up. "There's not much up there."

"There's not much down here either." He moved his arms in a sweeping motion.

Aimee looked around the small mall and smiled. "What's the matter?"

"Nothing with me. I'm just going up the stairs for exercise. What about you, little lady? What is it that you want this time?"

"My feelings are hurt." Aimee wrinkled her nose. "What would make you think I want anything at all?"

"You're a reporter." He continued going up the stairs. Aimee followed him. "Reporters always want something or are looking for somebody. So which one is it?"

They reached the top of the stairs and Aimee held back to see what Jose would do. Without hesitating, he turned around and began to head back down. She took out the picture and showed it to him.

He barely glanced at it. "Don't know. I'm an old man now. My memory isn't what it used to be."

Aimee had expected that answer. She knew how he operated. She opened her purse and took out a ten-dollar bill. She held it up, just above his grasp.

"Of course I might have seen him." He stopped and scratched his chin. His eyes never left the bill.

"Where might you have seen him?" She handed him the money.

He plucked it out with the speed of an animal eating out of the hand of someone he didn't quite trust. "I can do one better. I can tell you exactly where he lives."

Fantastic! All that waiting around had paid off. And who said being stubborn was bad? "Oh? Where's that?"

"Let's see." He scratched his chin. "My directions seem to get all confused."

Dang it! She hadn't been casual enough. She retrieved another ten dollar bill from her wallet and held onto it. "Where is he?"

"He's got a small motor home, and he parks it in the woods above Emerald Bay on the other side of the road."

Emerald Bay. Aimee brought her hand up and covered her mouth. She saw Jose looking at her through narrow eyes. She lowered her hand. "Could you be a bit more specific?"

"You know that dirt road almost directly in front of the bay?"

Aimee stood frozen, her eyes quickly blinking. She breathed hard and through her mouth.

Jose took a step toward her. "What's wrong?"

"My mom--the man with the devil eyes killed her!" She blurted out the answer before she realized what she said.

"What man? What are you talking about?"

"That man--the one with the devil eyes." Didn't Jose understand? Why didn't he help her?

"Lady, I have no idea what you're talking about."

Help her. Help me!

One horrid detail after another flashed in Aimee's mind. The knife dripping blood. The man with the devil eyes stabbing Mommy over and over.

The blood.

The knife.

The devil eyes following her. Haunting her. Forever.

She wanted to scream. Instead, she

whimpered.

Jose tried to touch her, but Aimee pushed him away. She had to escape. Run. Run as fast as she could. She ran back up the stairs and looked around.

She was in the mall.

Not the woods.

Her entire body shook. "Oh God!" She covered her face with her hands.

By now Jose stood next to her. "Aimee?"

"That bastard killed my mother!" *Beloved Mother*. If only Aimee could breathe.

"Who? What are you talking about?" His face remained impassive, but the eyebrows knit.

She focused on the old man. What had happened? His wide and alert eyes told Aimee she had frightened him. She took several deep breaths. "Jose, I'm sorry. I just remembered something that happened a long, long time ago."

"You gave me a fright." His normally brown skin had turned the color of a vanilla shake. "What brought that on?"

"When you mentioned that road, it was the same one we took when--" So that's why I fear Emerald Bay. I thought it was because my father had died close to there. But it was Mom's death I was remembering. It's always been Mom-- *beloved Mom*.

Jose rubbed his arms as though warding off some evil. "You're trying to say that some guy killed your mom up there?"

Aimee nodded.

He licked his lips. "While you were watching?"

"Look, if you don't mind, I don't want--"

"When did this happen anyway?"

"A long time ago. I was only seven. This man appeared out of nowhere, and he had a knife and--" Aimee cleared her throat. She could still see the knife dripping blood. And the eyes--the same devil eyes of her nightmare.

"Did they catch him?"

Aimee remained quiet, her head hanging low. "No."

"Why not? Didn't you see him? Couldn't you identify him?"

Aimee shook her head. All she could remember were the devil eyes. Why couldn't she remember more? Aimee swallowed hard and pushed the memory aside. Later, she could focus on this new development. Now, she had other business to tend to. She tried to breathe deeply. "You mentioned the dirt road, Jose. What about that road?"

"What about the man you're talking about?"

"Forget it. Tell me about that road."

"Not much to say about that road, except that he's dry camping about a mile in or maybe less. You'll see the motor home there."

"Dry camping?"

"Yeah, using the motor home without any plug-ins. No electricity, water, sewer. That sort of thing."

"I see." Aimee handed him the ten that she still clutched in her hand. "What else can you tell me about him?"

"Nothing else."

Aimee opened her purse.

"Forget it, little lady. I'd love another ten, but anything else I'd tell you would be a lie. Only reason I know what I do is because it seems mighty strange to me that someone like him would be living like that above the lake."

Chapter 36

The scenery between the mall and Aimee's house fused together until it became a constant blur. Quaint cafés, casinos, the various lake views, residences, and businesses all blended together until Aimee couldn't tell one from the other.

Tears pearled in Aimee's eyes. She let out a long sigh and the tears streamed down her cheeks.

Time had erased her mother's features from her memory.

Beloved Mother.

Aimee massaged her temple and looked through the rearview mirror. Seeing no cars, she made an illegal U-turn, heading away from home and toward Aunt Rachel and Uncle Ray's home. They had raised her. They had answers.

She stepped on the gas pedal and drove above the speed limit, reaching her aunt's house in record time. Once there, she sat in the car, stared at nothing, and tried to remember the drive. Part of her knew she should be concerned, but she had reached her destination. That was the important part. The hard part.

The rest would be easy, like having her teeth drilled.

She swung the car door open. Even before she got out, she spotted Aunt Rachel standing at the doorway. Her short, brown hair clung to her head as though she had just gotten up. She wore faded jeans and a pale yellow oversized T-shirt that read "Lake Tahoe, Lake of the Sky."

She held her hands together at her chin as she watched Aimee approach. "Oh my God, you're here. You're here. You actually came to visit."

Guilt and regret settled in Aimee's heart. Aunt Rachel lived about a thirty-minute drive from her, depending on traffic conditions. Yet, Aimee hardly ever went to visit her. It's not that Aimee didn't want to see her aunt. She was always too busy with her work, or her writing, or her projects. Oh yes, she was much too busy doing important things like watching the clock tick the minutes away. She needed a lesson on what's really important.

Aunt Rachel met her half way up the driveway and threw her arms around her.

Warmth and comfort engulfed Aimee. "Hi, Aunt Rachel. It's so good to see you." Aimee promised herself that she wouldn't allow so much time to lapse between visits. "It's been a while."

"And whose fault is that?" With her arm wrapped around Aimee's shoulder, she led her inside her house. "Here, sit. Sit. Make yourself comfortable." She pointed to the brown couch covered with fluffy throw pillows depicting snow scenes. Aimee sat down and Rachel sat beside her, an awkward silence spreading between the two. "Is it John again?"

Aimee shook her head. "That's over, and I really don't miss him at all."

"God made kitchens for talking." Aunt Rachel stood up and as though Aimee were still a little girl, she grabbed her niece's hand and led her into the kitchen. "Care for something to drink?" Even before she answered, Aunt Rachel had already reached for the glasses.

Aimee nodded.

Aunt Rachel filled the glasses with ice. "I'll fix your infamous mixed drink. It's so reassuring to know that some things don't change."

Aimee attempted a smile.

Her aunt watched her with eyes that seemed to miss little. "When you're ready to talk, I'm here to listen." She poured the sodas. "I've been reading your articles about poor Lauri. How's that murder investigation going?"

Aimee shrugged. "Complicated. Wish I could solve it now."

Aunt Rachel set the glasses on the dinette table. "Is that what's bothering you?"

Aimee shook her head and reached for her drink, not so much because she felt thirsty, but because it gave her something to do.

"Tell me what project you're working on now," Aunt Rachel said.

"I can't seem to grow real flowers."

"That's nothing new."

Aimee smiled and took a sip. "So I'm making paper ones."

"Different colors? Different shapes? Different sizes?" Aunt Rachel's eyes sparkled with anticipation.

Aimee nodded and drank her soda.

"Then I want a bunch to brighten my place."

Aimee could always count on Aunt Rachel to say the right thing. "I'll make some extra beautiful bouquets just for you."

Aunt Rachel wrapped her hand around her niece's. "I'll look forward to receiving them."

Aimee nodded and looked around. "Is Uncle Ray here?"

"Nah, and he's going to be real sorry he missed you. He was asking about you the other day." She squeezed Aimee's hands and released them. "He's out of town. Won't be back until tomorrow."

"I'm sorry I missed him. I wanted to talk to you both." With her free hand, Aimee played with the rim of the glass, willing herself to stay calm. She swallowed hard and breathed slowly. Might as well get it out. "When I was little, I used to have nightmares."

Aunt Rachel closed her eyes and let out a long-drawn sigh. "Oh God, no, Aimee. Don't tell me they've returned."

"Tell me about them."

Aunt Rachel smiled, but it came out looking forced. "What can I say? They were just nightmares. All children have them."

"What were my nightmares about? Monsters and witches?"

Aunt Rachel reached for her drink and swallowed very slowly. For a long second, she studied Aimee. She looked away. "Wellll. . ." She set the glass down and stared at it. "Not exactly."

"Then what?"

Her aunt remained quiet.

"Let me help. Maybe I dreamt of devil eyes and a knife dripping blood."

Aunt Rachel rubbed the bridge of her nose. When she opened her eyes, Aimee read the pain in her face. "When did the nightmares return?"

"So we're talking about the same nightmare."

Aunt Rachel looked down at the beige carpet. Aimee wondered if the answer lay there. "Probably."

"How old was I?"

"Seven."

"Tell me about my nightmares."

"You had them for almost a year after you came home from the hospital. Each time I would run to your room and comfort you."

"Why was I in the hospital?"

Aunt Rachel continued to stare at the carpet. "You know why."

"I know what I've been told, and I know what gossip says. Now I want to hear it from you."

Aunt Rachel took a deep breath and began, "Annie took you on a picnic up in the mountains." Her soft voice came barely above a whisper. "It had been raining and the road must have been slippery. There was an accident. You were in the hospital for six months. Annie wasn't as fortunate."

"If a car accident killed my mother, then why do I have nightmares? What's the connection?"

Aunt Rachel switched her gaze from the Aimee's face to her hands, which rested on her lap. "Maybe there's no connection."

No more lies. She had come to learn the truth. "Can you repeat the same story, but this time, look me in the eyes?"

Aunt Rachel gasped and covered her mouth. Centuries later, her gaze met Aimee's. "What are you saying?"

"I remembered."

Aunt Rachel scooted her chair next to Aimee's. She wrapped her arm around her. "Tell me what you remembered."

* * *

Mommy and she had just finished exploring the woods and were emptying the picnic box when someone arrived.

Mommy looked over Aimee's shoulder and gasped.

Aimee froze.

She wanted to see what scared Mommy, but fear caused her to lock her gaze on Mommy's face. The sounds of crushed leaves and twigs in the intruder's wake magnified themselves.

Mommy screamed.

Aimee turned and stared at the man's eyes. They seemed to float away from his face and move toward her. The eyes grew in intensity as they focused on her. These eyes were huge.

Cold.

Harsh.

And still they moved forward, closer to her. If she reached out, she could touch them.

Any minute now, they would embrace her and drag her to a bottomless black pit of forever.

The sky opened and a powerful lightning bolt lit the area. Then she saw it. The knife, covered with blood.

The eyes laughed. Aimee screamed. The eyes burned with hatred, mocking her terror. Mommy was dead.

"Oh God! No, no! No!" Aimee sobbed. "Mommy!" she cried.

* * *

Warm arms reached for her.

Beloved Mother.

"Mommy?" The arms held her. Comforted her.

A gentle voice said, "You're safe." The gentle arms continued to hold her close. Whose arms?

Aimee searched her surroundings for

anything familiar. She was . . . sitting in Aunt Rachel's warm kitchen, not out in the woods. Aunt Rachel sat next to her. Not Mommy. Not ever again. Aimee raised her head and blinked several times. She wouldn't cry.

She wouldn't.

Aunt Rachel wrapped her arms around her, held her like she had done so many years ago.

Aimee's head rested in the comfort of her aunt's shoulder. "Why didn't you tell me the truth? Why did you lie to me?"

Her aunt's body stiffened. "I'm sorry, Sweet Aimee, I had to. For your own sake."

Aimee pulled away from the embrace. "I don't understand." She noticed Aunt Rachel's cheeks streaked with tears.

Her aunt took a deep breath. "There were no witnesses to what actually happened, but this is what the police think." Her words came out sounding sharp, betraying her pain. "After this man . . . killed our precious Annie . . . he, uh, went after you. You ran. Somehow, you found the dirt road. He got in his car and chased you some more . . . He, uh—" She stopped and cleared her throat. "He ran you over. He must have assumed you were dead. He took off." Tears swam in her eyes. "You almost didn't make it. You were in the hospital for six months. Five of those were spent in a coma. When you woke up, you had forgotten everything that happened that day."

"Almost everything." Aimee had always remembered the devil eyes.

"Yes, almost everything. The nightmares followed. For several months, they came daily, and after that, they only came once or twice a week, then monthly until they finally disappeared. You were seeing a doctor then. We followed his instructions. He seemed to be helping you."

"I remember him--Dr. Paul Keller. Short, black hair with glasses."

Her aunt nodded. "You were so traumatized that we thought it best to give you some time to adjust. Then, slowly, we could start piecing the puzzle together. But you repressed the memory, and no matter what Dr. Keller tried, you wouldn't remember. He said not to worry, that in time you'd probably recall every little detail."

"He was right."

Aunt Rachel wrapped her hands around Aimee's. "Oh Sweet Aimee, I'm so glad you remembered. I hated not telling you the truth!"

In the safety of her aunt's house, Aimee began to feel warm and comfortable, like she had as a child. She opened her mouth to tell her aunt that, but changed her mind. Something in her aunt's eyes whispered of yet further doubts. "What's wrong?"

Aunt Rachel shifted positions. "I hate to ask you this, but I have to. Annie's death--it's still unsolved. We're sure you saw the . . . man. Can you identify him?" She bit her lip, waiting for the answer.

Aimee closed her eyes and saw the hand holding the knife. Then the eyes--the devil eyes. Always the devil eyes. The man had no face. Slowly, she shook her head. She wanted to remember. The bastard was out there somewhere enjoying life while her mother lay dead. Why couldn't she remember his face?

"No, I can't." She recognized the anguish in her own voice. "I can't remember what he looks like, but give me time. I swear I'll remember." *Please, dear God, help me remember.* "Now that I know the truth, I'll get hold of the news reports and police records that deal with Mom's murder. Maybe some fact in there will trigger my memory." Aimee wrapped her hands around her aunt's. "I promise, Aunt Rachel, I will avenge my mother's death."

Beloved Mother.

Chapter 37

When Aimee pulled into the driveway, she saw Dolphine sitting in her car, waiting for her. Aimee turned off the engine. Dolphine bolted out of her car. "Soon as you called, I knew something was wrong. What's going on?" Dolphine's forehead creased with concern.

Aimee led her inside the house and both flopped down on the couch. "Remember I told you about my nightmares?"

"Don't tell me they're back."

"It's worse than that. They weren't nightmares. They were memories."

Dolphine opened her mouth but nothing came out.

Aimee told her what had happened. "The worst part is not remembering what this--this monster--looks like. He's out there somewhere enjoying life, and my mom is . . . dead."

Dolphine hugged her. "What can I do to help?"

Aimee laid her head on her friend's shoulder and cried. She cried for her mom and for her inability to bring her justice. She cried for lost time. She cried because her heart ached.

Dolphine held her tighter and stroked her hair until Aimee's tears turned to sobs. Still she rested her head on her friend's shoulder. "I want . . . to remember, but I don't know how."

"We'll take it one step at a time."

Aimee straightened up. "We?"

"You're not alone in this." Dolphine flashed a reassuring smile. "We'll start rebuilding your past, one step at a time. Maybe something will trigger a memory."

Aimee sat, her hands neatly folded on her lap. She'll remember. She would remember.

"Aimee?"

Aimee stared at the brown carpet under her feet, the same color as dirt. The dirt that separated her from her mom. A tear rolled down her cheek.

"Aimee?"

Aimee's glance slowly traveled to her friend's face. There, she found love and compassion. But that wasn't enough. She stood up. "You're right. I need to take this one step at a time. I'll begin with the police station. There's got to be records about my mom's death."

"The newspaper, too. I can print out the newspaper stories and put them on your desk." Dolphine stood up. "Want me to go with you to the police station?"

Aimee shook her head. "Thanks, but no. I need to be alone on this. I can focus better."

"I understand." Dolphine reached for Aimee's hands. "You'll be okay?"

"You bet." She tried to smile but it faded like

a wilted flower.

"Promise me you'll call if you need anything?"

"You bet." They looked at each other and hugged. "Thanks. I know I can always count on you."

Dolphine nodded, raised her eyebrows, and cocked her head.

Aimee knew what she was about to say.

Dolphine took a deep breath. "You bet."

They giggled and Dolphine headed out.

Aimee stood by the window, watching her best friend drive away, leaving her only with one memory: *Beloved Mother.*

Chapter 38

"You sure you want to see this file?" Detective Tom O'Day held the box that contained all the information involving Ann Brent's murder. "After you called requesting this file, Marie and I took the time to acquaint ourselves with this case. I'll have to warn you. It contains some disturbing pictures."

"I know."

Three desks away from Tom's desk, Marie half sat, half leaned against the front lip of her desk. She folded her arms and focused her attention on the discussion at her husband's desk. Tom caught her eye and signaled for her to join them.

She pulled up a chair and sat. "I want you to know that even though we never solved that case, it's still active."

Aimee nodded.

Tom's eyes narrowed, pleading with his wife. "Help me here. Aimee wants to look at the contents of this box." Tom pointed to the evidence box on top of his desk.

"It's her mom. She's got a right."

Tom threw his arms up in the air.

Marie leaned over and held Aimee's hands. "We want to make sure you know that the pictures and reports in there aren't sugar-coated."

"Thank you. I understand that."

Tom frowned. "And you still want to do it?"

Aimee nodded and pulled her hands away from Marie's grasp.

"Okay, but only if you're sure."

"I am."

Tom looked around the police station for a private place for Aimee to go through the box. Marie stood up. "Follow me."

Tom grabbed the box and followed Aimee and Marie down a long corridor. Marie opened the door at the end of the hall. "This interrogation room has no one-way mirrors like the ones you usually see on TV." She pointed to the camera mounted in the corner of the wall. "That's what we use instead." She reached up and turned it so it wouldn't focus on Aimee. "You have full privacy."

"Thanks."

Tom set the box down on the plain wooden table with one chair on one side and the other three facing that first one. "I'm out of here." He gently closed the door behind him.

"He's feeling bad for you." Marie's lips trembled, as though she were trying to smile, but forgot how.

"He shouldn't. I'm a big girl."

"We know that, but if you need anything, we're just right down the hall. Take all the time you want." Marie let herself out, leaving Aimee alone with the box.

Aimee stared at the closed box. Her breathing came in short, loud gasps. She massaged her temples, took a deep breath and a small step toward the box. Her hand trembled as she reached for the box's lid.

She opened it.

Two files. One with reports, the other with pictures. Neither was thick. Her mom's life had come to this. Two skinny files. Tears pearled at the corners of her eyes.

Beloved Mother.

She read the reports first. Then re-read them when she realized the words made no sense.

A tourist--Clara Aguero, now deceased--had come across the body in the woods above Emerald Bay.

The body. Like an object, not a once living, breathing person. *The body.* Her Beloved Mother.

These were the same woods where supposedly Lauri's stepfather dry camped in his camper. She wet her lips and turned her attention to the papers she held in her hands. Ann Brent had suffered multiple stab wounds. She had dragged herself fifty-two feet before she surrendered to death. Her right arm stretched out, as if trying to reach for something.

Aimee set the report down. In her mind, she could feel her mother's anguish. She took a deep breath and continued to read. She read the autopsy reports, the toxicological results, the coroner's report. She read every file, every word, three times. But nothing came to her. Not one flash, not one memory. They had scurried to the back of her mind, taking all secrets with them.

Aimee closed the file and returned it to the box. She reached for the second file, the one with the pictures. She hesitated. *Look at them.*

She opened the file and gasped. The eight by ten glossy showed her mother as Clara Aguero had found her. A puddle of blood by her body. The blood seeping out of her still fresh wounds. Her arm outstretched, reaching. *What were you reaching for, Mama?*

Then, *where was I? Why didn't I help you?*

Aimee forced her sight away from the picture. She studied the rest, each picture bringing tears to her eyes. Still, she continued until she had seen it all.

Aimee returned the files to the box. She waited a few minutes, hoping the time would ease the anguish from her mind. She worried her lip and stepped out.

"You okay?" Marie leaned against the wall as she waited for Aimee to approach.

"Probably not, but I'll be fine."

Tom joined them. "Anything we can do for you?"

"You've both done enough. Thank you. I know it's a lot to ask, but when you have a moment to spare, I'd appreciate it if you devote some time to this case."

Tom nodded. "You got it."

Aimee walked down the corridor she thought would never end and finally out the door. Somehow, she reached her car, opened it, and sat behind the steering wheel.

She knew what she had to do. Drive off and head for the woods above Emerald Bay.

Lauri's stepfather waited for her there.

And maybe even the truth about her mother's death.

Chapter 39

Aimee sat in her car, her hands trembling, her body shaking. I will remember.

I will.

She looked and saw Tom and Marie standing outside the police station, studying her.

She flashed them a timid smile and waved.

Tom waved back. Marie didn't. She gave her the thumbs up signal instead.

Aimee turned on the engine, her hand lingering on the key. The gauge in the dashboard told her the tank was empty. She drove off, pushing all memories of her mother aside.

The first gasoline pumps she encountered were on a convenience store's parking lot. She pulled in, but remained in the car, forcing herself to calm down. When she felt she could handle the world again, she got out and began to pump the gasoline.

The men on the other side of the isle talked in subdued voices. Aimee glanced their way and recognized Burley. He and the two men with him focused their attention on the paper Burley held in his hands.

She approached them. "Hi."

Burley looked up and slid the paper behind

his back, like a naughty child caught looking at his father's *Playboy.* "Aimee, hi. Gee, I hardly ever see you and I've seen you twice today."

"Count your blessings."

Burley laughed, reminding Aimee of Earl's good nature. Amazing how these two looked alike.

Burley pointed to his friends. "This is Andy and this is Lloyd. Guys, this is Aimee Brent, the reporter."

Andy averted his eyes and nodded. Lloyd smiled nervously and whispered a timid, "Hi." He looked at Andy. "Let's get some snacks."

Andy looked at the convenience store and back at Aimee. "Ah, sure," he said. "Excuse us, Ms. Brent." They walked away.

"Did I interrupt something important?" Aimee asked Burley.

"No, of course not." He threw the papers he held through the passenger's window.

Aimee glanced at them and saw a list of cities with Andy's, Lloyd's, or Burley's names next to the cities' names.

Burley followed her gaze. He inched over so that he stood in front of the open window, blocking Aimee's view. "Nice day today, isn't?"

"Yes, definitely nice." She looked at the gas pump. "I've already filled up my car, so I better go pay and move out of the way. But before I go, I wanted you to know that Earl and I will be having dinner tonight. I thought you would like to join us."

Burley's eyes twinkled. "It's very nice of you to invite me along, but if you don't mind, I'll take a rain check. Me and the guys, we've got some details to work out."

I bet you do. Aimee nodded. She had hoped to talk to both of them. "Sure, another time. It was nice seeing you again."

"Same here."

Chapter 40

For the next forty-five minutes, Aimee drove at a steady sixty miles an hour. Soon she'd reach Camp Richardson Resort. Once there, the road leading to Emerald Bay would begin with its many twists and turns, and she'd have to ease off the gas pedal, but not yet.

She looked at her speedometer. When had she slowed down to forty? Her nerves must be dictating her speed. They bound tight, as if ready to explode. She looked down again. The speedometer needle had dropped lower. At this rate, if she climbed on a turtle's back, she'd get there faster.

She shook her head and forced her foot to step on the gas. Go faster. Why not? After all, she hadn't seen any cars in quite a while. The road was in perfect condition, and she still had several miles to travel. Then why was she slowing again?

Because that's where that psycho is. Out there in the woods. Above the lake. He killed Mama, and left me with those haunting words: Beloved Mother.

Like a door slamming, her mind shut down, blocking the blossoming of further memories. Why? What had happened that day that made her, almost two decades later, still unable to remember?

She looked up toward the darkening sky. If she wanted to reach the forest before the rain arrived, she'd better hurry. Again, she ordered her foot to push down on the gas pedal, but it seemed to have a mind of its own. It refused to obey.

She was being careful, she told herself, because of the hairpin turns. A quote from Shakespeare popped into her mind, "This above all. To thy own self be true."

Frustration ate at Aimee's insides. She sighed, pulled off the road, and stopped the car. Only half a mile to go. She rolled down the window and took several quick breaths through her mouth. The fresh air invigorated her, calmed her. She could think logically now. She knew she should continue. Giving up was a sign of weakness, something she didn't want to possess. She had to be strong. For Mama's sake.

Aimee's hand rested on the ignition keys. Mama wouldn't want her to be foolish. After all, Aimee didn't know what she would encounter in the woods. There was safety in numbers. She started the engine, turned the car around, and drove back to the newspaper office. She'd be back, but she'd bring Dolphine or Rich with her.

Chapter 41

Rich greeted Aimee at the door. "Hi." He flashed a smile that covered his face, ear to ear.

Aimee's worries peeled away. "Hi." God! Couldn't she think of something cleverer to say? Some of her hair fell and covered an eye. She tossed her hair back with a shake of her head.

For a while, Rich didn't move. Aimee looked up and saw him staring at her, his eyes filled with tenderness. "You did it again."

"What?"

"You shook your head in that special way of yours." He gave her a small smile and looked away.

Aimee wished she had a snappy reply so she could ease his embarrassment. Instead, her thoughts strayed back to the woods that hid the killer's identity. She wrapped her arms around herself to keep from shaking.

A worry frown formed in Rich's forehead. "What's wrong?"

Aimee looked around. No one paid attention to them, but still the newspaper office didn't seem to be the appropriate place to open her soul. Later on, when they were alone, she would tell him.

"Aimee?"

223

She realized she hadn't answered him. "I'm having a horrible day."

"Oh?"

"I'll explain later." She recognized the don't-you-trust-me-enough-to-tell-me look he gave her. In a way, that helped her calm down. In spite of the turmoil brooding inside her, she knew Rich would help her work her problem out. Before he could pursue the topic, she changed it. "How about you? How's your day coming?"

"So far so good. I found some information I think you'll want. But I'm not sure if any of this stuff is related to Lauri's murder."

"Let's hear it." Aimee followed him into the war room, an eight-by-ten foot area. A large wooden table with twelve chairs was the only item in the room. A long time ago, someone had named it the War Room because this was the place where assignments were made and discussed. By the time the meetings ended, Rich had made sure all angles of the main stories were covered.

Aimee sat down and Rich sat beside her. "Shoot," she said.

"Do you remember Scott Kula?"

"The name sounds very familiar, but I can't quite place it."

"A while back one of the casino card dealers got caught stacking chips."

"Stacking chips?"

"That's where the top chip in a stack is good and the ones underneath are fake."

Aimee nodded and Rich continued, "When he saw the security people heading toward him, he knew he'd been caught."

Aimee recalled reading the articles. The drama had fascinated her and slowly the details came back to her. "I remember now. He got so furious that he reached for a player's drink. He meant to throw the glass at the security guard, but instead it slipped out of his hand and shattered when it hit the table."

"Right. Do you remember what happened after that?"

Aimee thought for a few seconds, recalling the events in chronological order. "Of course. Someone got hurt. Right?"

"That was Scott Kula. When the glass broke and splattered, one of the pieces of glass lodged itself in Kula's eye."

"And Kula is suing the casino for big bucks." Aimee took out her pocket notebook and reached for a pen. She wrote Scott Kula's name. "What does all this have to do with Lauri?"

Rich spread his hands out and shrugged. "A lot or maybe nothing. Tell me what you think. Guess who's defending the casino?"

"It's got to be Mr. Stockton or Mr. Teague, but I still don't see the connection."

"What if I told you that there's a certain Nevada senator who is sponsoring a bill that will put a limit on the recoveries in personal injury cases?"

"Let me guess." Aimee wrinkled her face, pretending to concentrate hard. "Hmmm . . . Let me see now. Could it possibly be the infamous Senator Nye?"

"The one and only."

"Interesting." Aimee wrote this information down. "It looks like maybe our senator is helping our two lawyers. What do you think?"

"I agree." Rich pulled out a small spiral notebook from his shirt pocket. He opened it to a list and handed it to Aimee. "Especially when we see that the senator has steered a lot of business toward our lawyers. Look at that list. Our illustrious senator referred fifteen out of those eighteen people."

"How do you know?"

"I did some snooping. Talked to some attorney friends and they told me that Senator Nye always sends people to Stockton and Teague--never to them. The more powerful or influential the client, the more likely he'll end up with Teague or Stockton."

Aimee examined the list. Most of those clients she recognized as being high-society people. All very wealthy. She handed him back his notebook.

Rich closed it and returned it to his shirt pocket. "There have been other political favors."

"So there's no doubt. These two lawyers and

Senator Nye are tight. I wonder why."

Rich leaned forward, obviously engrossed in the conversation. "My question too. Let's play the Suppose Game."

Aimee looked away, thinking. "Suppose," she said slowly, "that our lawyers have something on the senator."

"And suppose Lauri knew about it."

Aimee snapped her fingers. "That's why the lawyers would hire her--to keep her quiet."

"But suppose Lauri got greedy."

Aimee thumbed through her pocket notebook and stopped when she found the information she was looking for. "It says here that Lauri was hoping to get hold of fifty thousand dollars."

"Blackmail money?"

"Suppose it was."

"It could have led to her death. But the question is, who had her killed? The lawyers or the senator?"

Aimee's mouth suddenly felt dry. "Either way, we're dealing with heavy stuff."

Both fell silent, then Rich said, "If our thinking is right, then where does Lauri's step-father fit into this?"

"I'll find out soon." Aimee's voice sounded small, even to her own ears. She cleared her throat and felt, more than saw, Rich's eyes scrutinizing her.

"You found him, didn't you?"

"I might have, but I haven't followed through, yet. You see, he's--"

Robert stepped into the War Room. "Hope I'm not interrupting anything important, but Rich, are you ready?" He pointed to his watch. "We're going to be late. Let's get going." He glanced at Aimee. "Hey, there," he said as he straightened his tie.

"Hey, yourself," she answered. "Why the tie? What's going on?"

Rich stood up. "Haven't you heard? Warner is handing out the awards for photo-journalism and Robert's basketball picture has been nominated."

Smiling, Aimee turned to Robert. "Congratulations! I'm proud of you."

"Me, too." Dolphine joined the group. She leaned close to Aimee. "Are you all right?"

She nodded.

"I invited Dolphine to be my date and she agreed." Robert radiated with happiness. "We're even taking the day off tomorrow to celebrate."

Aimee and Dolphine exchanged glances. Dolphine's eyes twinkled. Dolphine and Robert. Who'd imagine? When had this happened? Aimee felt happy for her friend.

Robert looked at his watch. "We better hurry if we expect to find good seats. He wrapped his arm around Dolphine and turned to Rich. "Are you ready?"

"Sure am." Rich headed his way. At the

doorway, he stopped and turned around. "You follow up on that lead, you hear?"

"Only if you come with me."

"When?" He glanced at Robert who paused just outside the door.

"Tomorrow."

"Sorry, Aimee, I would love to but I can't. The governor is going to be in town tomorrow to dedicate the new hospital wing. I have an exclusive interview with him. But don't let me hold you up. You follow through, and if it's him, we'll go to the police. Then we'll go have dinner to celebrate."

"Rich, I--"

He didn't wait for her to finish. He was already halfway out the door. "I'll call you tonight so we can finish discussing this." He closed the door behind him.

She stared at the door.

Both Dolphine and Rich would be busy tomorrow. She knew she couldn't face the woods alone. Yet if she didn't follow through, she'd be failing as a journalist. She dreamed of being a Pulitzer Prize winning reporter. This was the first important assignment she had been given. If she didn't face her fears, they would control her and that meant failure.

Failure was not acceptable. She would return to the woods by Emerald Bay, by herself if need be.

The thought caused her to sweat.

Chapter 42

Dolphine had come through as promised. Aimee found the printout of the stories dealing with her mother's murder. She flopped down on her chair and read them.

Only one article named her. "Ann's seven-year-old daughter, Aimee, was run over by a car and found unconscious in the woods, not far from where her mother lay. She remains in a coma."

Aimee folded the newspaper articles and stuffed them in her purse. Tonight, in the comfort of her home, she'd digest them. She picked up her purse, intent on going to Emerald Bay, but first, she'd check on Fluffs.

She found the cat on top of the dining table. Aimee shooed him off and Fluffs bounced onto the floor and regained his proper cat stance of aloofness.

Since she was already home, she could devote a few minutes to her projects before leaving for Emerald Bay. Seconds later, she was deeply involved in her project. Seven flowers later, Aimee glanced at her watch and was horrified to find it was past six thirty. Where had time gone? She really had planned to go to Emerald Bay, hadn't she? Now it was too late.

At exactly seven, the doorbell rang. She grabbed her purse, flung the door open, and immediately stepped out. "I'm ready." She closed the door behind her.

Earl's face showed a mixture of surprise and amusement at Aimee's haste. "All right." He smiled. As they neared his car, Earl said, "Every time I come to visit Mom, I always go to Rojo's. I haven't had the chance to do that yet, so how does that sound?"

Aimee eyed him. "I was kind of looking forward to Alpine Sierra."

Earl opened the door for her. "Then Alpine Sierra it is."

She smiled, got in, and glanced out the window. Ever since late afternoon, clouds had gathered, and the smell of rain hung in the air like a dark, velvet fog. This kind of weather reminded Aimee of the day her mother died in the woods by Emerald Bay.

She heard the distant rolling of thunder and she knew any minute now the sky would open to drop parallel ropes of rain. That brought on the painful childhood memories. "Not now," she whispered in her mind. She rolled down the window, took in a deep breath and forced the cool, damp air into her lungs.

All around her, dark clouds gathered rapidly. The surrounding pines became ominous creatures, mocking her, dragging her back into her past. The wind howled and chilled her bare arms. She shivered and rolled up the window.

"Is anything wrong?" Earl stopped at a red light and took the opportunity to steal a glance at her. His forehead furrowed.

Aimee looked out the window. "I was just thinking."

The light changed and Earl took off. "What about?"

Aimee shifted positions, and then shifted again. "About some sad memories, but we don't need to talk about them."

Earl wrapped his hand around Aimee's. "Yes, we do. I can tell this is bothering you, and I want more than anything to help you."

Aimee crossed her arms and stared out the window.

"Talk to me, Aimee. I'm a good listener and I promise it won't go further than me."

Aimee hesitated. "It's my mom." She expelled her breath in an audible hiss. Had she really said that out loud?

"Is she ill?"

Aimee shook her head. "When I was seven years old, Mama and I planned a picnic." She looked up toward the graying sky. "It was threatening rain back then too. Dark clouds covered the sky. Even so, I insisted on having our picnic. Mama suggested that we wait, but I was too stubborn. I had a tantrum, and she finally agreed. Now she's dead because I was so dang stubborn." She stared at the darkening sky.

"This weather reminds me of that day."

By now they had reached the restaurant's parking lot. Earl turned off the engine, leaned back, and waited for Aimee to finish. When she didn't, he urged, "Go on."

"A man came out of the woods. He--" A lump the size of a lemon formed in her throat. She swallowed hard and cleared her throat. "He had a knife, and he, uh, put it--" This was a lot harder than she thought it would be. "He held the knife against my mom's throat and ordered me to go to him."

"What did you do?"

"I stood frozen." Her eyes widened and she gasped. "Mama told me to run, but I couldn't. I was so afraid. She tried to fight him and that's--" She wet her lips. "--that's when he slit her throat."

Earl closed his eyes and shook his head. He drew Aimee toward him, wrapped his arm around her, and placed her head on his shoulder. "How did you manage to escape?"

Aimee straightened up. "He kept calling me, urging me to come to him." Aimee placed her hand over her mouth, reliving the nightmare.

* * *

"Your mommy needs help. You can help her, Aimee. All you need to do is come." His voice had been as gentle as the bubbling stream. Aimee's lip quivered as she shuffled a few inches toward him.

She stared at the hand that clutched the knife. Blood dripped from its blade. "Put it back!" she hissed.

"What?"

"The blood. Put the blood back so my mommy can get up."

"That's what I plan to do. But I can't do it by myself. I need your help." He reached out for her, and that's when she saw his eyes. Eyes that housed darkness, hatred, and evil. Eyes like these could only belong to the devil himself.

In her head, Aimee heard Mommy's desperate wails. "Run, Aimee, run!" Aimee simultaneously screamed and bolted, blind panic fueling her flight. She was oblivious to the quaking aspen in front of her and the sharp rocks under her feet. The prickly manzanita reached out and scratched her, but she continued to run blindly.

Somewhere out here was the road. Mommy's car waited for her. She could hide there. But which way?

She hurdled over a fallen tree and dashed through the bushes. On the other side of the bushes was a clearing--no, the road. She found the road. But now which way? She stood in the middle of the road trying to spot Mommy's car.

She didn't see the speeding car until it was too late.

* * *

"The car hit you?" Earl asked.

Aimee nodded and plastered her hands to her face. "I was in the hospital for several months and during that time the psycho got away." She sighed, shook her head, and looked out past the window. "What kind of person am I? I stood there while he killed Mom. Then I ran away. I didn't even try to help her." She buried her face in his shoulder.

He comforted her by gently stroking her hair. "Think about it, Aimee." His soft tone reassured her. "You did the right thing. You were seven years old. What else could you do? He probably would have killed you too--or raped you. You did the right thing."

"But what if Mama was still alive?"

"Even if she was--which I seriously doubt-- you couldn't have done anything to help her. You were just a little girl."

"I could have been with her."

"Do you think that under the circumstances your mom would have really wanted that?"

At first Aimee didn't answer She shook her head.

"Well then? Knowing that her daughter is all right is the best thing for any mother. So by taking off the way you did, you gave your mother peace."

"I never thought of it that way." Tears swam in her eyes as layers of guilt peeled away, leaving behind a thick crust that would disappear only after the killer was caught.

As though reading her mind, Earl asked, "What about the man? Did the police ever catch him?"

Aimee bit her lip with the painful memory. She remained silent for the moment and let out a loud sigh. "I was the only witness."

"And?"

"And I can't remember what he looks like even though I stood no more than three or four feet in front of him. The only thing I remember were his eyes. They were so frightening, they still haunt me today. All I wanted to do was to get away from them. I ran away and permanently blocked his facial features. And now that I want to remember, I can't, for the life of me, do it."

"I can help you remember."

"How?"

"We'll go over the scene, over and over."

"I've done that, but no matter how much I think about it, I can't remember his face."

"Have you tried hypnosis?"

Aimee shook her head. "You seem to know a lot about psychology. Are you a shrink?"

Earl smiled and shook his head. "I read a lot, and because of Mom, I've talked to a lot of doctors. So I know what I'm talking about. If you want me to, I'll go with you to a hypnotist. I'll do anything to help you." He hugged her tightly.

Aimee's shoulders relaxed.

Earl raised her head and kissed her forehead. "Do you still want to eat? We don't have to if you don't want."

"I do," she said. "I finally feel I can conquer this, and that's given me an appetite." Besides, she still had to talk to him about his brother.

"That's what I like to hear." He smiled and helped her out.

They ordered and chatted about insignificant things. Moments later, the waitress returned and set a steak, baked potato, and salad in front of Earl. Aimee had chosen the pot roast. It looked good and smelled delicious. She cut a small piece of meat and slowly chewed, savoring each morsel. Her taste buds sang out.

She looked at Earl, who also seemed to be enjoying his meal. She squinted and cocked her head. "Earl, do you suppose you could help me with something else?"

He nodded. "For you, I'd do anything." The warmth of his smile reached his eyes and brightened his pupils.

Oh, oh. She hoped she hadn't been leading him on. She drew back in her seat. "I have a reason to believe that Lauri's stepfather has surfaced. He may be out there in the same woods where my mother was killed. He's staying in a camper. I've tried going by myself, but I turned back. You understand why."

Earl nodded.

"Will you come with me?"

"Of course. How about tonight?"

Aimee gasped. "No, not when it's dark or thundering. Tomorrow afternoon?"

"Tomorrow would be perfect."

Aimee buttered her biscuit. "I also wanted to talk to you about your brother."

Earl's eyebrows arched. "Oh? Why are you interested in my brother?"

Aimee shrugged and sipped her soda. "I'm just curious. What does he do for a living?"

Earl set his fork and knife down and frowned. "He's a drifter. He goes from job to job. Don't know what he's currently doing, and I don't care, either." He wiped his mouth and picked up his silverware. "Can we talk about something a little more pleasant than my brother?"

Ouch. She had touched a raw nerve. Next time she'd approach the subject with more diplomacy. "How's your mom?"

Earl smiled without any warmth. "You're going to think I have a screwed up family."

"Don't we all?" Aimee looked at the two elderly ladies who approached them. They smiled as they focused their attention on Earl.

"How are you?" asked the one to the right. She had thick white hair and wore a bright red dress. "Aren't you going to introduce us to your lady friend?"

"Sure." A look of confusion crossed Earl's face, yet he managed to smile pleasantly as he stood. "This is Aimee Brent, a very talented reporter."

Both of the ladies smiled. The one wearing the red dress offered Aimee her hand. "Hi. I'm Betty and this is Jo." She pointed to her friend before turning to Earl. "What did you do? Did you forget our names? Now it hasn't been that long, has it?"

Earl looked embarrassed and waved his hand as though dismissing the subject. "I think you ladies have me confused--"

Betty reached for a chair. "Now, Kevin, don't tell me you've forgotten us already."

Jo pulled her away. "Come on, Betty. We don't want to interfere with you young people. We just wanted to stop and say *hi*."

"That's right," Betty said, "but before we go, I have to tell you how thrilled I am to see you so happy. I thought you'd never find happiness again. At poor Juliet's funeral, you looked so miserable. I have never seen a man who loved his wife more than you, and the age difference didn't bother you none. That's what I told Jo, didn't I?"

Jo's forced smile was more of a nod. She tried to drag her friend away, but Betty refused to budge. Instead she continued, "I mean after poor Juliet's funeral, you packed up all of your belongings and left town, and I don't blame you. Uh uh, I don't blame you at all, Kevin Limbo. I turned to Jo here and I told her, 'This here man's heart is broken.' That's what I told her. Isn't that right, Jo?"

"That's exactly what you said, Betty." She grabbed her arm. "Now let's leave these nice people alone." She pulled her away. "Kevin, it was good to see you again. We're still in the neighborhood. If you're ever back in town, look us up."

Earl nodded. "Thank you, but like I said before, you have me confused with someone else. My name is Earl Dietz, not Kevin."

Jo's eyebrows furrowed. "I'm so sorry. Our mistake. You look very much like the man we know." She grabbed Betty's hand and led her away.

Earl sat back down and shrugged.

Aimee's eyes narrowed as she stared at Earl. "What was all that about?"

"They obviously had me confused with some other guy, but they did seem to be sweet old ladies."

"Yes, they did." She watched the two old ladies leave the restaurant. "You and Burley look so much alike. Do you think they thought you were him?"

Earl tightened his features, giving him an almost comical look. "No, silly. If they did, they would have asked for Burley, not Kevin. Besides, we said we weren't going to talk about Burley, remember?"

She remembered all right, but she hadn't

agreed. She needed to find out why Burley had so many aliases, and she wanted to verify the two ladies' story. "Sure. We'll talk about other things." They did and they finished their meal pleasantly. Earl paid and they stepped out.

When a bolt of lightning lit the sky, Aimee gasped and jumped back.

Earl took a step back, wrapped his arm around her, and moved his hand up and down her arm. "You're thinking of the woods, aren't you?"

Aimee nodded and leaned closer to him, relying on his strength to help her conquer her fear.

"It's all right, Aimee. Eventually you'll remember who did this to you and your mom. In the meantime, think of it as only a storm." He squeezed her and she looked up at him. Unexpectedly, he leaned toward Aimee and kissed her lips. She tried to pull back, but the kiss had been so unexpected, she didn't get a chance.

Aimee thought about saying something about the kiss. After all, she didn't want to mislead him. But when her eyes met his, she found so much concern and tenderness in his eyes, that she thought best not to mention it now. Once inside the car, they would talk about it. She smiled. "Thanks, Earl. Your vote of confidence really helps."

Chapter 43

Aimee hoped that a good night's rest would help her remember the killer's face, but the night came and left no footprints in her mind.

Determined not to waste the day, she grabbed her purse, phone, car keys, and headed for the newspaper office. She squinted when the sun hit her eyes. She eased her foot off the gas, pulled the visor down, and continued to drive.

The giant ponderosa pines gently swayed in the wind, as though keeping rhythm to a silent song. High above them, the blue sky promised a spectacular day. My, but what a wonderful day it promised to be.

Her thoughts turned to Rich. He wanted her. She knew it. Now all she had to do was make him admit it. Love nipped at the end of her nerves and a tingle ran down her spine. *I love you, Rich, and I know you love me, too.*

She pulled into the newspaper's small parking lot and got out. She knew she was a bit early, but she hoped to catch Rich before he had breakfast. She'd suggest McDonald's. Mmm. Yummy.

Much to her surprise, Aimee found the doors to the *South Shore Carrier* office locked. She retrieved the keys from her purse and unlocked the building. "Rich?" she called, even though she knew he wasn't there.

She headed for his desk. The top story revolved around the Truckee mystery.

From behind her, Rich said, "I've been making progress on that story. It seems to be taking some rather unusual twists."

Aimee nearly jumped out of her skin. Bummer, he caught her snooping at his desk. Pretending that was an everyday occurrence, she turned to face Rich. He looked nice, real nice. She smiled, but before the smile blossomed, it faded away.

His glacial eyes fixed on her.

"What's wrong?" She moved toward him.

"I've been thinking." His eyes never left her. "I owe you an apology."

Aimee came to an abrupt stop. "For what?"

"For the way I acted the other day at your apartment and the comments I've been making. It's very unprofessional. You are my employee and I am your boss. I shouldn't have taken advantage of that relationship. I'm sorry."

Her eyes searched his face, eager for him to assure her he was kidding. Instead, she found a face of stone. "Advantage? Is that what the evening meant to you?"

Rich looked away. "I'm sorry."

He was sorry. She was in love, and he was sorry. What had gone wrong? "Talk to me."

He sat down at his desk and picked up the

notes on the Truckee mystery. "About what, Aimee? I really need to do my work."

Aimee raised her head and thrust her chin out. "Am I going to continue working here, or will that make you feel uncomfortable?"

"Oh, no, please stay. I don't want you--" He paused and swallowed. "--to leave. You and Dolphine have always been my best reporters-- which reminds me, we better get to work." He pointed to a stack of papers. "There are some stories that need to be polished. Work on those before you continue working on Lauri's case."

"Yes, Sir." She reached for the stack, but lingered by his desk. "So how's your Truckee story coming?"

This time Rich looked up. "It's getting more interesting by the minute." His gaze slipped away from Aimee and down toward his work.

"Burley has some kind of a business in--" Rich continued to work. She clammed up.

Rich looked up. "What?" His voice came as a hoarse murmur. He cleared his throat. "You were saying?"

"Nothing." Like a stallion fleeing a burning stable, Aimee pivoted and stormed out of Rich's office."

By now, the other staff members had wandered in. They smiled. Aimee didn't. They saw sunshine. Aimee saw shadows. She sat at her desk, blindly staring at the Kleenex she slowly shredded in her hands.

"Aimee?"

Aimee's gaze drifted toward Dolphine, who attempted a smile, but failed.

"What's wrong?"

Aimee continued to stare at her friend.

"Is it because Robert and I are dating, and I didn't tell you?"

Aimee shook her head.

"Then?"

Aimee sat ramrod straight, staring at nothing.

Dolphine squinted. "It's okay if you don't confide in me. Just know that when you're ready to talk, I'm here for you. Can I give you a hug?"

Aimee nodded.

Dolphine hugged her and for one brief second Aimee wanted to blurt out how Rich had hurt her, and what a fool she'd been.

But then Dolphine released her. The moment was broken, and Dolphine walked away.

Someone called her.

Aimee turned.

Robert showed her some pictures and Aimee told him which she liked the most. After he walked away, she couldn't remember which picture she chose. She turned on her computer and buried her thoughts in her work.

A bit before noon, she stopped by Rich's desk. "I'm going to check out that lead on Lauri's stepfather."

"Fine." He didn't look up.

"Is there anything you want to say before I go?"

"Good luck."

"That's it?"

"Yes."

"Rich, I don't understand. What happened?"

Rich set the papers down. "Nothing happened. You're a reporter in this office and I'm your editor."

"And that's all there is?"

"That's all there ever was." He turned his attention to his workload.

Chapter 44

Aimee pulled into her driveway and looked at her watch. She had less than ten minutes before Earl showed up. She rushed to the bedroom and freshened up. She caught a glimpse of her reflection in the mirror. An angry, sad woman stared back. That wouldn't do. She straightened up watched for Earl's arrival through the living room window

Fluffs rubbed himself against her leg. She reached down and patted his head. "Are you finally accepting me, Fluffs? In a couple of days, your dad and mom will be back in town, and you'll be gone. I'll miss you."

Fluffs meowed and walked away.

Aimee wondered what that meant.

She looked up as Earl pulled into the driveway. Aimee grabbed her purse, stepped out, and arranged her features in what she hoped looked like a friendly smile. "Hi." She stepped into his car.

"You look very nice."

"Thank you." She buckled her seat belt. "Let's get this over with."

Earl nodded and drove off in silence.

Aimee stared out the window at the tall, ominous pines. Their needles swayed, creating a swishing sound. Aimee bit her lip and rolled down the window.

"Are you all right?"

Aimee nodded and bundled herself against the sharp wind.

"We don't have to do this." Compassion filled Earl's voice.

"Lauri's killer might be is out there."

"We can let the police handle it."

"And lose my exclusive? No way!"

Earl smiled. "You've got guts."

"I'm not too sure about that. Deep down inside there's a family of chickens living right in the middle of my gut."

A layer of clouds moved in and covered the earth with a gray blanket. Aimee shuddered. One of these days, she'd leave this place, its weather, and Rich behind.

Earl turned onto the dirt road and in less than five minutes, she spotted a small motor home, perhaps twenty-six or twenty-seven feet long. "Bet you that's it."

Earl drove on past the camper, around the curve, and parked. Aimee glanced around, trying to look behind each bush, each tree.

"Ready?"

Actually, no. If she were smart, she'd send someone else to do the dirty work, but no, she had to be stubborn. She had to do this herself. A faint, involuntary cry escaped her.

Earl looked at her. "You okay?"

She forced a smile and nodded. She stepped out of the car and headed down the hill.

Earl wrapped his hand around Aimee's. She felt comfort at this small gesture, but as illogical as it seemed, she continued to search the forest for her mother's killer.

When they reached the camping site, Aimee noticed a man, his back to them, sitting in a lawn chair reading. Occasionally, he'd raise his head as though keeping an eye on the approaching rain. Aimee looked down at the ground, pretending she hadn't noticed him.

Earl's elbow poked Aimee. She looked at him, and he tilted his head toward the man. He, too, had noticed him.

Aimee nodded once and braced against the threatening rain. Gigantic pines, white fir, and quaking aspens cast dark shadows. Aimee squeezed Earl's hand and plunged onward.

As they walked past the man, Aimee looked for a rifle or a knife. Not seeing one, she made a forty-five degree turn and headed toward the shadowy stretch of the woods the unsuspecting man temporarily called home. "Hi," she said.

Startled, the man looked up from his Clive Cussler book. "Hello."

"Mind if we join you?" Aimee asked.

"It's a state forest. It doesn't belong to me."

That much she knew. She wondered what other pearls of wisdom he would utter. She sat down on a fallen tree, and Earl stood behind her.

"I'm--"

"I know who you are. I enjoy reading your articles, and I recognized you from your picture." He stood up. "The question is, do you know who I am?"

Aimee didn't flinch. "Charles Boyd." Her voice came out, loud and clear.

Charles sighed and slammed the book shut. "In a way, I'm glad. Maybe it's finally over."

"What's over?"

"The lies, the game."

Ah, more pearls of wisdom.

Charles smiled, but there was no humor behind the smile. "My life the last couple of months would have read like a Dirk Pitt adventure." He pointed to the Cussler book.

"Care to tell me about it? Your life, not Dirk Pitt's."

He didn't smile at her attempt at humor.

Aimee said, "I'll guarantee that everything you say is off the record. Maybe later you'll grant me an exclusive."

He stared at Aimee and remained silent.

"Your wife needs you," Aimee said.

He closed his eyes, the pain etched on his face. "You guarantee it's off the record."

"You have my word."

He sighed and remained quiet. The intenseness of that silence felt surreal. The only sound heard was the shuffling of his feet. He cleared his throat. "I met a man who owns a fantastic hideaway in the Rockies. Once a month, he hosts some fancy parties. I was hired to fly his guests in and out." He stopped and focused his attention on Earl. "And you are?"

"I'm--"

"My photographer," Aimee finished for him. "He knows how to keep quiet. You were saying?"

Charles' face twitched. After a slight pause, he continued. "I'm not a stupid man. It didn't take me long before I realized what was going on. The parties served as covers for illegal gambling and drug dealing. So I went to the police and that's where I made my first mistake. I figured that the police in the small burg closest to the property would be the ones to contact. As it turned out, there was just a town constable with no real training. Of course I didn't find this out until it was too late."

"This small town has a name?"

"Yes, but bear with me for a while, okay?"

Aimee nodded.

He looked at Earl, then back at Aimee. "Anyway, I told the constable about the drug deals. He asked me to work undercover for him. I said, 'No.' He said the DA would press charges against me. I'd go to jail. That made me change my mind."

It'd make me change my mind too, Aimee thought. "How could he threaten you with jail if you weren't dealing yourself?"

"At that time, I didn't know any better, so I agreed to work for him." Charles shook his head. "He brought in a buddy, a deputy sheriff, who covered the county area around this little burg, I think. They thought they would make a big case and make a name for themselves.

"They showed me how to set them up. Guess that worked okay because several people in the ring started taking falls. It wasn't long before the leaders of the ring got suspicious. They put out a contract on me. Somehow the constable and the deputy managed to protect me--but just barely. They wanted to make up a story about me dying in an airplane crash, but that would cause the FAA to undertake a massive search. Of course no one would ever find my body or the plane.

"By now, the constable and the deputy sheriff realized they were getting in too deep, so they contacted the DEA. First thing DEA did was convince me to testify. They said I could go into the Witness Protection Program. I considered it, but the next thing I know, DEA and the constable and his buddy are into name calling and accusing each other of screwing up a big case."

Charles paused and took a deep breath. "I saw them as bumbling idiots and wondered what was going to happen to me. I got so fed up that one night I walked away. They didn't know about Karen, and I wanted it that way. I told them I was divorced. She'd be safe that way."

Charles cast his gaze downward. He picked up a stick and drew lines in the dirt. A few seconds later, he dropped the stick and looked at Aimee. "For all I know, I'm wanted by the law as well as by the bad guys." Charles paused, his eyes and thoughts somewhere else.

"You mentioned the ring. What exactly is the ring, and who's involved in this organization--or whatever it is?"

Charles shook his head. "No names, no details. When things settle, I'll answer any questions you have and I'll give you an exclusive. For now, that's all you need to know."

"Fair enough," Aimee said, glad that she had a small reprieve from her fast note taking. "What happened next?"

"I couldn't stay away from Karen. I love her too much. The problem was that she had no idea why I had deserted her and Lauri. It was hard staying away, especially when I heard that she had given birth to our daughter. I wanted to hold her, touch her. Then I heard our baby had been born with a defective heart. I feel so shitty. Poor Karen has to bear it all by herself. I should be there for her. This is as close," he gestured to the camp, "as I can get to her."

Far away a clap of thunder roared, and Aimee braced against the moving shadows. Earl placed his hands on her shoulders.

Charles rubbed his eyes. "I couldn't just pop

in and say, 'Hi, honey. I'm home.'"

"That's where Lauri came in."

"Exactly."

"What I don't understand is, why Lauri? Why didn't you go directly to Karen?"

"Karen has somewhat of a temper. If I showed up, I was afraid she'd be furious with me. She wouldn't let me explain. I was hoping that Lauri could pave the way." He balled his hand and pounded it against his opened palm. "What a mess."

"Maybe if you had become part of the Witness Protection Program and you hadn't lied about your marital status, things would have worked out differently."

"I know." Charles ran his fingers through his hair. "To make matters worse--not that I'm blaming you--your paper ran that story about me and kind of made it look like I died. After that, I couldn't very well have a miraculous recovery. If I did, and if the few surviving ring members got a whiff of it, they'd come after me, or worse, after my family. I can't exactly run to the DEA either. The only one I could turn to was Lauri." Charles cast his eyes down and shook his head.

"Why couldn't you go to the DEA?"

"I told you. They're a bunch of bumbling idiots and besides, they're probably so angry at me for taking off, they'll immediately arrest me. I don't want to do any jail time for this. All I wanted to do was the right thing, but things got so messed up, I no longer know what's what."

Aimee gave him a moment to compose himself. "Tell me what happened with Lauri."

"She was thrilled to see me. We got to talking and she casually mentioned that she feared that her boyfriend might be a small time pusher, even though the real dealer is Blade."

"Who?"

"Some guy named Blade. I forgot his last name, but supposedly this guy is a biggy in the local drug trade. I figured if I can hand Blade over to the police, the DEA would tend to be more forgiving and would let me go."

"It doesn't work that way," Aimee said. "I'm sure they would be happy to get Blade out of circulation, but the DEA may still want you to testify, and that won't change. At this point, I think your best bet is to contact DEA and see if they want you as a material witness, and by the way, they're not all a bunch of bumbling idiots. The ones you dealt with could be the exception to the rule."

Charles sighed. "I guess you're right. I was grasping at straws, trying to find a way out of this mess. That's how Lauri got involved. I asked her to persuade Gary to set Blade up. I know she talked to him about it, but that's as far as it went."

"Did you ever ask Lauri what happened?"

"Well, yeah, I mentioned it, but I was more

interested in finding out whether she'd be willing to ease the news to Karen about my return." He looked down and frowned. "It seems like everyone used Lauri, including me."

Yep, you're a real asshole. Aimee allowed the silence to speak for itself.

Charles squirmed. "I knew Lauri was running around with the wrong crowd. I could have helped her. Instead, I pumped her for information about Karen and our new daughter. I wanted to know every little detail about them. Like the unselfish person she was, Lauri told me all about them. Very seldom did she talk about her problems." Charles hung his head for a few seconds, before returning his eyes to Aimee's face. "Oh, by the way, I read the story you wrote about my wife's financial need. It was a very well written piece. Thank you for helping her."

"You're welcome. Karen told me the donations keep pouring in." She studied Charles' features. "What are your plans now?"

"I'm not sure. All I know is that I feel so damn guilty." He looked away and Aimee was surprised to see his eyes glistening with tears. "I think I'm responsible for Lauri's death."

"How?"

"This drug thing. Lauri told me Gary didn't like her meddling in his drug business. She didn't say, but I think Gary went to Blade and that's what led to her death. If Gary didn't kill her, he knows who did." He shook his head and closed his eyes. "If only I hadn't asked her to get involved, she might still be alive." He rubbed his neck and bit his lip. "Look, I'm telling you this because I feel I can trust you. I think you'll be willing to help me."

"I'll do whatever I can. Just exactly what is it that you'd like me to do?"

"Not now, but maybe when the time is right, talk to Karen. Let her know about me. I'll do as you suggest. I'll go talk to DEA and if I get in trouble with them, maybe you could get your police contacts to help me. All I want is to get out of this mess so I can get back to Karen and my baby girl."

"Just one question: was that you at Lauri's funeral? Were you the one we all chased?"

He nodded. "I wanted--I needed to say goodbye to Lauri."

Aimee handed him her business card and wrote down her cell number. "Here's how you can reach me. I always check my messages. Let me know what happens with the DEA."

He thanked her and put the card in his shirt pocket. "Maybe, just as soon as we get this mess with Gary straightened out, things will start working for me. I know Gary knows something that he's not telling."

Aimee remembered Gary knowing that Lauri was dead even before her body had been found. She turned and walked away, Earl following close behind.

Chapter 45

"He's a real jerk," Earl said once they were inside the car.

"That's putting it mildly," Aimee answered. "All that stuff he said about what happened in that small burg didn't make much sense. I wish I knew which small town he's talking about, then I could contact my police sources and get their version. Of course if I knew where in the Rockies this happened, I could probably come up with the name of the small burg." She paused. "And I'd like to know where he got the money to buy the camper." She stopped and turned around. "In fact, I'm going to go find out right now."

When Charles saw her heading toward him, his knees buckled, causing him to stumble. He straightened himself and waited for her to approach. "Is there something else?"

"Yes. You said you'd fill me in on all of the details later, but there's something I need to know. Where did you get the money to buy that camper?"

Charles looked at the camper, then back at Aimee. "You're not thinking I kept some of the drugs and sold them, are you?"

Aimee stared at him and remained silent.

"You don't know me. It's natural that you'd

be suspicious." He took a deep breath. "It's a used unit. One of the guys I'd frequently flown to the Rockies got a divorce. He sold me the unit dirt cheap, $2,500 to be exact. That was one less thing his wife would get, he said."

Aimee nodded. "Thank you for the information. I'll be in touch." She turned and headed back to Earl's car.

Aimee's cell rang. She flipped it open and read the caller I.D. Dwayne Strokes. She didn't recognize the name, but decided to take the call anyway. "Hello?"

"Is this Aimee, the reporter?"

"Yes it is. What can I do for you?"

"I'm one of Gary's friends. I know he talks to you a lot. I thought maybe you'd be able to help him."

"Help him? How?"

"The cops came and picked him up and took him away in handcuffs. Everyone but me is saying he killed Lauri."

"Why not you? Why are you different?"

"Me and Gary grew up together. I got two real brothers, but it's different between me and Gary, and I just know he couldn't have done it. You know what I mean?"

"I'm sure Gary appreciates your loyalty."

"Will you help him? Nobody else will."

"I'll do my best, Dwayne. Thanks for calling. I'll follow up on the lead." She disconnected and stared ahead, her mind reeling with questions.

Chapter 46

Earl drove slowly out of the forest road and turned onto the main highway. He paused long enough to look at Aimee and a concerned look covered his eyes. "Are you all right?"

The weather. The woods. Mama. Rich. Now Gary. Her heart was ready to explode into thousands of tiny pieces. Her head hosted an entire marching band, complete with a drum line. The sky promised to release its fury in the form of a downpour any minute now. *Oh yes, everything was all right. Just peachy keen.* She nodded.

Earl stroked her cheek. "You don't have to be tough for me."

She nodded and gave him a small smile. They remained silent the rest of the way.

When Earl pulled into her driveway, his hand lingered on the ignition key. "I'd like to see you again." His voice sounded small, timid.

Had Aimee intimidated him that much? Earl had never been anything but nice to her. "Call me." She stepped out of the car. "And thanks for coming with me today."

"You're welcome, and you bet I'll call." He put the car in reverse and left.

Aimee glanced up at the sky and retrieved

her car key from her purse. No sooner had she gotten in her own car than the rain began. By the time she neared the newspaper office, rain and wind swept across the street with such ferocity that Aimee's car shook.

She looked at the front and side parking lots. Rich's car wasn't in its usual parking place. Well, good. She didn't feel like facing him now.

Raising the collar of her jacket, Aimee ran into the office. She picked up the first available phone and asked to speak to Tom or Marie. She was put on hold for what seemed to be an eternity. She drummed her fingertips against the top of the desk.

"O'Day here."

"Hi, Marie. Aimee Brent. I'm in my scoop mode. What can you tell me about Gary?"

"Sorry. I really don't know much, so I can't tip you off."

"Can you at least tell me if you have Gary in custody?"

"We have Gary, but not in custody. We're only questioning him. We don't have enough to hold him. But just give us time. People like him hang themselves soon enough. We'll keep him here for maybe another hour. Maybe longer."

Aimee thanked Marie. An hour from now, she planned to be sitting in the police station. In the meantime, she'd work on the stories she had been neglecting.

She checked the assignment sheet now

located next to Rich's desk. Her gaze wandered off to the yellow tablet on Rich's desk. On the top line in bold letters it said: TRUCKEE MYSTERY. Aimee picked up the pad and began to read:

#1 Fargo, N D: Barbara Marcil, age 71
Died in car accident.

Husband, possibly early to mid-thirties, originally from Truckee,

Disappeared after receiving insurance money.

(Source: *Fargo News*, via conversation with editor Ed Long.)

#2 Davenport, Iowa: Harriet Sue Buller, age 70
Accidentally drowned.

Husband, possibly early to mid-thirties, traced back to Truckee, withdrew all of Harriet's life savings before disappearing.

(Source: *Davenport Herald Post*. Editor: Jeff talked to *Fargo News* Editor, Ed Long.)

#3 Albany, GA: Daniela Hilda Loom, age 69
Died from apparent heart attack.

Husband, age 37, suspected to have ties with Truckee.

Was sole heir to Daniela's bonds, savings accounts.

Husband Ernie withdrew money and disappeared.

(Source: *Albany Evening News*, talked to Ed

and Jeff at Editor's Convention--I should have gone!)

Truckee, California

Check on possibility of an organization existing.

Possible leader sends young men to marry wealthy to semi-wealthy elderly women.

Shortly after wedding (three to nine weeks), wife accidentally (?) dies.

Husband inherits money, vanishes, returns to Truckee (?)

Check on possibility of similar cases in
Fresno, California
El Paso, Texas

May be more: check on two more apparently unrelated deaths.

Aimee set the notepad down. The Truckee Mystery seemed to be a lot more complicated than she had originally thought. No wonder Rich found it so fascinating. She would love to work on this after she wrapped up Lauri's case. She'd ask Rich if she could do that--provided he was still talking to her.

She returned to her desk, but halfway there, she stopped. She went back and re-read Rich's notes. Men--all apparently from Truckee-- married elderly women who shortly after their marriages died an accidental death. The widower then vanished, taking with him all of his wife's wealth. Was it possible that these men returned back to their headquarters--say Truckee--to resume their normal lives?

It would be so simple. All the Truckee men would need was an alias and a list of cities where these rich, elderly women lived.

Aimee thought of Burley, his aliases, and the list of cities he and his buddies had the day she saw them at the gasoline station. It all made sense. It fit.

She thought of Grandma Louise's frail condition and Earl's loving devotion. If Burley was one of the Truckee men--or worse, if he was the organizer--the news would destroy both Grandma Louise and Earl. They deserved better, but Aimee had no choice. Those elderly ladies were probably killed for their money. Someone had to fight for them.

She would verify her suspicions before mentioning anything to Rich or to the police. If she was wrong, she would have hurt Grandma Louise, Earl, and Burley for nothing.

Chapter 47

Aimee caught Gary as he was leaving the police station. He saw her and frowned. Aimee ran toward him. "I want to talk to you," she said trying to catch her breath.

Gary continued walking. "Yeah? Well my lawyer says I shouldn't talk to nobody, so go away."

"Don't you trust me? I thought we were friends."

"You're not my friend. You just want a story."

"I would like to think of you as my friend, and although it's true that I want the story, I also want to help you, provided you're innocent."

He paused and stared at Aimee. "Well, I am, and I thought between you and me, we had already established that."

"We have, so let's go get a Coke and talk about it." Maybe she should throw some french fries into the deal. "I promise that everything you say is strictly off the record. Besides, if you help me catch Lauri's killer, that'll clear you."

He continued to stare at her. "I don't know why, but I trust you, lady."

They drove down to McDonald's in Aimee's car. On the way over, Gary sat with his chin resting in the palm of his hand, his eyes glued to the passing scenery. They ordered, remained quiet while they waited for their food, and when it was ready, they sat at one of the outside patio tables. Gary continued with his silent brooding, which he accentuated by frequently stirring his Coke with the straw. He hadn't even touched the super size large order of fries.

A brief moment of silence followed. Then, "Do you know what pisses me off the most?"

Aimee shook her head. "What?"

"My old man. They had to call him three times before he finally came to the station. He was having a big important meeting with his clients. That's a hell of a lot more important than me." He wrapped his hands tightly around the cup, his knuckles turning white. "Lauri's the only decent thing that's happened in my life. Why do they think I'd kill her?"

"Because of the drugs."

Gary's face paled, but he quickly recuperated. "Shit! Who have you been talking to?"

"Tell me about the drugs."

"I don't do drugs."

"I've been told you smoke pot."

"So? Pot ain't no drug."

Aimee slammed her open palm on the table. "Listen, if you expect my help, you've got to be straight with me. Now tell me about the drugs, all the drugs."

Gary leaned back and focused his attention on a chirping bird. Slowly, his gaze shifted toward Aimee. "It's nothing big, you know. A little pot. Now and then, some acid. I don't use it--the acid, I mean, but it brings in good money. Better than asking that asshole for money. It used to bother Lauri though. She threatened to walk if I continued to sell. It pissed me off--her trying to run my life, especially when she runs off at night to do some secret job for those fancy-ass lawyers."

"Did this lead to a fight between you and Lauri?"

"A big one, almost broke us up. But I knew she was right. I traded her. I told her I'd stop selling if she stopped whoring."

Aimee's eyes popped opened and her eyebrows arched. "Stop whoring?"

Gary shrugged. "It was just something that came out. I don't even know why I said that. Maybe in the back of my mind, I suspected something. I don't know." He reached for the necklace he wore. Nervous fingers worked the chain.

Aimee noticed that it held a cheap key. "That's an unusual necklace."

Gary dropped it down underneath his shirt. "It's Lauri's. She told me it was the key to her heart. I looked around the house and found an old key. I gave it to her. She wore it too, just like I do mine." He smiled at the memory. "Man, I

267

miss her."

His eyes clouded and for a second Aimee thought he was going to cry. Instead, he cleared his throat. "I shouldn't have told her that."

"What?"

"That she should stop whoring around."

"What was her reaction?"

"She started crying and told me it wasn't what it seemed. Man, that scared me. I really didn't mean that she was a whore. I was pissed and blowing off steam. But she took it seriously, like I really meant it."

"What did you do?"

Gary frowned. "Not much to do. I told her I didn't mean it and she calmed down some. She said it was just a job, a temporary thing and she guaranteed me she was still a virgin."

"How long did this job last?"

Gary shrugged. "A couple of weeks, I guess. But on the last day, she was really freaked out. Like something happened. I tried to comfort her, but when I tried to put my arm around her, she pushed me away. I'm not sure, but after what you've told me, and going back to that night, I'm thinking that might have been when she was raped."

"Do you think her mother knew this?"

"I'm sure she knew Lauri was doing whatever she was doing, but I don't think she knew about that last night. Like I said, her ol' lady spent most of her time worrying about the baby and ignoring Lauri."

Aimee leaned forward. "I need to know what Lauri did, and I think you know. Why won't you tell me?"

Gary chomped on some ice and seemed to consider answering the question. He frowned. "She was setting someone up." His voice was barely above a whisper.

"Who?"

"Dunno." He scooped up some ice and ate it.

Aimee glared at him.

"I swear. I really don't know." He squeezed ketchup on his fries and shoved a handful of them into his mouth. What a charmer.

"What else can you tell me?"

"That's all," he said then added, "for reals."

Aimee was not satisfied. "Let's see if we can come up with some possibilities. Was there someone Lauri was afraid of?"

A mouthful of fries later, he said, "Nah." Again, the charm oozed out of him.

"Someone she hated?"

This time Aimee had to wait until Gary washed down the fries with a large gulp of his drink. "Nah." He reached for a fry and his hand froze halfway there. "Yeah, but that's too far-fetched." He shoved more fries into his mouth.

"Who?" More drink. More fries. Did he ever not eat? And why wasn't he fat? Maybe there was a story there. "Who?" Aimee repeated before he had a chance to grab more fries.

"Don't remember his name. Some senator or a governor or something like that."

"Senator Nye?"

Gary's face lit up. "Yeah, that's it. She started talking about him all of the sudden--like she knew him. And the stuff she said about him!" He blew some air through his mouth. "I've never seen Lauri like that. She really was a real cool chick, except when it came to that dude. Do you think she actually knew this senator, like personally?"

Aimee shrugged. "Did Lauri ever ask you to do anything for her?"

Gary's eyes met hers and immediately looked away. "Dunno what you're talking about."

"Yes you do."

His gaze didn't waver away from his drink, as if it were the most fascinating item on the table. He remained silent.

Aimee said, "Let's go back to the drugs. Tell me about them."

"I already did." He still didn't look up.

"Tell me something you haven't told me before. Isn't there anything else you can add?"

"Nah."

"What about Blade?"

This time his gaze snapped to meet hers. He recoiled back into his seat. "Who?"

Aimee leaned back and shook her head. "I don't think you understand the gravity of your situation. The police are looking at you for murder, Gary, and I don't think you did it. You can't afford to protect anyone."

Gary mumbled something that ended with "Blade." Aimee leaned forward. "What?"

"I said I wasn't protecting Blade. He's an asshole."

"Tell me something about him."

"I did. He's an asshole."

"Give me something else."

"Like what?"

Aimee took out her pen and opened her reporter's notebook to a clean page. "Let's begin with his real name."

"Jack Lawson, but nobody knows him by that name. It's just Blade."

"Why the nickname?"

"He collects knives."

She wrote down *Jack Lawson/Blade/has knife collection.* Lauri: stubbed to death. She looked up at Gary. "Tell me more about Blade."

Gary swept a handful of fries, dipped them in the ketchup, and stuffed them in his mouth. "Can't," he mumbled through a mouthful of fries.

Aimee looked away. She couldn't stand all this charm. "Why not?"

"I talk, he kills me."

"Like he did Lauri?"

"I . . . didn't . . . say that." His gaze darted from object to object and his fingers twisted imaginary items.

"Gary, talk to me."

He withdrew the straw from his drink and drummed the table with it.

"Did he actually threaten to kill you?"

Gary remained silent but his drumming increased in tempo.

"I hope you know you can talk to me." Should she bribe him with more food? "Blade will never find out we talked. If you know something please tell me. You owe Lauri this much." She noticed his Adam's apple bobbing.

Several seconds passed before he spoke. "Blade sells to all the users at school. He's the main pusher." A thread of nervousness ran through his voice.

"And?"

"And Lauri wanted me to set him up."

"Did you?"

"No way, but that didn't keep Blade from finding out what Lauri wanted to do. When Lauri turned up dead, Blade came to see me. He was afraid her death would lead to him and his business. He said that if I mentioned anything about him, he'd get word to the police. He'd make it look like I'm the big-time pusher and that Lauri found out about it, so I killed her."

"Do you think he did it?"

"I used to, but now I know he didn't."

"How's that?"

"I found out that on the night Lauri

disappeared, Blade set up a big deal. There's no way he could have had the time to kill Lauri." For a few moments he sat perfectly still, thoughtfully studying Aimee, his fingers steepled against his lower lip. "I'll make you a trade."

"What kind?"

"I'll give you names, places. You take Blade out of circulation."

"What's in it for you?"

"If my name pops up maybe you could tell the police I helped you. Maybe I won't do any time."

"A little while ago you pretended you didn't even know Blade. Why the change of heart?"

"Like you said, I owe Lauri. Besides, I'm in enough trouble. Why add more?" He reached for the key around his neck and played with it. After a while, he dropped it back under his shirt collar. "So can we do that?"

Aimee turned to a new page in her notebook. "Give me some names."

"Let me do a little research. I'll get back to you."

Aimee eyed him.

"I promise."

She put her notebook away. "All right, if Blade didn't do it, then who did?"

"Had to be them lawyers. They used her to set someone up--maybe that senator. Then something goes wrong. Two weeks later she's dead."

"Did you tell the police?"

"I tried, man, but my . . . uh, stupid lawyer keeps telling me to shut up. My old man is about ready to kill me for disrupting his meeting. The police are pressured to find the killer, and I'm it. Innocent or not. Case closed."

"What's going to happen to you?"

"Only thing that saved my ass is that they want to try me as an adult. So they're waiting and watching. That's what O'Day told me. Sooner or later, I'm going to slip up, O'Day said. That's probably them over there, eating their hamburgers."

Aimee glanced at the two middle-aged men seriously involved in devouring their Big Macs. They didn't look like police at all.

Abruptly, Gary stood up. "Look man, I told you everything I know. If Blade's guilty, leave me out of this. I never talked to you about him. As far as I'm concerned, all we talked about were those wonderful lawyers."

"Wait, Gary, before you leave, is there someone Lauri would have talked to about that job she did for Mr. Stockton and Mr. Teague?"

Gary considered this for a while. "She was closer to me than anyone else, and I told you all I know."

"What about that girlfriend of hers who moved away?"

"Anyah, you mean?"

"Yeah, that's the name."

"I don't think she'll be much help. She was Lauri's best friend, but I don't think she even knows about Lauri's death."

"How can I get hold of her?"

"Anyah's grandma died and left them a house somewhere in West Virginia. Some real small town. So they moved there."

"How long ago?"

"About two, three days before Lauri died."

"So Lauri could have talked to Anyah about the job."

"I guess so."

"You wouldn't happen to have Anyah's address or phone number, would you?"

"Yeah, she gave it to me and Lauri before she left. I don't know if I still have it though. I'll check. If I do, I'll call your office and give it to you." He turned and glared at the two men. They ignored him.

In fact, they did a very good job of not seeing him. They had to be cops. Aimee's concentration broke when Gary continued to speak. "Look, I gotta go. Okay? I'll get Anyah's number for you. One way or the other. Also, those names." He turned to leave.

"Gary, wait."

He stopped.

"I brought you here. I'll take you back."

"Don't bother. I want to walk. I need to be alone, okay?"

"Okay."

He left, and Aimee stayed behind. The man with his back to her stood up, got in his car, and slowly turned in the same direction Gary had taken. The remaining man continued to eat. He nonchalantly cast his eyes toward Aimee's direction, then down again.

Chapter 48

Aimee stood up, dumped her drink in the trash, and leisurely strolled toward her car. Using the window as a mirror, she saw the second man stand up. Walking with a slight limp, he headed for the parking lot.

Damn! Gary had been right. She opened her purse to retrieve the cell, paused, smiled, and closed her purse. Using the public phone, she punched in the appropriate numbers. On the third ring someone said, "South Lake Tahoe Police."

Aimee recognized the voice as belonging to one of her police contacts, an older officer named Marc Corbett. "Hi, Marc. This is Aimee. I'm in a bind, and I need you to bail me out."

"I'll try." His voice sounded a bit guarded.

"There's a detective I need to talk to, but I can't remember his name."

"What does he look like?"

Aimee pivoted and looked at the man who pretended not to follow her. He had busied himself buying a newspaper from the machine by McDonald's back door. How convenient. She said, "He's got olive skin, about five-eight or so, wears glasses, a bit on the dumpy side. He walks with a slight limp."

"Oh, you must mean Detective Ariel Kirkwood--that jerk. Does he usually wear pullover type shirts?"

The man was now tying his shoe. How creative could he get? What would he do next? She looked at his shirt, a white, long-sleeved pullover type. "Yeah, that's him. Is he there?"

"No, but I can leave him a message."

"Don't bother. I could probably get the same information from Detective O'Day. I hope he's there."

"He sure is. Let me connect you."

As soon as Aimee realized she was on hold, she yelled out, "Hey, Ariel! Ariel Kirkwood!"

The startled man looked up.

Aimee pointed to the phone. "Detective O'Day wants to speak to you." She set the phone down.

As they passed each other, the embarrassed man kept his eyes glued to the floor, but Aimee couldn't resist the temptation. "Hi, Ariel." She used her friendliest tone. "How are you doing today?" She thought she heard him mumble something, but she wasn't sure.

When she reached her car, she tried to spot Ariel. Instead, she saw an elderly woman sitting inside McDonald's. Her hunched shoulders and hanging head spoke of defeat, emptiness. Aimee winked and looked again. *Grandma Louise.* She had aged so much since she had last seen her at Lauri's funeral. Aimee went inside and sat down in front of her. "Hi. How ya' doing?"

Grandma Louise didn't answer. Instead she glanced up at Aimee through glassy eyes. Her eyebrows knitted slightly in puzzlement.

"Grandma Louise? Is everything okay?"

The elderly woman's face remained impassive.

Aimee leaned toward her. "Is Earl with you?" Aimee scanned the place for him. Unable to find him, she dug into her purse for her keys. She planned to take Grandma Louise home and stay with her until Earl arrived.

"No, he isn't."

Startled, Aimee looked up and closed her purse. "What?"

"You asked if Earl was with me. I'm telling you, he's not here." Her voice sounded squeaky, like a rubber squeeze toy. "He's at home with his wife back in Fresno, California."

Aimee gasped. "His wife?"

"Yes, Dawn, I think that's her name." She looked around curiously. "Or is it Daniela? No, that was the one before--or am I thinking of Burley? Sometimes it gets so confusing." She smiled widely. "Well, it doesn't matter. Earl's happy. That's important. Don't you agree?"

Not sure what to say, Aimee nodded.

Grandma Louise cast her eyes toward the parking lot, then up toward the sky. "Burley, he's his own man. Cares only about himself. Always been that way. But Earl . . . Earl . . . he's a good boy. Do you know him?" Grandma Louise's forehead furrowed and her eyes were as vacant as a deserted house.

"Yes, I do."

"Then you know what a nice person he is." She smiled with the memory of a mother bragging about her son. Her tone came out bright and cheery. Her eyes no longer carried the polished-button look, but instead sparkled with life. "He's dating, you know."

Didn't Grandma Louise say he was married? "What?"

Grandma Louise leaned closer to Aimee as though ready to reveal the world's best-kept secret. "I heard Earl's dating. Now, let's see. Who's he dating? Oh yes, that reporter: Aimee Brent."

Aimee gasped. That was news to her. Why hadn't someone told her? She was about to say something--she wasn't sure what--when she heard Grandma Louise giggle like a high school girl.

"Why that's you, isn't it?"

Aimee smiled and nodded. "Yes, Grandma Louise, that's me."

"Good. I'm glad he's seeing you. I want him to settle down. He's never done that, you know. He's such a playboy." The curve of her lips could hardly be called a smile.

Aimee retrieved her keys, but stopped when Earl came down the aisle leading from the men's room.

"What a pleasant surprise." He smiled. Then he saw his mom and his eyes narrowed with curiosity. He turned to Aimee, "Hey, why the worried frown? What's wrong?"

Aimee stood up. "I'm thirsty. Let's go order a drink."

"I'll get it for you. What do you want?"

"I think we should both go get it."

"Oh . . . uh . . . yes, of course. Mom, we'll be back in a second. Will you be okay, here by yourself?"

"Of course, don't be silly."

Aimee and Earl made their way toward the order counter. "What's wrong with your mom?" Aimee waited until they were out of hearing range.

"Why?"

"First she said you were married to a Dawn or a Daniela, and you were both living in Fresno, California. Then she thought it might be Burley she was thinking about."

Earl stiffened.

"Then she said that you were dating me and asked if I knew that."

"I'm sorry, Aimee. I never told her anything like that. She's seen us together, and maybe she was hoping . . ." He gave her a half smile that seemed more of an apology. "Mom's not well. This thing with Lauri getting killed has really worsened her condition. She's constantly making up stories. I swear, Aimee, I don't have a wife in Fresno or anywhere else--and to the best of my knowledge, neither does Burley." He rubbed his forehead as though he had a headache. "I don't know what to do."

"Have you taken her to a doctor?"

"Yes, I have and they told me that physically, she's fine. Mentally--well, they're not so sure. I'm beginning to think Mom has dementia." He looked down at the floor.

"Anything I can do?"

"Say a prayer for her and completely ignore anything she tells you. I've been trying to find someone who can take care of her on a full-time basis. Unfortunately, I haven't found the right nurse yet, although I've interviewed several people."

They moved up in the order line. They would be next. "You never told me what your brother does for a living, other than drift from job to job. There must be something he does on permanent basis."

"Burley is into music. He composes. He sings--that kind of stuff."

"So that would require him to travel a lot?"

"I suppose so."

Aimee remembered that one of the places on Rich's list was El Paso. "When you lived in El Paso, did your brother visit you?"

Earl's eyebrows furrowed. "As a matter of fact, he did. He was there for a couple of months.

Why do you ask?"

Oh, oh. She had raised Earl's suspicions. She shrugged. "I don't have any brothers or sisters, and I wonder what it's like. Do you get to see each other a lot?"

"We keep in touch, but not often enough. We're not very close." The people in front of them finished ordering and moved to the side.

Earl asked, "Do you want something else beside a Coke, or should I say, a mixed Coke?"

"No, thanks. In fact, I don't want a drink at all. I'm following a lead, and I was on my way out when I saw Grandma Louise."

"You sure you can't stay, not even for a little while?"

"I really must go." She looked at the pimple-faced youth behind the counter. "Sorry."

They returned to the table where Grandma Louise waited for them.

Aimee looked out the window and saw Detective Kirkwood get in his car and drive off. His firm chin, tight lips and narrow eyes revealed his anger. She smiled and hoped she didn't get him into too much trouble.

"What happened to your drinks?" Grandma Louise asked when Earl and Aimee returned to the table empty-handed.

Earl smiled. "I forgot to ask you what you wanted."

"And I didn't realize it was this late." Aimee looked at her watch. "I have an appointment with Lauri's mom, so I need to take off."

"Is it about that lawyer thing?" Earl asked.

Aimee nodded and wondered if he or Burley had ever been married. She glanced down at Earl's ring finger and thought she saw a different shade of skin where a wedding ring had once been. She looked back up at him, hoping he hadn't noticed. "Yeah, same old thing. Sorry about not being able to join you."

"How about supper then?"

Aimee considered the suggestion. She could use the time to press him for more information. "I'm making some spaghetti tonight. I'd love for both of you and Burley to join me." The least she could do was invite Earl and his family for dinner. After all, they were dating. "Say about seven?"

"That's too late for Mom, I'm afraid, but I can make it, and if I were you, I wouldn't count on Burley. He's unreliable. I'll find someone to stay with Mom while I'm gone, but how about meeting at six instead of seven? You might even be able to talk me into helping you cook. When it comes to the kitchen, I've got a couple of tricks up my sleeve."

Aimee nodded, her mind still on Earl's wedding ring finger.

Chapter 49

The first thing Aimee noticed when she stepped into Karen's living room was Lauri's small picture, the type school-age children exchange with their friends. Still, the picture marked a victory for Lauri. She had, at long last, earned her place on the family's mantel. A bit late, but hey, at least her picture adorned the room.

Aimee recalled the other picture of Lauri, the one where she was a small girl, sitting on the swing. She wondered where it went.

As though reading her thoughts, Karen said, "I did some more digging and found an older picture of Lauri. I still plan to put up the other one, soon as I get a frame."

Aimee nodded and both stared at Lauri's picture. What would her life have been like?

Karen's voice interrupted Aimee's thoughts. "I fixed tea." She pointed to the couch. "Please make yourself comfortable while I get it." She dashed toward the kitchen.

Aimee sat down and for the first time noticed that Baby Karen rested in her infant seat at the foot of the couch. She wore a soft, pink, one-piece outfit and, surprisingly enough, she had a round, healthy-looking face. A sense of loneliness stirred in Aimee, and she wondered what Rich and her baby would have looked like. The empty hollow feeling surprised her.

"She's absolutely beautiful, isn't she?"

Aimee looked up and noticed Karen balancing two glasses of iced tea, a sugar bowl, a teaspoon, a plate containing lemon wedges, and three packages of Sweet n' Low on a tiny, plastic serving tray. One thing Aimee could say about Karen, she was prepared.

"Yes, she's beautiful. I hadn't seen her before. Won't she wake up with us talking?" Aimee whispered.

"No, she's used to noise. Lauri always had her radio blaring with that weird music of hers." She set the tray down on the imitation wood coffee table. "Please help yourself."

Aimee smiled a "thank you" and began fixing her tea.

"I'm glad you stopped by. I've been meaning to call you and thank you for the story." Karen's face lit up. "I've already collected several thousand dollars--and it's still pouring in. Between what my caseworker can provide and that money in the bank, I have enough for a down payment, so I've already contacted Houston. In less than a week my baby will get the help she needs." She shook her head as though she found it hard to believe. "I would like to thank all of the people who donated money."

"It'll make a good follow-up story. Maybe when you get home from the hospital, I could write a story about--" She was going to say about a father, mother, and baby being reunited, but she couldn't tell her that. "--a successful operation due to the readers' generosity."

"It will be successful, won't it?"

"I'm sure it'll be."

Karen picked up her tea and took a sip. Her complexion turned the color of ash and her hands began to shake. She set the glass down. "She's got to make it. She's all I have left."

Maybe not, Aimee thought. "We'll all be praying for you and her." She paused and continued, "I came over--"

Karen bolted up. "To talk about Lauri." She reached for Lauri's picture. "I was thinking. The picture here looks silly. Unframed. So tiny compared to Karen's. I want to get it framed, but I haven't had a chance to go to the store." She put the picture back and turned to face Aimee. "What do you need to know about Lauri this time?"

"Same thing. I have to know about that job she had."

Karen reacted as though Aimee had thrown her a ton of bricks, and she was falling under their pressure. Her shoulders sagged, her face became livid. "I . . . I told you before . . ."

Aimee stood and walked toward her. "Please, Karen, the truth. I'm not here to judge you. All I'm trying to do is piece together the events leading to Lauri's death. If it comes to that, Gary is willing to testify that Lauri worked illegally for Stockton and Teague."

Karen rubbed her hands. "No one's going to believe him, are they? I mean, he's just a junkie, right?"

Aimee shrugged. "Who knows what people will believe. But, unless you set it straight, there'll always be that bit of doubt in everyone's mind."

Karen bit her lip and her hands played with the edge of her pale blue T-shirt. "Wh-what doubts?"

"People will always wonder why you encouraged your daughter to become a whore."

The look of shock on Karen's face made Aimee wonder if Gary had misinformed her. Karen's next statement erased her doubts.

"It wasn't like that. They promised me it would never go anywhere near that." She opened and closed her palms in rapid succession.

"By *they*, I suppose you mean Stockton and Teague."

Karen slumped down on the recliner, closed her eyes, and nodded. "There's a senator who--"

"Senator Nye?"

Karen opened her mouth in surprise, but soon recovered. "Yes," she said, "Senator Nye. He gave George and Marvin a lot of static. Then somehow one of them found out that the senator likes young girls. They asked me if Lauri--well, you know." She sat, hunched forward, her hands clasped by her knees. "I was horrified. But they offered to pay me ten thousand dollars. Normally, I wouldn't have considered it, but I had to think of my baby--and Lauri said she didn't mind. I could tell she really wanted to do this, for her sister. I thought it would teach Lauri responsibility. It'd be good for her. I really didn't see any harm in it."

"What were the arrangements?"

"Lauri was to meet the senator and flirt with him."

"Where were they meeting?"

"At the apartments on Blackridge Road."

"An apartment? That didn't worry you?"

"They promised Lauri was only going to flirt with the senator. They took me to the apartment and they showed me how it was going to be. How they had arranged it so they could protect Lauri. They assured me Lauri would only flirt. That's all. If things started getting out of hand, George and Marvin would be there within seconds. They were to watch them through those two-way mirrors. You know, the kind they use in police work."

Aimee nodded. "How did Mr. Stockton and Mr. Teague define flirting?"

"I--well, uh, just flirting, I guess."

"You mean to tell me that you didn't ask

them to tell you exactly what Lauri was supposed to do?" Aimee tried to keep the edge of sarcasm out of her voice, but she noticed that some escaped anyway.

"I didn't think it was necessary." Karen shot her a defensive look. "They promised. They're lawyers."

"But you didn't ask?" Aimee didn't repeat the question so she could hear the denial again, but because she found it so hard to believe.

"When Lauri came home that first night, I asked her how it went. She said *fine*. I knew it couldn't have been bad because she wanted to go back. I didn't force her to." She folded her arms in front of her and pouted, like a child reproached. "She did it on her own. She wanted to help her sister. She did help her sister."

"And you trusted your employers?"

"Of course! I would never let Lauri put herself in a situation like that if I couldn't trust them." She stood up, folded her arms, and looked down at Aimee.

"These are the same two trustworthy lawyers who were planning to use an innocent girl to blackmail a senator."

Karen flinched. "Politics is a dirty business which most of us choose to ignore. Besides, it doesn't involve either one of us." Her eyes blazed with a sudden fury. "You have no idea what it's like knowing that your baby is slowly dying because you're too poor to afford the surgery. There were no options. We did it only for little Karen. And, besides, Lauri was one-hundred percent safe!"

Safe? Lauri was safe? Was Karen really that naïve, or was she just plain blind? Aimee remembered something that Aunt Rachel had told her a long time ago. As a preteen, Aimee had suffered her first heartbreak. She was in the sixth grade and she had fallen hard for the star quarterback, an eighth grader. Aunt Rachel told her he was no good. He enjoyed breaking girls' hearts.

Aimee wouldn't believe her. It wasn't until she caught her supposedly best friend with him that she realized Aunt Rachel had been right. "Why didn't I see that coming?" she asked her aunt as she wiped away her tears.

"I suppose that's because people only see what they want to see."

Now those words echoed in her mind. Maybe that had been the case with Karen. "Didn't the police tell you that Lauri might have been raped--or at least there's evidence of rough sex?"

"Oh God, no!" Karen covered her mouth, and her eyes became two huge round, wild balls. "No, no." She took two steps backwards. "I didn't ask George and Marvin for details. I didn't want to know. I was so afraid to learn the truth. I figured that if I didn't know, I wouldn't hurt--and Lauri wouldn't be hurt. They promised. Oh my God, they promised." She wiped tears away. "The rape or rough sex, could that have been. Gary? He probably did it."

"He denies it. And I believe him."

"You don't know him. He's a drunken junkie who would lie to God."

That didn't sound like the Gary Aimee knew. Sure, he was short in the charm department and his mother should have washed his mouth out with soap a long time ago. But a drunken junkie? Hardly. "I'll stand by Gary on this."

Karen's eyes widened with surprise. She opened her mouth, changed her mind, and closed it. She focused on her baby. "Please don't judge me. I only did it for her. I closed my mind to any bad possibilities. I didn't ask any questions. I didn't want to know. All I wanted was to raise the money for my baby."

"It's not my job to judge you. I only want to find out who killed Lauri."

Karen raised her eyes to meet Aimee's. "When the police first found Lauri's body in the woods, they came here to search the house. They found no sign of a struggle, so they let me move back in right away. Maybe if we go through Lauri's room again, we'll find something that will nail those two bastards. Maybe the police missed something."

"Like a diary?" Aimee knew she was reaching for straws, but she needed something tangible.

"I have no idea if . . ." Karen paused, then continued, ". . . my daughter kept a diary. Supposedly, most teenagers do. Let's hope Lauri was one of them."

They searched Lauri's desk and bookshelf, but their efforts proved fruitless. Next, they looked under the bed and found a large storage box. They pulled it out and opened it. Halfway through, Karen straightened up. "We may be too late."

"What do you mean?"

"The day after Lauri died--I think it was, all of those days are hazy--Marvin came to see me. He said something about giving Lauri some papers to type, and he wanted them back. It didn't make much sense, but he said it made Lauri feel important. Like a fool, I believed him." She ran her fingers through her hair. "I let him come in and rummage around in Lauri's room."

"Did he carry anything out with him?"

Karen wrinkled her forehead, trying to remember. "I don't think he did. Nothing I could see, but he was alone in this room for a while."

"Why's that?"

"The phone rang. In fact, it was George. Now that I think about it, he didn't have anything to say, but he kept me on the phone. How could I have been so stupid?" She slammed the box shut. "Nothing here. Whatever it was, Marvin must have taken it."

"No, I don't think so. The police were here first. They would have found it. That means that if there's something hidden, it's still here. Lauri would have hidden it in a very safe place, and I don't think Mr. Stockton or Mr. Teague took that into consideration." Aimee studied each detail in the room. If she read Lauri correctly, she left some kind of clue. It was up to her to find it. But where? Where?

Her hand reached down and clutched Lauri's covers. Filled with inspiration and perhaps a bit of hope, she got on the floor, rolled on her back, and scooted under the bed. The only thing she found was a pair of wadded up socks and a lot of dirt.

Even though Aimee hadn't expected to find much, the sting of disappointment in not finding anything between the box spring and the bed frame stung her. She stood up and dusted herself off.

"I guess that's it." Karen's flat tone spoke of her feelings.

Aimee stood, analyzing every item in the room. "Maybe not. In the movies someone always hides things between the box spring and the mattress. Maybe if Lauri watched enough TV--"

"That she did."

Together they pulled up the mattress and searched the area. Again, they came out empty-handed.

"Dammit!" Aimee said. She helped lower the mattress, and as she did, she felt a slight bump under the fitted bed sheet. Taped to the bottom of the mattress was a business size envelope. "We've got something!"

Karen scooted over beside Aimee and looked over her shoulder. She held her breath.

Before Aimee could stop her, Karen grabbed and opened the sealed envelope.

Chapter 50

Aimee eased into her driveway, turned off the engine, and stared at the envelope resting on the passenger seat. It contained a single sheet of paper with only one word printed in large block letters: ANYAH.

Aimee grabbed the envelope and stepped inside. As soon as she walked in, Fluffs jumped off the table. "Caught you. You know you're not supposed to be on the table." He had knocked over the bottle of glue, and a small trickle poured out. The petals she had so carefully sorted by size laid scattered on the floor, the chairs, and on the table.

Fluffs looked at her and meowed.

She stood the glue up, cleaned the mess, and looked at her phone. No blinking light. No messages. Her cell phone hadn't rung. Why hadn't Gary called? She called Dolphine, asking if she had any messages at the office.

"No, sorry. If you get one, do you want me to forward it to you?"

"Nah, thanks. It can wait. I'm heading for work."

"See you in fifteen, then."

"A bit longer than that. I'm stopping by Lauri's grave. I feel that my first bouquet of homemade paper flowers should go to Lauri." Aimee reached for a handful of flowers she had made, a couple of buds, and some leaf clusters. "I'll see you in about half an hour." She disconnected and twisted a green, stem wrap tape around the paper flower arrangement.

Aimee reached for her purse and car keys. Before closing the door behind her, she said, "Okay, Fluffs. I'm leaving. You can jump back on the dining room table while my back is turned."

Fluffs meowed.

* * *

When Aimee returned to work, she checked her e-mail. No messages from Rich. Well, phooey, but she really hadn't expected to hear from him. Gary, however, came through and left two messages. The first one gave her Anyah's address and phone number. The other was a set of names and deals Blade had supposedly conducted. She worked on that for a few minutes and then typed up her notes. At a bit past two o'clock, or five o'clock Eastern time, she called Scott Depot, West Virginia. She asked to speak to Anyah.

"Yeah?" came the youthful-sounding voice over the phone.

"Anyah? My name is Aimee Brent, and I'm a reporter for the *South Shore Carrier.*"

"Wow! Really? You're calling from California? What do you want with me?"

"I understand you're Lauri's best friend."

"Yeah, so?"

"Have you heard about Lauri?"

"Heard what?"

"Then you haven't kept in touch with her."

"Nah, I've been meaning to write, though. But that's like schoolwork. You know what I mean? I thought maybe I'd call her instead. I don't have a cell so I can't text."

"Anyah, I'm afraid I have some bad news for you."

"She ran away again, huh? Well, if you're wondering if she's here, she's not."

"Anyah, Lauri's dead."

Anyah gasped. "Oh, God! What happened?"

"She was murdered."

Aimee recoiled as the phone hit the floor, followed by some commotion. Someone-- probably Anyah--wailed. This was followed by the sound of footsteps. Someone picked up the phone. "May I help you?" a different voice asked.

"My name is Aimee Brent, and I'm a reporter for the *South Shore Carrier*. I--"

"What is it that you want?"

"I need to talk to Anyah. Is this Mrs. Platt?"

"Yes, it is, and Anyah's quite upset. What's going on?"

"Mrs. Platt, Lauri Evans was murdered several days ago."

A long pause followed and Aimee wondered if Mrs. Platt had set the phone down and walked away. Aimee thought of saying *hello* when she heard Mrs. Platt say, "The way that child ran wild, this doesn't really surprise me. What did you say your name was?"

"Aimee Brent."

"Why do you want to talk to my daughter? We don't live in California anymore."

"I thought maybe before you moved, Lauri might have told Anyah something that--"

"I seriously doubt that. Anyah hasn't had any contact with anybody from back there since we moved, and she certainly would have mentioned something if that girl was in trouble again."

"Anyah might not realize she knows something. Please, could I speak to her?"

"We moved to get her away from there. We don't want to see it starting all over. I'd appreciate it if you don't call again."

The line clicked and a dial tone started before Aimee could answer. She slammed the phone down. That hadn't worked out the way she wanted. Maybe if she called back tomorrow, she'd have better luck. If not, she would have to tell the police. If it came to that, she'd make sure that she'd work up some kind of agreement with Detectives Tom and Marie O'Day. Aimee wasn't about to give up an exclusive.

She sat at her computer and re-read her notes. Her cell rang. "I just hung up the phone," Gary said. "Anyah called. She said that her mother had hung up on you. So she called from a public phone. She wants to help."

Super. "How's she doing?"

"She's upset. I guess I should've called her. I wasn't thinking."

"It's hard to remember everything when you're mourning."

"Yeah, I guess so, but I still feel real bad that I forgot." He sighed. "Anyway, she told me something that I think you should know."

"What's that?"

"Before Anyah left, Lauri gave her a box."

"A going away gift, you mean?"

"That's what I thought too, but Anyah says that when Lauri handed it to her, she asked her to please guard it with her life. Then Lauri said that if anything unusual happened, she was to use her judgment. Anyah didn't know what to do, so she called me."

"She did the right thing. Did she tell you what kind of box it is?"

"Yeah, she said that it's a fairly small, wooden box."

That's not exactly what she meant. Her fault. She'd rephrase the question. "What's in it?"

"She doesn't know."

"She doesn't know? Didn't she open it?"

"No. Lauri asked her not to, and you gotta know Anyah to believe this, but she's not going to open it. She refuses to break her word."

"Oh, for Pete's sake." She wished she had been able to talk to Anyah.

"And besides," Gary continued, "it's locked."

"Locked?"

"Yeah, Anyah says it's a small lock, and Lauri didn't give her the key. That means it's got to be somewhere in Lauri's room."

Aimee thought for a second, then said, "Or around your neck?"

"Damn! I never thought about that." Aimee imagined him fingering the key. "That girl had everything worked out, didn't she?"

"Apparently. But that didn't help her any."

A long pause followed. "No, it didn't."

"Can you call Anyah back? I'll pay for the call."

"Don't sweat it. My cell's got free long distance and even if it didn't, my ol' man is loaded. What do you want me to tell her?"

"Ask her if she can send the box by Federal Express. Tell her I'll pay for it when I pick it up. We don't have a branch here, so she'll have to mail it to Carson City. I'll drive over there tomorrow and get it."

"Will do."

"Thank you. I'll need to borrow that key from you, just in case."

"No sweat, but I'd like to have it back."

"You'll get it back, I promise." She hung up the phone and wondered what was so important that Lauri would go to such a great length to hide.

Or was it to protect?

Chapter 51

Earl washed the tomatoes, diced them, and tossed them on top of the lettuce he had previously washed and cut. He reached for the carrots. "So what did you find out about our lawyer friends?"

Aimee stopped buttering the French bread and looked at Earl. She hesitated for a moment. "I think I finally got them."

"Oh? How's that?"

Aimee opened a bag of noodles. "Lauri's best friend, Anyah, moved to West Virginia, but before she left, Lauri gave her a box."

Earl stopped peeling the carrots and looked up at Aimee. "What's in the box?"

"I don't know. What I do know is that the lawyers searched Lauri's room after her death. I bet you they were looking for that that box."

Earl looked down at the carrots. "Seems that way. When will you find out?"

"First thing tomorrow morning, I'm heading for Carson City. Anyah sent it FED-EX."

"You're not going alone."

"No, I'm--"

Earl interrupted her. "I'm driving you. What time do you want me to pick you up?"

"Oh, that's sweet, but no, thanks. I've already

called Lauri's mom, and she definitely wants to come." She checked on the pot of water heating for the spaghetti.

"I'll pick her up, too."

"I appreciate that, but it's not necessary."

Earl finished peeling the carrots and began to cut them. "Look, Aimee, I'm not going to let you go by yourself. It's too dangerous. Whatever's in that box could have led to Lauri's death. Our lawyer friends could easily be watching every move you make."

"Oh, Earl, if I were being followed, don't you think I would realize that?"

"Not if they hired a professional. Remember, these are powerful men. They have connections in high places. I wouldn't trust anyone."

Not even Detectives Tom and Marie O'Day? Were they connected somehow? How powerful were these lawyers anyway?

"Aimee?"

Startled out of her stupor, she said, "Sorry. What did you say?"

"I said I really don't want you and Karen to go alone. Really, I don't mind driving you." He placed the sliced carrots to the side and grabbed an onion.

"We'll be careful. Don't worry."

"The reason you don't want me to drive you is because Rich is doing that?"

Aimee took a long time in placing the spaghetti in boiling water. "Rich is busy working on another story."

"Oh really?" He continued to cut the onion. "What's he working on?"

"He calls it the Truckee Mystery, about several men whose elderly wives died, and the police are looking for their much-younger husbands. It seems like they're all from Truckee."

"Damn!"

Aimee gasped when she saw that Earl had cut his finger. "I thought you said that when it comes to the kitchen, you're an expert."

"I am, but I've never been good at cutting things. I hate violence!"

Aimee smiled. "Come on, let's take care of that before you bleed all over the salad. I never cared for red lettuce." She led him to the bathroom.

"So tell me about that Truckee mystery." Earl tightened his face as Aimee poured hydrogen peroxide over the cut.

"Sorry, can't. I'm not working on that story, so I really don't know any of the details." Did he also suspect Burley? How much did he know? "Why the interest?" She put a Band-Aid around his finger.

Earl shrugged. "Oh, I don't know. I guess maybe it's because I'm originally from Truckee and because I like hearing the news before it hits the newspaper." He looked at his bandaged finger. "It feels a lot better, thanks."

Aimee nodded as she put the items back in

the medicine cabinet.

"What do the police have on the Truckee men?" Earl asked as he followed Aimee back to the kitchen.

"Not much, I think. Like I said, Rich is the one working on that. Not me, but I would love to talk to Burley."

Earl stiffened. "Burley? Why?"

"He does music, right?"

"Yeah."

"Thought maybe our paper could run a small feature on him. You know, local music man does good. I'd like to hear about his accomplishments, what cities he has visited, you know, stuff like that."

"I'm afraid I don't know much about my brother's business. He pretty much keeps to himself, but I'll let him know you want to talk to him."

"Thanks. But before you do, I need to know. Has he done tours in other cities?"

"Why would you want to know that?"

"Because if he has, I can make a big deal about it. He's not just a local celebrity."

Earl nodded. "I know that at times, he's gone for a couple of months."

"Where to?"

"I'm not sure. I know there have been several places. Sometimes he stays gone for five, six months."

Just long enough, Aimee thought.

Chapter 52

The next morning at seven, Aimee drove to Gary's house and honked. He ran out, removed the key from his neck, and handed it to Aimee. "Don't forget to call me and let me know what's in that box, and take real good care of that key. It's the only thing I have left of Lauri."

If the contents of the box proved to be important to the case, she would have to hand them over to the police. They might even request that she not mention it to anybody. "I'll call if I can. Thanks for the key." She gave him the thumbs-up signal.

As she drove away, she heard Gary yell, "Hey, why can't you call?"

Too late to answer. She had already driven off.

Half-an hour later, Karen, the baby, and Aimee headed out of town and down the highway. Aimee glanced out of the driver's window and caught a glimpse of the lake. She stepped on the accelerator and longed for the desert that was still several miles ahead of her.

"Are you all right?" Karen asked.

"What?"

"I was wondering if you're all right."

"Oh yeah. Sure. Why do you ask?"

"You seem preoccupied, and you're going rather fast, aren't you?" Karen cast an anxious look at the back seat where Baby Karen, strapped into a car seat, slept.

Aimee looked down at the speedometer. She was doing almost eighty-five. She eased her foot off the gas pedal. "I guess I'm just anxious to get there." She carefully watched the speedometer for the rest of the way.

* * *

The package, approximately the size of a brick, felt empty. Aimee signed for it, paid, and returned to the car where Karen waited for her.

"Is that it?" Karen asked when Aimee slid in beside her. She eyed the bundle.

Aimee nodded and unwrapped it. She found a small, wooden box. She shook it. "Sounds like maybe a piece of paper's in there."

"An explanation, maybe? A letter?"

"Maybe." Aimee retrieved Gary's key and inserted it in the keyhole. The box opened with ease. Inside, Aimee found a sealed, blank envelope. Pushing the envelope's contents to the left, she carefully ripped one-eighth of an inch off the right hand side. She peeked inside and saw a single strip of negatives. Who still uses regular film, she wondered? She shrugged and took it out.

Aimee glanced at Karen who cocked her head like a bird paying close attention. Holding the strip by the corners, Aimee put it up to the

307

light. The color negatives had been severely underexposed and neither Aimee nor Karen could make out any of the contents. The best they could do was spot some unidentified odd-looking shapes.

"Now what?" Karen asked. "I don't think we'll be able to get anything out of those."

"Don't count on it. I just happen to know someone who can help."

"Great! Who's that?"

"Robert, our staff photographer. He is quite a determined young man. I'm sure he'll work with them until he gets some kind of an image."

Before leaving Carson City, Aimee pulled into the convenience store parking lot. "You sure all you want is coffee?"

Karen nodded. "Black with a little bit of sugar. None of that sugar-substitute junk."

"Got it." Aimee glanced at the baby. "What about for her? Tequila? A rubber boat? Maybe some juice?"

Karen smiled. "She's fine."

Aimee grabbed her purse and stepped inside the store. She poured the coffee before heading for the self-serve fountain, where she mixed a Coke and Diet Coke. She paid and returned to the car.

About twenty miles down the road, Aimee spotted a car speeding toward her. Its bright lights flashed on-and-off several times. Instinctively, Aimee looked down at her speedometer. She slowed down. As the approaching car neared her, she could hear its horn honking.

Karen's face pinched in alarm. "Who is it? What does he want?"

Aimee wished she knew. The good thing was that they were heading in opposite directions. By the time the other car turned to follow, she'd be far away. She slowed down a bit. Maybe she'd get a good look at the driver. She breathed easier. "It's okay," she said, slowing down even more. "It's only Earl. According to Grandma Louise, he and I are sort of seeing each other." She thought about how silly that sounded. How do you sort of see someone? Do you close one eye and squint through the other?

"Oh, thank God. I thought--"

"I know." Aimee pulled off to the side and watched Earl make a U-turn. He parked behind her and rolled down the window.

"Please don't be upset." Earl spoke even before he reached Aimee's car. He nodded at Karen and turned his attention to Aimee. "I was just worried about you. I called your office. They told me you'd already left. So I hurried over. Are you all okay?"

Was he trying to be her boyfriend or her mother? "We're fine."

"Well, I feel rather foolish, but I'm glad everything turned out all right. Did you get your package?"

Aimee nodded. "Yeah." She pointed to it.

"Good!" He smiled. "So what was it?"

Before Aimee could answer, Karen blurted out, "It's a strip of negatives, but they're so underexposed, we might not be able to get anything."

"That's a tough break, but at least you're both okay." He tapped the car. "If you don't mind, I'll follow you back to make sure you get home safely, and once we reach South Lake Tahoe, I'll go on my way."

Aimee nodded. She waited until he started the engine before turning to Karen. "I wish you hadn't told Earl about the negatives."

Karen's eyebrows rose in an arch. "Aimee, I'm sorry. I thought you two were an item. You said so, didn't you?"

Not exactly, Aimee thought.

When Aimee didn't answer, Karen said, "I'm sorry."

"Don't worry. I can handle Earl."

"Why didn't you want him to know?"

"We're not sure what's going on. The less people who know, the better."

Karen nodded. Aimee drove off and watched Earl follow them.

Aimee vaguely wished Rich had been her knight on a white horse. Instead, Earl came to the rescue. Give Earl two points. Rich got zero. Aimee sighed. Such was life.

Bummer.

Chapter 53

"I can work with this." Robert held up the strip of negatives and studied it. "I'll use different grades of filters and overdevelop the paper a little to bring up the contrast. If that doesn't do it, there are other things I can try." He nodded. "I can't guarantee results, but I'll give it my best." He stepped into the darkroom and closed the door.

Karen and Aimee exchanged glances. Aimee smiled and went to her desk. Karen followed her, found a chair, and sat down. She set the infant seat on the floor beside her. Baby Karen had once again fallen asleep. "I wish she wasn't sleeping. I could play with her. It would give me something to do. I hate waiting," Karen said.

"I know what you mean." Aimee handed her a newspaper.

"Thank you." She opened the newspaper and fingered her necklace. She soon gave up on reading. She set the paper down and focused her attention on the far corner of the wall.

Aimee gathered her notes on Blade and handed them to Dolphine. "Sure you want to do the leg work on this?"

Dolphine cocked her head. "This is me you're talking to. Of course I want to follow up on the leads we have on Blade. I've already made an appointment with the school counselor." She grabbed the papers out of Aimee's hand. "See ya." She threw her a kiss.

Aimee pretended to catch it.

As Dolphine walked out, Earl walked in. Instinctively, Aimee's eyes traveled to Rich, hoping to see a sign of jealousy. Something. Anything.

Without smiling, Rich waved at Earl and pointed to Aimee.

Earl thanked him although Rich probably didn't notice. He had buried his face in some paperwork.

Earl smiled at Aimee, but since she didn't return his smile, he hesitated, his eyes begging for forgiveness. "I'm sorry. I just had to come." Earl spoke loudly enough so only Aimee could hear.

"It's all right. I'm not really that busy." Aimee leaned against her desk and looked at Karen who had preoccupied herself by playing with the baby. Aimee guessed Karen had awakened her. Aimee's eyes strayed toward Rich. He was doing an excellent job of ignoring her. "What brings you here?"

"I was worried."

"Worried?"

"I was afraid you were upset with me for trying to follow you to Carson City. I'd hate for you to be mad. I just came to talk about it. Is this a bad time for you?"

Before Aimee could answer, the door to the darkroom opened and Robert stepped out. "I did it!" He beamed like a one-year-old who had just learned to walk. "It's a bit grainy, but you can definitely tell what's going on."

Karen bolted up. "And what's that?"

"Just hold on," Robert said. He signaled for Aimee to join him.

Aimee jumped off her desk. "Hold that thought, Earl. I'll be back." From the look on Robert's face, Aimee prepared herself for the worst. "What gives?"

"I was only able to get an image from one negative. The rest were no good, but the one I got, it's a doozey." He scratched his chin, a custom he had when feeling uncomfortable. "It's a picture of Lauri in a . . . uh, compromising position with Senator Nye. The picture certainly doesn't leave much to the imagination. After you've seen it, you can decide what you want to do about Karen."

Aimee followed him into the darkroom. "It's that bad?"

"I'd rather you form your own opinion." He opened the door wider.

The safety light barely lit the room. Robert turned it off and flipped the regular switch on. Instantly, the small, crowded room flooded with light.

"Are you sure you want to see this picture?"

Robert looked apologetic.

"Of course. I'm a big girl. I can handle it."

"It's not a nice picture."

"I gathered that and I'm prepared." She stood by the developing trays and looked down. The picture lay face down in the fix.

Using tongs, Robert turned the picture. Aimee looked down, stared at it, and closed her eyes, trying to make the image fade away. She heard someone behind her gasp. Karen had followed them into the darkroom. Her complexion had turned pasty and she stood trembling.

Aimee tried to hug her but Karen pushed her away. "That wasn't supposed . . . they promised . . . flirting, they said. Nothing more than that. They promised." Karen covered her face with her hands and a sorrowful wail escaped her lips. "How could I have been stupid enough to believe them?" She turned away and formed a fist. She banged the air. "Why didn't Lauri come to me?"

Aimee bit her tongue to keep from saying the obvious.

Karen lowered her head. "I know what you're thinking. She couldn't come to me because she thought . . . she thought I . . . didn't love her. But I did, except, I guess, I didn't show it."

Aimee led Karen out of the darkroom and back to the chair by her desk. As she handed

Karen a tissue, Aimee noticed Earl had waited and went to him. "I'm kind of busy right now. I'll call you later."

Earl nodded. "I gather you found evidence against Senator Nye, and perhaps even on Stockton and Teague. Am I right?"

Aimee shrugged and led him outside. The nippy wind caused her to wrap her arms around herself. "I'm not quite sure what we have."

"I think what you have is the solution to the case. The senator and/or the lawyers are guilty as hell."

"Maybe so. It does look that way."

"And you're not mad at me for following you?"

Aimee smiled. "No, Earl, I'm not mad at you. I must admit, though, I felt like you were smothering me. Then I got to thinking about it and realized how sweet it was of you to be so concerned."

"But?"

"There's no *but.* It's just that all of a sudden, I got busy, you know, with the picture. I don't want to waste any time. I'll call you later."

Earl leaned over to kiss her lips, but Aimee moved just enough to offer her cheek.

Earl frowned. "I'll be waiting."

After Earl left, Aimee headed for Rich's desk.

He looked up at her and he, too, smiled, surprising Aimee. She had been sure he would never smile at her again. She fought the urge to throw her arms around him. "We got 'em."

Rich nodded. "Robert just showed me the picture. Go for the story." His eyes sparkled with pride, causing Aimee's heart to break in two.

She wanted to smile, but if she did, she knew it would probably come out looking fake or worse, it would turn to tears. Rich must have noticed it, as he glanced away. Aimee said, "I'll go write that story." She turned, walked toward the darkroom, and knocked on the door.

"Come in. I'm just cleaning up."

Aimee let herself in. Robert rinsed the tray that held the developer. "What can I do for you?"

"I need to take the picture and negative with me."

"Not until I make a copy for my own personal files!"

Seldom did Aimee find herself at a loss for words. She searched her mind for something witty to say.

"I'm just kidding," Robert said. "Boy! You should see the look on your face." Pretending to be hurt but actually looking more pleased than hurt because he had put one over on Aimee, he retrieved the negative from the enlarger and the picture from where it hung to dry. He handed them to Aimee and pointed toward Karen and her baby. "Do you want me to take them home?"

Aimee glanced at the solemn-looking mother and noticed that she resembled a worn-out doll. "I'd appreciate that, but let me talk to her first."

Aimee headed toward Karen and pulled a chair beside her. "You know that I'll have to take this picture and the strip of negatives to the police."

The woman's focus slipped away from Aimee and she nodded. Baby Karen, resting on her infant seat by her mother's feet, began to fuss. Karen ignored her. "I guess I should be thankful they didn't use a digital camera and the picture isn't plastered all over the Internet." She looked at Aimee. "Why do you suppose that is? It seems to me it would have certainly been a lot easier to go digital."

Aimee shrugged. "I wondered that too. All I can think of is that the person who took those pictures felt more in control if he actually had a hard copy. Things aren't always as safe in a computer. A hacker who knows what he's doing can gain entrance and destroy the evidence. That's just my guess. That's something your boss will have to answer."

"You're probably right. I'm glad it's not on the Internet. Hopefully there's only that copy floating around. I'd hate to think otherwise." A small tremor escaped her body and Karen hugged herself.

Aimee glanced down at the envelope that contained the eight-by-ten picture. "I'll talk to you in a minute." She turned around and returned to the darkroom. She knocked on the door.

Robert stuck his head out. "You, again? Now what?"

"Can you make an extra copy of this picture?" She handed him the negative.

"Aimee, I swear. I was just kidding. I don't collect stuff like that."

"Ease off, Romeo-With-a-Dirty-Mind. I have a reason to believe that maybe the picture and negative will disappear. If they do, I want to have a back up. Now, can you do it?"

"Sure. Of course. But what about Karen and the baby?"

"Don't worry about them. I'll take them home while you work. Just do me one more favor."

"Anything for my gal's best friend." He bowed and touched his forehead as though saluting.

"Don't breathe a word to anyone about the back-up. The fewer people who know the better."

"Not even to Dolphine? You're asking me to keep a secret from my own future wife?"

Really? When had they gotten so serious? "She's my best friend, but this is work related. So, no, not even Dolphine."

Robert nodded. "I can dig it, but if Dolphine uses her sweet charms on me, I'll squeal every detail."

Aimee smiled.

She drove Karen and the baby home. Neither Karen nor Aimee spoke, which pleased Aimee. After viewing the picture, words seemed inadequate. Once they reached Karen's house, Karen said, "That picture, will the newspapers and TV stations receive copies of it?"

Aimee glanced her way. Karen looked frightened, like a lost child. Aimee's heart went out to her. "The story will, but not the picture."

"So nobody is going to see Lauri naked . . . and . . ." Karen looked away, unable to hold Aimee's eye.

Aimee shook her head. "That kind of picture cannot be printed in the newspapers nor be aired. It will probably be used in a courtroom and shown to the jurors. It will make national news and some terms like 'graphic sex scene' will probably be used."

"Any way around that? For Lauri's sake?"

"I'm afraid not. But if there's any consolation, this will bring down the lawyers and Senator Nye."

"You would think that would provide some kind of comfort, but it doesn't." She picked up the baby and stepped out of the car.

Chapter 54

A small reception area greeted South Lake Tahoe Police Station visitors. The area was empty except for a young man talking to Officer Duffy through a counter window.

Aimee stood behind and to the left of the young man. Duffy signaled for her to come in. Aimee thanked him and opened the door to her right. She found Detective Tom O'Day at his desk.

He motioned for her to join him. She pulled a chair next to his desk and waited for him to finish talking on the phone. When he hung up, he looked at her and gave her a small smile. "Are you mad at me?"

Aimee idly drummed her fingers on one knee. Seconds later, her eyes widened. "You're talking about the tail you put on me."

Tom nodded. "I'm curious. What was it that gave him away? I didn't think you'd recognize him as he has just been transferred to our unit, and he's not here in the mornings when you come in for your daily updates. How did you know who he was?"

She raised and lowered her eyebrows several times. "Let's just say I have an expert's eye." Aimee wasn't about to tell him that the expert eyes were in Gary's face. "Ariel didn't get in trouble, did he?"

"Don't worry about it. He's a jerk nobody likes. Everyone here at the station considers you their new heroine." He leaned back. "But to answer your question, at first, yes. When he came to the phone, I was pissed. Then it struck me as being damn funny." He shook his head and smiled. "I'm sorry I sent him after you. I'm getting desperate, and I'm sure you and Dolphine know more than you're letting on."

Marie O'Day pulled up a chair and joined them. "To what do we owe the pleasure of your company?"

Aimee raised the manila folder containing the picture and the strip of negatives. She handed it to Tom.

Marie scooted her chair so she could see better.

Tom opened the envelope and retrieved the print. He let out a loud whistle. "Well, I'll be damned! So that's what all the blackmailing was about."

"I told you it'd be something like that," Marie said.

Aimee sat up straighter. "So you knew about the blackmail?"

"Hey, we may be a small town police department, but we're not hicks."

"I'm sorry, Detective O'Day--"

"Tom. Call me Tom, remember?"

"Tom. I didn't mean to insinuate that--"

"We know," Marie said. "My husband was teasing you. He does that whenever he can. Eases off tension."

Tom continued to study the picture. When he looked up, he noticed that both Aimee and Marie stared at him. He stuffed the photo back in the envelope, smiled sheepishly, leaned back in his chair, and focused his attention on Aimee.

"Mind if I ask what you plan to do with the picture and negative?" Aimee asked.

Tom and Marie exchanged looks. "The DA will probably go for statutory rape, sexual assault, and on the lawyer's side, conspiracy. As of now, the senator and the lawyers are our prime murder suspects. We don't have the evidence to file any murder charges, but we'll be working toward that goal." He picked up a pencil and tapped his desk. "Your turn. Tell us what you know."

Aimee swallowed a deep breath and narrated every detail in chronological order. When she finished, Aimee leaned back in the chair. "Basically, that's it. Do you have any questions?"

"A couple." Tom took time to read through his notes. "Tell me again how you managed to get hold of the picture."

"Lauri gave the strip of negatives to her best friend."

Marie flipped a page in her notebook and

found what she sought. "Anyah, the one in West Virginia."

Aimee had never mentioned that Anyah lived in West Virginia. This team of detectives was really on the ball. She was impressed. "Right."

"And how do you suppose Lauri got her hands on this?" Tom pointed to the negative.

"I don't know, but Lauri was very resourceful."

"She was resourceful all right, maybe a little too much for her own good." Marie shook her head sadly and shrugged. "Let's do a bit of theorizing. I want to see if we're thinking alike."

"I'm game."

"Why do you think Lauri wanted that negative?"

"Because she wanted to blackmail either the senator or the lawyers or all three."

"I follow you, but I don't think it would be that easy for Lauri to get hold of the senator. I'm sure all arrangements for meeting with the Senator were made through the lawyers." Tom's earlier easy-going attitude left him. He was all business. "On the other hand, the lawyers are easily available."

"They knew she could expose their scheme, so they killed her."

Marie shifted to a more comfortable position. "It all sounds good, but there's one minor problem."

"What's that?"

"At the time of Lauri's death, both Stockton and Teague were conveniently out of the city attending some lawyer thing."

"You said it, *conveniently.* First, they hired somebody to do it, and then went out of town for the perfect alibi."

"And it will remain the perfect alibi until we find that somebody."

"Do you have any leads?"

"I thought I did that day in the cemetery, but that turned out to be Lauri's stepfather trying to visit his daughter for the last time." Tom shook his head with the sadness of the memory.

"Then there's T. J. Bryan." Marie stood up, opened a file cabinet, and searched for a file. She looked at her husband. "I thought we had a picture of him."

"We do, but I gave it to Duffy to make some copies we can circulate."

"Who's T. J. Bryan?" Aimee wrote the name down.

"As often as you're here, I'm sure you know him." Marie closed the cabinet and sat back down. "But you probably know him as The Ape." She paused and studied Aimee's face. "He makes the rounds of the casinos, and he's got a record longer than both your arms put together. Right now he just happens to be working for one specific casino which--"

"--happens to be the one Teague and

Stockton are currently defending in the Scott Kula lawsuit," Aimee finished for her.

"You're a sharp cookie," Tom said.

"I'd rather be called an observant reporter."

"Which reminds me." His eyes pierced hers. "All of this is off the record."

"Of course." She showed him her opened hands. "Now tell me about this T. J. 'Ape' guy."

"He doesn't have an alibi for the time Lauri was killed," Tom said.

"Oh?"

"In our book, that clears him."

Aimee frowned. Shouldn't it be the other way around?

Seeing her confusion, Tom added, "If he was hired to kill Lauri, he'd make sure he had a tight alibi. Besides, there's nothing to connect him to Lauri. However, he's still a possibility. A weak one, but nevertheless, a possibility we plan to pursue."

"So where does that leave us?"

"Looking for the missing link," Marie answered.

"I'll check around."

"You do that, but this time, if you find something, don't withhold the information. You wouldn't want us to put Ariel on your tail again, now would ya?" Tom smiled as he spoke, but his tone was serious.

Aimee eyed him. "You held back."

"Hey, we're the police. We can do that."

"Well, I'm the reporter, and I've got a story to wrap up."

"You're going to write about the lawyers and the senator."

"That's all right, isn't it?" Her eyes squinted, analyzing both of the detectives.

"Of course, but I thought since you broke the story, you'd like to be there when we bust our illustrious lawyers. Then we can use whatever we get from them against our prestigious senator. You may want to hang close to the lawyer's office, if you want to get an exclusive." He stood and reached for his jacket.

"I'd love to," she said, but remained sitting.

Marie stood up. "All right, let's go."

Aimee's glance traveled to meet Marie's eyes. "I have more."

"Like what?"

"Information which proves Jack Lawson--better known as Blade--is knee-deep in drugs. Dolphine, as we speak, is gathering all of those details."

Marie nodded with approval. "You and your buddy sure are on the ball. If Rich isn't careful, I'll steal you both away from him."

Inside, Aimee beamed, but she put on a poker face.

"I guess that means that you're not interested in working for us." Tom put on his jacket. "We want to hear what you have to say about Blade, but first, let me notify our boss. Afterwards, we'll head to the DA for warrants. Once we have those, we'll bust those lawyers and make arrangements with the Nevada police to arrest the senator. We will, of course, file for an extradition. Let's get going before any of them get a chance to run. You can ride with us and fill us in on Blade on the way over there."

Aimee nodded. "Can do," she said, "but I'd also like to call Robert, our photographer and have him meet us there."

"We have no problem with that."

Chapter 55

Pride swelled inside Aimee. TV, radio, and newspapers all over the United States carried her story. She picked up a copy of the *New York Times* and re-read the article carrying her byline.

All modesty aside, she and Dolphine had done an outstanding job. Sexual charges were slapped on Senator James Nye, who faced extradition to California. He was expected to resign in the midst of the scandal.

The lawyers needed their own lawyers to defend themselves of the blackmail charge. Rumors spread that Stockton, Teague, and Senator Nye had hired lawyers whose reputations were as unsavory as theirs. It figured. Some people never learn.

She found three more congratulation cards on her desk, and her heart once again filled with pride. She had exposed some ruthless, powerful men. She glanced at her desk and became painfully aware of the lack of flowers. This story, more than the Cat Lady's story, deserved a reward. Maybe it was time to move on.

She went to Rich's desk to look for a resignation form. Instead, she found scattered on top of the desk his notes on the Truckee story. She would have time to work on it now. If she stayed.

The front door opened, and Rich walked in, carrying an arrangement of yellow carnations. When he saw Aimee, he faltered. "I was going to set these flowers on your desk, then take off. But since you're here . . ." He handed her the bouquet.

"Thank you." Her tone, she knew, sounded non-committal, but if she had found the nerve she would have hugged him. She buried her nose in the flowers and sneezed. *Good going, Aimee. You really know how to ruin the perfect moment.* "They're beautiful." She set them down on Rich's desk and without looking at him asked, "Where were you going?"

"Just out."

Aimee let the comment pass and focused her attention on the bouquet. "I'm not sure I deserve them. No arrests for murder have been made in Lauri's case."

"But you still exposed a very nasty operation--no pun intended. And I'm sure that it won't be long before the police make an arrest charging the lawyers and the senator with murder. In essence, your assignment is over."

"No, I don't think so. If you don't mind, I want to keep working on it." What was she saying? Wasn't she going to quit? Well, maybe later. Yes, definitely later. "I feel that there's a missing piece. Something I'm overlooking."

"Such as?"

Aimee shrugged. "If I knew, the police would be making more arrests."

The phone rang and both Rich and Aimee turned to see if one of the reporters would answer it. Dolphine picked up.

Aimee said, "Even though I'm still working on Lauri's case, I'll have plenty of time to pick up another story."

"What were you thinking of?"

"I thought maybe we could work on the Truckee story. We talked about it once."

Rich remained silent, and Aimee looked away.

Dolphine, or the phone, or both, rescued her. "Aimee," she called from the other room. "The phone's for you. Line two. It's Grandma Louise."

Aimee feigned a smile. She pointed to the phone. "May I?"

"No need to ask. You work here."

Was this his way of letting her know she was just an employee? She picked up the receiver. "Grandma Louise, how are you?"

"Much, much better, thanks to you. I know your article never mentioned a connection between Lauri's death and the lawyers, but the article said that a strip of negatives had been found. It won't take the police long to put the facts together. It's just a matter of time before they're charged with murder. Right?"

"I can't speak for the police."

"But they will arrest Stockton and Teague.

They're guilty, right?"

"The police did arrest them, but not for Lauri's murder. There is no definite proof that links them to Lauri's death."

"Sounds like you and the police have doubts."

"Let's just say that the case isn't closed. The police will continue to work the two cases."

"And you? What do you plan to do?" Grandma Louise's voice sounded harsh.

"I plan to continue investigating until--"

The room brightened as though someone had turned on a power light and aimed it at the newspaper building. The lights flickered on and off and back on again. Seconds later, thunder shook the room and sent a chill running down Aimee's back. She nearly dropped the phone.

"I hate lightning." She remembered a recent story about a boy in New Jersey who had been killed during an electrical storm as he talked on the phone.

A long silence followed at the other end of the call.

"Grandma Louise? Are you still there?"

"Yes. I guess the lightning shook me up, too. It was so sudden. But before the lightning hit, you started to say something about continuing with what?"

"The investigation."

"Listen to me, Aimee. I'm an old woman now, and I know what I'm talking about. You need to distance yourself from this story. You've worked too hard on it. If you continue, it will swallow you whole."

Aimee smiled. This was the Grandma Louise she remembered. She must be feeling better.

"Thanks for the advice, but I'm fine. I can't let it go unless I know for sure that Teague and Stockton are responsible for Lauri's death."

"They are--them and that senator. For your sake, drop the story."

The phone went dead and Aimee hung up. The storm probably knocked the lines down. She looked around the office. Rich had left. Aimee walked over to the window. Massive clouds changed the sky from gray to gray-black.

She hated storms, hated them. She wrapped her arms around herself. The thunder roared around her and once again she was a little girl, running through the woods. Running for her life. The trees loomed high above her. Their branches reached out and grabbed her. She screamed and spun around.

"Aimee, I'm sorry." Dolphine said, withdrawing her arm. "I didn't mean to scare you. I called you. I thought you heard me."

Good going, Aimee. First, she made a fool of herself in front of Rich. Now she did it again. This time with Dolphine. She was batting zero. "No need to be sorry. I didn't hear you. My mind was far away. What can I do for you?"

"The phone."

"What?"

Her fingers formed the symbol for horns. She put the thumb by her ear and her pinkie by her mouth. "It's for you."

Great. Everyone and his mother wanted to talk on the phone during an electrical storm.

"Didn't you hear it ring?" Dolphine asked.

"No, I didn't. I thought all of the lines were dead." Still feeling foolish, she tried to ease her embarrassment by smiling. "I'll take it." She went to her desk and pushed the button for line one. "This is Aimee Bent. How can I help you?"

A pause.

"Hello?"

"You got it all wrong." The voice, raspy and guttural, sounded slightly familiar but Aimee couldn't quite place it.

"I beg your pardon?"

"I have the information you want."

Aimee paid close attention to the voice, the way the words were stressed, but that didn't help. "What information?"

"About Lauri."

"What about Lauri?" If only she could get the caller to talk in more complete sentences.

"Meet me."

"Where?"

"In the woods above Emerald Bay."

Aimee remained still, her eyes wide open, her lips trembling. She reached for the wall to help her maintain her balance. Did this voice belong to Lauri's stepfather? She decided to take a chance. "Charles Boyd? Is that you?"

A pause. Then, "I'll be waiting."

Outside, the thunder roared. "No, not today. I can't possibly do it today."

"Yes, today. Right now. I'll be there." The dial tone followed.

Aimee pushed *57, but the call couldn't be traced. She slammed the receiver down, her hand lingering on it.

"Aimee?" Dolphine reached for Aimee's arm. "Is anything wrong?"

"This person wants me to meet him in the woods above Emerald Bay."

Dolphine's face pinched with alarm. "Right now?" She looked out the window. "We're in for a pretty nasty storm. You're certainly not going, I hope."

"I have to. He knows something about Lauri."

"Who is he?"

Aimee shrugged. "I'm not sure. I think it's Charles Boyd. But the voice wasn't quite right. It was too soft." A sudden gust of wind rattled the windows.

"You can't be serious about going out there." Dolphine focused on the darkening sky beyond the window. "Especially with your past history."

"I have to." She, too, eyed the threatening darkness. "But I'm not going alone."

Dolphine stepped back. "Oh no! Don't ask

me to do that."

"I wasn't thinking about you."

Dolphine relaxed. "Oh, you mean Rich." She pointed to the door. "But he left, just a little while ago, and he didn't say where he was going. He seemed rather upset. What's going on? Did the two of you have a fight?"

"I almost wish we had fought. Then I would know what's going on."

The normally bright newspaper office dimmed and turned gloomy. A cloud shut out the last of the sun's rays. "Aimee, please don't go out there."

"I don't have much of a choice."

"Yes, you do. You can call the police."

She could do that, but that might scare off the informant. Besides, if she kept on relying on others, she would never face her fear. "You're right. I shouldn't go."

Dolphine's eyes narrowed as she stared at Aimee. She turned and walked toward her own desk.

Aimee reached for the phone. After she punched in Earl's number, she retrieved the card attached to the flowers. It read: *Congratulations, R.*

The impersonal message caused tears to swim in her eyes. She quickly wiped them away. She heard someone pick up the phone.

"Earl?"

"No, it's Burley."

"Hi, Burley. It's me, Aimee. Can I please speak to Earl?"

"Yeah, sure, but first I need to tell you something."

"What's that?"

"Earl told me he told you I'm into music and you mentioned doing a piece on me and the guys."

"Yes, I'd like that."

"Great, how about now? I could show you the master plan we have for doing concerts at different cities. That's what we were working on that day we met at the gasoline station."

Oh, really? "I would like to see that list, but right now I'd like to speak to Earl."

"Sure thing, but first you've got to hear this. We, each of the guys in the group, have our own stage names. Take my name for instance: Burley Dietz. What kind of a name is that? So I use Phillip Fillini. Now that's a classy name and--get this--when I sing solo, I have another name, Allan Albey. Now, how cool is that?"

"So you have two stage names?"

"More, depending on whether we do country western, or hard rock, or classics."

That explained the aliases and the list of cities she had seen. She needed to digest this new information and verify the facts. But right now she needed to take care of this other matter. "I'll call you and set up an interview."

"When?"

"Soon, but not right now. I've got a minor emergency here and I need to talk to Earl."

"Hold on. I'll get him."

A few seconds later she heard, "Aimee, Burley says you have an emergency. What gives?"

"I just got this strange call. Someone wants me to meet him in the woods above Emerald Bay. I can't go there alone, especially now with the storm around us."

"I'll come pick you up. Where are you?"

If she walked out with Earl, Dolphine would know what she was up to and would insist on going. "I'll be at home."

"I'll pick you up there. Will half an hour be okay?"

"Half an hour's fine, and Earl?"

"Yes?"

"Thanks."

"Don't mention it. You know I'd be upset if you went alone."

Aimee hung up and wished Rich had been the one who said that. She grabbed the flowers and started out the door.

"Not so fast," Dolphine said. "I'm changing jobs from reporter to your personal secretary. Phone for you, again. Line three."

Aimee set the flowers down and picked up the phone. "This is Aimee Brent."

"Aimee, Tom here. I wanted to let you know that we've arrested Jack Lawson, alias Blade, on drug distribution charges. All that information you and Dolphine gave us really helped. Thanks."

"You're welcome. How much can we print?"

"Just that he's been arrested. We don't want details getting out. We want to use them at the trial. Make sure it sticks. If it does, and there's no reason why it shouldn't, hopefully, we can lock him up for good, and then you can print whatever you want."

"What about Gary?"

"The judge will probably give him a lecture, and let it go at that. I made sure the district attorney knows Gary is cooperating."

Aimee thanked him and cradled the phone. She looked up and saw Dolphine standing in front of her desk. She gave her a high five. "They've arrested Blade."

"That's great news."

"It is, and I'm going to celebrate by going home early and working on my project."

"You're sure that's what you're going to do?"

"Would I lie to you?"

"Under these circumstances, yes."

Aimee grabbed the flowers. "I'm going home." Which was true.

Chapter 56

The clock ticked another minute away. Aimee stood in front of the living room window, watching her driveway. When Earl's car pulled up, she grabbed her purse, an umbrella, and a raincoat, and then hurried out.

Earl smiled when he saw her. He opened the car door for her and waited until she got in. He frowned as he cast his gaze toward heaven. Lightning flashed across half the sky, followed an instant later by thunder.

"Thanks for coming." She squeezed his arm. "Looks like we're heading for a bad storm, but at least it's not yet raining."

"Give it time. The rain will come." He closed the door and went around toward the driver's side. "It's going to be one heck of a storm. Are you sure you want to go there now? Can't it wait?" He put the car in reverse.

Aimee shook her head. "I wish it could wait, but whoever called made sure I understood I was to meet him today." Thick, dark clouds continued to roll across the gigantic pines, white fir, and quaking aspen.

She forced her focus away from the trees and toward the road. Gradually, the city faded from the side mirror's image, and the woods lined both sides of the highway. The deep shadows cast by the clouds enveloped the forest and made her shiver. She pushed her fear down.

Earl reached out and squeezed Aimee's hand. "I won't allow anything to happen to you."

"Thanks. That makes me feel better, but unfortunately, this is something I have to face on my own."

For a while they drove in silence. When Earl finally spoke, his voice came out barely above a whisper. "I want you to stay in the car. I'll meet whoever it is that's waiting for you."

Aimee smiled appreciatively, but shook her head. "He'll probably only hide. He's expecting me." The first drops of rain began to fall, tiny drops like pins falling from the sky. "He didn't say anything about meeting him alone, but you being with me might spook him."

"Are you saying I shouldn't have come?" An edge of irritation crept into his voice.

"No. I need you. I couldn't have done this on my own. But once we get there maybe you could wait in the car."

"No way, Aimee. That guy could very easily be the murderer, and that's the only reason he wants you there. He wants to make sure there are no loose ends." As the rain began to pound harder against the windshield, Earl switched his windshield wipers to high. "I'm not letting you go there by yourself."

"Please, Earl, I have to."

"Then why the hell did you ask me to come? To be your damn chauffeur?" He no longer bothered to hide his resentment.

The anger in his voice startled her. She wondered if he was yelling because he wanted to be heard above the pounding rain or because he was upset. She turned so she could face him. "I'll be all right. I really don't think this has anything to do with my past."

Earl remained quiet for a minute. "You're sure now." His voice no longer sounded anxious.

She nodded.

He continued to drive until they reached the area above Emerald Bay. Aimee expected Earl to turn into the dirt road, but instead he parked across the street from it, turning the car so that it faced the dirt road. He let the car idle. "I'm still worried about you. We should call the police. Did you bring your cell phone?"

Aimee nodded. "It's in my purse, which I'll leave here. Use the phone if you have to."

Earl frowned.

"Don't sweat it." Aimee squeezed his arm. "I've done this before. I get a strange call, I go meet a complete stranger, and *voila*, I've got a story. This is no different than any other time."

"It is different. This time you're dealing with a lunatic."

"We don't know that. The person out there could very easily be the friendliest man in the world. In fact, now that I think about it, do you know who he probably is? I think it might be Jose. He's that Navajo who led me to Lauri's father. You took me to see him. Remember?"

Earl nodded.

"Jose is very nice and very gentle. We have nothing to worry about."

Earl faltered. "Didn't you tell me that you thought Lauri's stepfather was the one who called?" Earl focused his attention on the dirt road before him, perhaps trying to see if he could spot somebody.

Aimee followed his gaze, but all she saw was a deserted road. "It could also be him."

"The truth is, you don't know who it is."

"No, I'm not sure. The voice sounded familiar, but I couldn't quite place it."

"Describe the voice."

"Everything was whispered so it was hard to tell too much. The words came out throaty, as if someone was purposely trying to lower his voice. And it was soft."

"Soft?"

"Yeah, like a kid's." The realization startled Aimee. Gary. It must have been Gary. If he had called, and if he was the murderer, did this put her in danger? He was stronger than she. To ease her worries she added, "It could also have been a woman's voice."

Earl shook his head. "I don't like this. I don't like it one bit."

"It's sweet of you to worry, but I'll be fine."

Lightning exploded and thunder followed within seconds. Aimee's heart landed in her throat. She wished she wasn't such a chicken. "I'll be fine," she repeated.

He turned and raised her chin to meet his face. "You promise me, Aimee Brent, that if you think there's the slightest chance of danger, you'll come running back here immediately."

Aimee nodded.

Earl stared into her eyes. "Aimee, I have to tell you something before you go. I didn't mean for this to happen, but it did. I'm . . . . I'm falling in love with you. You'll be careful?"

She knew she should acknowledge his feelings, but the truth was she fancied herself in love with a man she would never have. Why was she such a fool? She smiled and squeezed his hand. "I'll be careful." She reached for the door handle.

"Wait, at least let me drive you part way. There seems to be a clearing up there wide enough for me to park." He pointed to the dirt road.

Aimee removed her hand from the door handle and nodded. As Earl started up the dirt road, the tires sloshed through the mud. Aimee rested her head against the window, her gaze glued on the thick, concealing shadows. "Somewhere in this area my mother died." She formed a fist and blew in it.

"Please let me go with you."

Aimee shook her head. "I'm not going to lie to you. I'm very afraid. But it has nothing to do with meeting this man. It's my past haunting me again. I keep remembering my dream. I look at these woods, and I see those devil eyes and that psycho. I can almost hear him laughing at my fear."

Earl wrapped his arm around her and pulled her closer.

Aimee continued, "That's why I have to go there. Today. By myself. I've got to prove that he's long gone. Can you understand that?"

Earl nodded.

Aimee took a last look at the woods. "The rain, the circumstances, the woods--all of these remind me so much of my childhood. I've got to face my past sometime."

"Aimee--"

She put her index finger across his lips. "Shh. I wouldn't have come this far if you hadn't brought me. But I must face this alone. Just knowing that you're here, waiting for me, has given me the strength I need to do this."

Aimee put on her raincoat and checked its pockets to make sure she had her notebook and a pen. She grabbed the umbrella--it might serve as a weapon, if need be--and stepped out into the hard, relentless rain.

* * *

Earl watched as Aimee disappeared over the crest of the hill. Watching her walk away made him think that the woods had opened its mouth and swallowed her whole. Earl slammed his open palm against the steering wheel.

He shouldn't have let her go. Something wasn't right. Aimee had said this seemed like a repeat of her childhood, her mother's killer waiting for her.

His eyes widened in horror. "Oh God!" He jumped out of the car and ran, not bothering to close the door.

Chapter 57

Aimee squinted and pulled up the hood of the raincoat, forcing the water to run to the side of her face. She stared at the shadowy stretch of the woods, listening to all the creature sounds. From the bushes beside her, a low guttural noise emanated. Above her, the leaves rustled in the wind.

She looked around. There, behind the trees, someone . . . No, over there, behind the bush. She took a deep breath and forced her voice to come out strong. "I'm Aimee Brent. You wanted to see me. Here I am."

She remained perfectly still, listening, waiting. A streak of lightning snaked to the ground, and the thunder crashed all around her. "If you don't show yourself, I'm leaving." In spite of the cool rain, perspiration drenched her back.

The bushes swayed. Aimee moved toward the clearing, away from the bushes. Crackling sounds surrounded her. Aimee froze. She knew she should run, but the contact between her brain and her legs had shut down.

She stood in a vacuum as the forest went deathly quiet. Even the relentless rain slowed to a drizzle. All she could hear was her steady breathing and pounding heart. Her eyes darted from tree to tree.

A streak of lightning brightened the entire area and sucked Aimee's breath away. She looked up as thunder exploded within the light. In that second of brightness, she got a glimpse of an image. Framed like a still picture ten feet away, a shadowy figure scurried between two giant ponderosas. A black cape covered the entire body, even the head.

As the lightning flashed again, Aimee caught a glimpse of the figure's eyes. The vision lasted only a second, but for Aimee, it might as well have been an eternity. The wild eyes housed an anger filled with venom. These were the eyes of her nightmare, except that this time, they were real.

They were here, and they wanted her dead. Like a soldier ready to deliver that final blow, they advanced toward her.

The layers of years peeled away from Aimee until she was seven years old again. Her eyes burned with blinding tears. Her body trembled with abject fear. She pushed her fear aside, forcing her mind to travel past the devil eyes. She saw a nose. The eyebrows. A mouth. She gasped. She recognized the face.

"Daddy!"

He didn't answer. Instead, a whisper of graveyard breeze reached her ears. "Come to me," it said. "Come to me."

"No," Aimee whispered. She wanted to bolt,

but fear froze her. She became a frightened animal caught in the beam of light. All around her thunder erupted and lightning crackled into life.

"Your mother needs help. You can help her, Aimee. All you need to do is come."

Could she still help Mommy? She inched forward and noticed the knife dripping blood. "Put it back!"

"What?"

"The blood. Put the blood back so Mommy can get up."

"That's what I plan to do. But I can't do it by myself. I need your help." He took several steps toward her.

Whimpering, Aimee lowered her head and closed her eyes, willing herself not to see the knife Daddy held, the knife that dripped with Mommy's blood.

The sloshing sound of his water-soaked shoes revealed his proximity.

Aimee tightened her face like a fist when she felt him raise the knife. She shuddered with fear as a slap of cold wind hit her.

She wanted to run, but terror rooted her to the spot. She opened her eyes, raised her head, and faced Daddy.

His eyes glinted with the evil that lived in his mind. This man couldn't possibly be Daddy, but an evil man, the devil of her childhood years.

Aimee steeled herself for the pain she would feel when the knife sliced through her flesh. She closed her eyes, but popped them open when a splashing sound filled the air. She saw the bad man lying face down in a puddle of mud.

Aimee's breath escaped her. Mommy had dragged herself toward them, reached for his legs, and pulled them out from under him.

He fell with a loud thump. He moaned and stayed down. He blinked several times.

Aimee went to her mother's side. "Mommy?"

She opened her eyes and slightly moved her index finger indicating that Aimee should run. Blood streamed from her shattered veins.

"Run!" Mommy seemed to beg. She went limp as her life drained away. She remained motionless like a broken tree limb. Somehow, Aimee knew, Mommy was dead.

Her anguish echoed in the sky. It responded with angry, rolling thunder. It thrust against Aimee's eardrums like a cannon barrage.

"Aaamieee!"

Someone behind her called. *Mommy? Is that you?* Even as she asked herself this, she knew it couldn't be. Mommy died--*eighteen years ago*. Now, someone else behind her called, and someone else stood in front of her.

A new terror seized her when she realized that the figure ten feet in front of her was real. She backed up a pace, as though she'd been punched full in the face. From behind her, a voice like a wispy wind reached her. "Oh, God! No! Aimee, run!"

Something snapped inside Aimee. With an agility that surprised her, she pushed the figure away. Not waiting to see what effect her shove had, she plunged on into the wood's threatening darkness.

The rain began again in earnest. Aimee ignored it. Tears stung her eyes. She sucked in her breath. The water she inhaled choked her and slowed her progress. She continued, terrified. Where was she heading?

She slowed down. Quarter-sized raindrops beat down on her. The groan of thunder forced her childhood fears to surface like monsters in the black recesses of her memory, nudged on by the relentless rain and low, menacing thunder. She pushed them away.

She broke into a run, wanting only to get away, not caring which direction. Her water-filled shoes and wet socks felt like bricks that slowed her progress. Her heels hurt, demanding that she stop, a luxury Aimee couldn't afford. She felt clumsy as she dodged the fallen timber and climbed over rotting trunks that blocked her path. She had to stop. The piercing pain in her side and aching muscles screamed at her. She leaned against a tree, gasping for air.

From behind her came a distinct sound. The menace of thunder accompanied by something else.

Footsteps!

Someone closed in on her.

Renewed panic tightened her chest, making it almost impossible to breathe. Like a trapped, desperate animal, she felt a scream gather in the pit of her stomach. She forced it back down and blindly pushed on.

"Aimee!"

Panic fueled her, and she pressed on faster.

"Stop! It's me."

She stumbled over a rock. Pain shot up her leg in sharp flashes as she tumbled down. She glanced over her shoulder and saw someone almost on top of her.

She remembered the umbrella. What had she done with it? She half-crawled, half-dragged herself, desperate to escape.

Strong arms reached out and grabbed her.

Aimee screamed.

"It's okay. It's me. You're safe."

The grasp was firm. Aimee couldn't escape, yet she resisted. She wiggled. She squirmed. Her entire body shook, but she continued to fight.

"Aimee!" He shook her. "It's me. Rich. You're safe now."

Aime's eyes widened. Rich? How could that be? She blinked and stared at the familiar face. "Wh-what are you doing here?" Something in the back of her mind, an image not quite in focus, attempted to form.

"Dolphine got me on my cell. I'm glad she

did."

The pounding rain ceased, leaving the woods swirling with mist. Aimee recalled the bit of folklore Aunt Rachel had taught her. The bigger the raindrops, the shorter the storm. She didn't know if that was true, but she did feel grateful for the reprieve.

She squirmed into a sitting position, but the world around her continued to spin. Rich offered her his hand and assisted her up. He held on to her.

"I'm okay," she said at last, but spoke too soon. The suffocating pain overwhelmed her. Had Rich not held her, she would have plunged to the ground.

"Are you sure you're okay?" He wiped away the rain water that dripped from his wet hair and down his forehead.

Aimee breathed slowly through her mouth. After a moment, she nodded. "I need to calm down." She waited for a few seconds before adding, "I'm okay. Really."

"Damn, Aimee. You scared the shit out of me."

Aimee stared at Rich. As long as she'd known him, she'd never heard him curse.

"What happened?" Rich asked.

"I took a trip down Memory Lane."

"Huh?"

"Remember that day at my house when you made breakfast for me, and I woke up screaming?" That seemed like ages ago.

Rich nodded.

"I've acted out my nightmare, and it finally makes sense." Her entire body shook, and she wrapped her arms around herself. "Eighteen years ago in these woods, someone killed my mom."

"Oh Aimee."

"I watched as that beast slit my mother's throat." Aimee gasped for breath. Mom. Oh, Mom. *Beloved Mother.* "All of these years, I've blocked his face from my memory. Until today. I saw him, back there." She pointed with her head.

"He's here?" Rich's eyes wildly searched the area behind them.

"No, he's not here. It was all in my mind. I saw him in my mind." She rubbed her arms as though she could rub the chill away from them. "Where are we?"

"The road is just behind those trees." He pointed to the cluster of ponderosas directly in front of them.

Aimee almost smiled. She had been so sure she was lost. She headed toward the road, and Rich walked beside her. "A year before mom . . . died, my dad was also killed in a fiery crash right over there at Emerald Bay." A shuddering spasm racked her body.

Now she understood why she had been so reluctant to find out if Lauri's stepfather had returned. Deep down she knew it would lead to the truth about her father, a truth she didn't want to face. She held her head up high. He would no longer intimidate her. "Except that my father didn't really die. He set the whole thing up to make it look that way. You see, he had another family which he . . . loved better than us, if he ever loved us at all." She dropped her head, but refused to cry. Rich wrapped his arm around her.

"My mom and I saw him several months later in Disneyland. When he realized we had recognized him, he came back to kill us." She shook the memory away. "The ironic part is that Mom really loved him. She never would have told. She even convinced me that the man in the amusement park wasn't my father, only someone who looked like him. Except that I know better now. That was him I saw." Tears flooded her eyes, and she angrily wiped them away. "He didn't have to kill her."

Rich shook his head. "No, he didn't." His soft voice contrasted to the fury of the storm that dissipated.

"I guess I loved him too. I thought that if I couldn't remember his face, then he really didn't kill Mom, and he didn't try to kill me too. I blocked those images, but today--just now--they surfaced."

Rich stopped. "Why? What happened out there that made you remember?"

Aimee continued walking. "Someone put on

a play for me which brought back the memories."

Rich jogged to catch up with Aimee. "I don't understand."

"You will. It's all perfectly clear to me now."

Chapter 58

Aimee eyed the sun peeping out from behind the thinning puffs of clouds. She was in the passenger's seat, drying her hair with the towel Rich had handed her. Next to her was the crumpled, soggy blanket both she and Rich had used to dry themselves. She had protested when Rich had begun to use it to wipe off most of her caked-on mud.

The least she could do was apologize. "I'm sorry your blanket got all dirty."

"It'll wash." He drove slowly down the dirt road. "By the way, where's your car?"

"Earl brought me."

Rich raised his eyebrows. "So where is he?"

"He left, I suppose."'

"That son of a bitch left you here by yourself in the middle of a rain storm when he knew you had gotten that weird call?"

Wow! Rich must be setting some type of world record. This was the second time within the hour he had cussed. Aloud, she said, "He had no choice."

"Don't give me that. I can't believe you're still defending him. You really love him." He swerved the car to avoid a pothole, but in only found a deeper one. "Dammit!" he said.

Change that from world record to galaxy record.

Rich leaned toward the windshield so he could see better. "So you do love him."

"Love him? What makes you think I love him?"

Rich almost went off the road when he turned to gape at Aimee. He over corrected and fishtailed. "You . . . don't--?"

"No, I don't." *I love you.* This she kept to herself. "What gave you the idea I did?"

"When you were together at the office, I could see those sparks flying between you and him. At first I thought they were harmless. So I didn't say anything. Then over at Alpine Sierra, when he kissed you, and you leaned toward him, I knew I stood no chance of ever getting you to . . . love me."

Aimee closed her eyes. "Were you there?"

"Yes."

She nodded and bit her lip. "So when you gave me the brush-off, it was because--"

"I want what you want. If Earl makes you happy, then go with him."

Aimee leaned over and squeezed his arm. "Oh, Rich, I don't want him."

Rich's smile radiated like the sun's warmth. "When I thought I lost you . . ."

Funny, she never knew she was lost. "When was that?"

"When I realized you went out with Earl,

and I thought you loved him."

"I didn't go out with him. It was a business meal, and the kiss was a reassurance kiss. There's nothing between Earl and me."

"He loves you. I know. I can tell."

"I know that too." Men! She might as well take the plunge. She'd be an old lady before he did. She bit her lip and added, "He knows that I could never love him because of how I feel about you."

Rich's face beamed with a smile that spread from one side of his face to the other. He brushed the tip of her nose with his finger. "And how do you feel about me?"

She hesitated for a second. *Go ahead. Tell him.* "I think . . ."

"Yes?"

"I think I'm in love with you."

He swallowed hard and barely nodded. "I have loved you since the first day you walked into my office."

She swallowed hard and barely nodded. Today turned into one heck of a day.

Rich threw her a kiss. "Think maybe we should go out and celebrate? Where would you like to go?"

"I've had just about all the adventure I want to have. I'm emotionally and physically drained. Mind if I go home and rest? Maybe later tonight we could celebrate." She closed her eyes and leaned her head on Rich's shoulder.

"I'll take you home and call you later today."

Aimee's eyes snapped open. "I can't rest. We need to finish this."

"What are you talking about?"

"Let's play the What If Game."

Rich's face remained impassive, but his eyebrows knit slightly. "You start because I have no idea where this is leading."

"What if Burley is telling the truth?"

Rich's eyebrows further pinched together. "That didn't help at all, but I'll play along. Then we know he didn't lie."

Aimee shot him a frown.

"Sorry. I need a bit of information here."

Aimee told him about meeting Burley at the gasoline station and about his list of cities. Then she told him about his aliases and his constant trips to Truckee.

Rich nodded. "Hmm. Are you thinking what I'm thinking? Burley is part of the Truckee Mystery?"

"At first that's what I assumed, but now I'm not so sure."

"And why's that?"

"I talked to him a little while ago and he cleared each of those suspicions. Apparently, he and his friends from Truckee formed a musical group and they go from city to city. They have different stage names and that's why the aliases. I haven't had a chance to verify this, but my gut feeling tells me Burley has nothing to do with the Truckee Mystery."

Rich nodded. "Your gut feelings have always been right. Let's go with that for the moment. What if he's telling the truth? Then that would mean . . ." He looked at Aimee for help.

"That Earl--not Burley--is the Truckee Man."

Rich's glance strayed toward Aimee and almost, once again, drove off the road. He immediately corrected his mistake. "Earl?"

"Yes, Earl."

"Okay, you've got my mind going in whirls. I'm all ears."

"One day I was talking to Grandma Louise during one of her not-so-lucid moments, and she accidentally spilled the beans. She let out that Earl had been married before, several times."

"Oh really? That's interesting in itself, but hardly a reason to think he's the Truckee man."

"I have more."

"Go on."

"Remember that day when I went to eat with Earl?"

"Oh yeah, I remember." Rich rolled his eyes.

Aimee almost smiled, but the smile never reached her lips. "After dinner, two old ladies approached us. Apparently, they had recognized Earl, but they called him by a different name. They talked about his wife and how Earl looked so sad at her funeral." A chill covered Aimee's body and she wrapped her arms around herself.

"Cold?"

"A little bit. We are soaking wet." Aimee looked out the window at the warm sunshine. "Maybe the sun will dry us off by the time we get home."

Rich turned on the heater.

Its warmth cut through Aimee's chill. "Thanks."

Rich adjusted the sliding control. "I've had some trouble with my heater. I've been meaning to fix it, but since it's summer, I'm not in much of a hurry. Are you getting warmer?" He banged on the console with the palm of his hand.

"It's fine." She fell silent, lost in her thoughts.

Rich's voice interrupted her. "You were saying about Earl?"

"Because Earl and Burley look so much alike and because I knew that Burley has several aliases, I immediately assumed the two little old ladies got Burley and Earl confused."

"Natural assumption."

"Yes, but a wrong one."

"Explain."

"One day when you weren't in the office, I went to your desk and read your notes on the Truckee Mystery."

He eyed her, but remained quiet.

"Sorry," she said, "by nature reporters tend to be nosy. Now that I've had some time to think it over and digest all of the information, little pieces started fitting in this giant puzzle I've been carrying in my mind." Aimee looked out the window, toward the trees. "First of all, the old ladies called Earl, Kevin."

"One of the names the killer used."

"I know." She paused, trying to form her ideas. "He's also planning to move here. He used to live in El Paso."

"That's where one of the murders occurred."

"Mighty coincidental, wouldn't you say?"

"You know how I feel about coincidences."

"Same way I do. That's why I think Earl is the ending to your Truckee story."

Rich slowed down as he started maneuvering the car through the hairpin curves. "Boy, was I off. I was sure it was the work of a group." He looked at Aimee. "Warm now?"

She nodded.

He turned the heater off. "Explain to me how this leads back to Lauri."

"Today, in the woods, Grandma Louise--"

Rich's eyebrows arched. "Grandma Louise was out there?" His eyes lit up. "Was she the one who called to set this meeting up?"

Aimee nodded. "Yes, that was her, but her voice sounded so strong, it never dawned on me it was Grandma Louise. Today when I saw her, she was strong and lucid. The way we remember her. I think she's been playing us all along."

Rich rubbed his forehead. "Unbelievable. I fell for her act."

"If it makes you feel any better, not all was an act. She's really beginning to lose it, but not in the grand scale we all thought."

Rich took a curve and slowed down. "Tell me what happened."

"Earl apparently told her about my past. Grandma Louise decided to use that information to scare me out of digging deeper. She hoped the lawyers or the senator would be blamed for Lauri's death."

"Are you saying they are innocent?"

"Of that account, yes. They did use Lauri to blackmail the senator, but neither the lawyers nor the senator killed her."

Rich rubbed the bridge of his nose. "If they didn't kill Lauri, then who?"

"What I think happened is that somehow Lauri found out about Earl and she blackmailed him. Earl killed her to keep her quiet."

"Can you prove any of this?"

"Maybe if I talked to Earl--"

"No way."

"I'll call the detectives, Tom and Marie, and tell them to meet us." She shrugged. "Rich, I left my cell in Earl's car. Can I borrow yours?"

Rich's eyes met Aimee's. She quickly looked away. He handed her his cell.

Aimee punched in the numbers, spoke softly, snapped the phone shut, and returned Rich the cell.

"No luck?" Rich asked as he put the cell on the floor beside him.

"No, but I left a message."

Chapter 59

Rich pulled into Aimee's driveway and turned the engine off.

"Thanks for coming to my rescue." Aimee leaned forward and kissed Rich's lips. She reached for the door handle.

Rich stopped her.

Aimee looked at him. "What?"

Rich released his grasp on Aimee's arm. He opened the driver's passenger door. "Let's go."

"Go? Where?"

"You're going to bed to rest. I'll wait in the den. One of the O'Days should be returning your call. I'll fill him or her in. I'll even wake you up if you want me to."

Aimee's emotions had played havoc on her. She could use a small nap or at least a few minutes rest--if she could wind down. "Are you sure?"

Rich nodded.

Aimee stepped out of the car, and Rich led her up the driveway.

She squatted and from under the welcome mat, she retrieved the house key. "I left my purse in Earl's car and lost my umbrella somewhere along the way. Glad I decided to hide a spare key."

"You also left your cell in Earl's car, don't forget."

Aimee smiled. "That, too."

Rich waited for Aimee to open the door.

She stepped in and heard Rich close the door. The first thing she noticed was the umbrella she had dropped in the woods and then, her purse. It took her mind two seconds to process the information and grasp its meaning.

She gasped, took a step backward, trying to warn Rich, but by then, it was too late.

Chapter 60

As soon as Rich closed the door behind him, Earl stepped out of the hallway and into the living room. Aimee's eyes focused on the gun Earl aimed at her. She held her breath and stood taller.

"Put the gun down." Rich's firm voice vibrated with authority. This was his editor's voice. "If you love Aimee, you won't shoot her."

With one single sweep to his right, Earl swung the gun toward Rich. "No reason I can't shoot you. One false move from either one of you, and you're dead." His voice dripped with ice. His gaze darted toward the closed door down the hallway.

Aimee followed his glance. "Grandma Louise is there, isn't she?"

Earl's forehead knitted. "What if she is? Leave her alone." He pointed to the couch. "Sit."

Aimee's lips went suddenly dry and she wet them. She and Rich both sat down. "This is about Lauri, isn't it?"

Earl nodded. "I'm sorry she had to die. She was an innocent bystander."

"What happened?"

He looked at Aimee with the warmth of a glacier.

"She found out, didn't she? And she tried to blackmail you."

Something flared in Earl's eyes, but Aimee couldn't decipher it. Within seconds, the hollow look in his face returned. "Yeah," he whispered, "and Mom tried to protect me. That's why she was out there in the woods. She never meant to hurt you, only to scare you."

Aimee's mouth continued to be as dry as desert dust. She swallowed hard. "Or drive me insane. I was on the edge."

"I wouldn't let--" Earl looked at Rich, then at Aimee. "--anyone harm you."

Aimee took in short, shallow breaths. "Then why did you agree to drive me to Emerald Bay?"

"I swear, Aimee, I didn't know. I really thought it was some weirdo--or maybe someone had actually gotten some information. I had to go, to protect you or to keep you from learning more. It wasn't until after you walked away that I realized it was Mom."

Aimee sat up straighter. She filled her burning lungs with air. "Actually, I'm glad she did that. She did me a favor."

"How's that?"

"When I saw her there, I felt I was seven years old again, and every detail came rushing back to me. I was finally able to see the killer's face. I know who he is, and why I blocked the memory."

Earl's eyes widened. "It's someone you

know, isn't it?"

Aimee nodded. "I saw . . . my father's face."

"Your father? Man, this is a screwed up world. You know why he did it?"

Aimee felt Rich inch forward on his seat. If only Earl wasn't so far away, they could jump him. "He was a bigamist. I guess he was afraid Mom would expose him."

"Wouldn't a divorce be easier?"

"I would imagine so, but obviously he didn't. He had his reasons, I guess." She stood up.

Earl immediately raised the gun, pointing it at Rich. "I didn't say you could stand, not unless you want your lover dead."

Aimee sat back down.

Earl visually relaxed. "Good. I really don't want to hurt you." He continued to point the gun at Rich.

"Just like you never wanted to hurt Lauri." She recognized the bitterness in her own voice.

"I had no choice. She threatened to go to the police."

"If you didn't pay her. You could have paid her."

"Where would that lead? She would only have wanted more."

"Wouldn't that have been better than killing her?"

"No."

Aimee's features tightened and her lips

quivered. "You son of a bitch. You never cared for anybody but yourself."

Earl flinched and Aimee's eyes widened. Using a softer tone, she continued, "I bet you anything that the only reason you wanted to date me was to find out how much I . . ." She looked at Rich. ". . . we knew about the Truckee story."

Much to Aimee's surprise, Earl nodded. "Yeah, that's how it started, but believe me, Aimee, something happened along the way."

Aimee studied Earl. "There's something I have to know."

"What's that?"

"Yesterday when Karen and I went to Carson and you followed us, it wasn't because you were concerned about our safety. You had to find out what Lauri left behind and whether it implicated you. Am I right?"

Earl stared at Aimee.

"Answer me!"

"I won't lie to you." He stared straight into her eyes. "I had a gun with me."

Aimee gasped.

"If it helps any, I don't think I could have gone through with it. I could have easily killed you several times, but I didn't. I knew you would eventually figure it out, and I would end up going to jail. I couldn't let that happen, and that's when I considered--" He paused, and when he spoke again, it was barely above a whisper. "--killing you."

Aimee folded her arms in front of her. "The reason you didn't kill me was because there was always a witness, and you couldn't afford that."

"That's not true, Aimee. I had a lot of chances, but I never acted on them."

Earl's words gave Aimee hope, but what of Rich? Would he hurt Rich? "Oh sure, like when?"

"Like the time I was inside your house."

"When you came over for supper?" She stole a quick glance at Rich. He shrugged.

"Then too, but I was here, earlier."

"When?"

"That night Rich came to pick you up. I was hiding in the furnace closet. You kept staring at it, like you knew."

Aimee remembered the feeling of being watched. A chill, like fog, smothered her.

"Aimee, I'm only telling you this to prove that I had plenty of opportunities to kill you."

"Is that supposed to make me feel better?"

"It doesn't matter."

Earl's flat tone refueled Aimee's fear. Where were the O'Days? Why hadn't they called? "You know those innocent, elderly women trusted you, yet you killed them just to get their measly savings. I don't suppose it mattered how they felt."

"They never suffered. The last few months of their lives were the happiest they'd ever been. I made sure of that."

Rich said, "You bastard. Do you really think it's okay to kill people as long as you show them kindness first? You're nothing but a crazy, hypocritical, pompous ass." He spoke with the same rancor Aimee felt.

Earl's eyes narrowed and his face turned bright red. For a minute Aimee thought he was going to walk across the room and belt Rich. Maybe this was part of Rich's plan. Together, they could jump him.

"Does that make you feel good? Gives you a sense of power?" Rich egged him on. His hand tightened into fists by his side.

Earl took three steps forward, and then stopped.

Aimee's face paled.

"Enough," Earl said. "You." He pointed at Aimee. "Come here."

Chapter 61

Perspiration drenched Aimee. She glared at Earl, and cast Rich a pleading look. She remained glued to her spot.

Rich held her back. "Don't do it, Aimee. Stay where you are."

Drops of sweat formed on Earl's forehead. His chin hardened as his eyes reflected his determination. Still aiming at Rich, Earl cocked the gun.

Aimee bolted to her feet. So did Rich. "Don't shoot!" Aimee gasped.

"Then get over here."

Aimee ran to Earl, Rich close behind her. "Here I am," she said.

"You." Earl waved the gun at Rich. "Get back."

Rich froze. Aimee hesitated.

"Do as I say or I'll shoot you. Stay put." Earl pointed at Rich. "Aimee, you come."

"What are you going to do?" Aimee heard the quiver in her voice.

"We're leaving."

"Where are we going?"

"Away." Earl pulled Aimee in front of him and put the gun to her temple. He glared at Rich. "You follow us," Earl told Rich, "and she's dead.

And believe me, I'll shoot her. Then I'll kill myself--I have nothing to live for. But before I die, I swear, I'll kill her."

Earl dragged Aimee to the door. She stumbled backwards in Earl's grip, her eyes glued to Rich's face. His complexion paled, his nostrils flared, and his fists shook at his side.

Earl let go of Aimee temporarily as he reached for the doorknob, the gun at her temple. The instant Aimee felt that little bit of freedom, she stomped on his foot as hard as she could and bent down. She swung her elbow back, aiming for the groin. Instinctively, Earl stepped back, and Aimee's elbow connected with his thigh.

Rich grasped the opportunity and charged. Earl half-straightened and pulled the trigger. Aimee gasped as the sound of the gunshot deafened her. All color washed from Rich's face. Time stopped.

Rich raised his arm as though reaching for Aimee. "Aa . . . Aimee." He crumpled to the floor. A puddle of blood formed where he lay.

"Riiiiich!" Aimee bolted toward him, but Earl yanked her back.

"You're coming with me!" He dragged her out of the house and into the street.

In the near distance, Aimee heard the wail of sirens closing in on her house.

Earl dragged Aimee down the block and shoved her into his white Pontiac. He got in after her and handed her a set of keys. "Drive," he said cocking the gun.

Aimee stared at the Pontiac. Didn't he drive a Toyota? The police wouldn't know about the Pontiac. They'd be looking for the Toyota. Whose car was this? Where were they going? How's Rich? *Oh God, please let him be all right.*

Earl noticed Aimee's hesitation. "The Pontiac is mine. The Toyota belongs to Mom. I drive it as much as possible when I'm here. Now, quit stalling and drive."

As Aimee slowly drove away, her thoughts remained with Rich. "Where are we going?"

"To the airport."

She sneaked a glance away from the road and toward Earl. "You know you won't be able to get on a plane with a gun."

"I'll guarantee there'll be no problems boarding this plane."

"You . . . you have a plane?" Aimee's heart sank.

Through the rear view mirror, Aimee saw a car advancing toward them. She held her breath when she realized it was similar to Rich's car. Was he--?

No, of course not. Even if he were still alive, he'd be in no condition to drive. The thought pulled at Aimee's soul, causing her to tremble. The best she could hope for was that it was an unmarked police car.

But more than the police, Aimee wanted to see an ambulance rushing toward her house.

Then Rich would get help--if it wasn't too late. She fought back the tears and turned her attention to Earl. "Won't the pilot stop you? He'll get in trouble if he knows you're carrying."

"I pilot my own plane."

Aimee bit her lip. If they reached the Douglas County Airport before the police caught them, she wouldn't be able to escape.

When she reached the area where the roads met to form a Y, a place where the locals shopped, she turned up Highway 89 instead of staying on Highway 50, the road that would take them to the airport.

Highway 89 not only snaked along the lake's shores, it also took them farther away from the airport. Earl squinted at the changing scenery. They were now leaving the city behind. He sat up straighter and poked the gun at her. "You missed the exit, didn't you?"

Aimee shrugged. "Depends on whether you're a local or a visitor. Tourists take 50, which is more congested. I prefer this. It's faster." Aimee wiped the sweat off her forehead. "Is that what you did with all that money? You bought yourself an airplane?"

"Partly. I also made other large purchases."

"Such as?"

"I've always liked England. I bought some land and a house. Paid cash. It's all clear and very private." He glanced out the window and frowned. "I don't remember any other road leading to--"

Aimee cut him off. "Does Grandma Louise know about you?"

"I wish she didn't, but she does."

"How do you know?" Aimee casually glanced at the rear view mirror. The car had gained some distance and kept itself approximately twenty to thirty car lengths behind.

"She told Lauri."

"Why did she do that?" As she spoke, she noticed a car in the next lane in front of her. If she bumped into it, it would give the police--if it were the police behind her--a chance to catch Earl.

Earl said, "I don't think she meant to. You know how Mom just rambles on some--"

Earl didn't finish his statement. At that moment, Aimee threw the steering wheel to the left and stepped on the gas pedal. The tires screeched and the car swerved.

Aimee braced for the impact of bumper meeting bumper. It never came. At the same moment Aimee switched lanes, the car made a left turn. The tires on the white Pontiac squealed as Aimee came to an abrupt stop.

"What the hell are you doing?" Even though the car swerved several times, Earl held onto the gun. He shoved it against Aimee's ribs. "You straighten out this car right now." He let out the air he'd been holding when he noticed that other than a few angry motorists, no one paid attention to them.

Aimee did as told. As she pulled away, she noticed that the car she had assumed belonged to a policeman had disappeared. Bitterness stung her eyes. She drove on as darkness swallowed her.

Chapter 62

Aimee felt detached, a bystander where dream-like events revolved around someone else. A madman pointed a gun at the stranger driving a car along the lake. That driver's life was in danger, not Aimee's.

Aimee was somewhere else. With Rich. He had his arms around her. She felt safe. And he was safe. He wasn't lying on the floor with blood gushing out of him, stealing his life away. A shuddering spasm racked her body. She couldn't go on. She wouldn't go on. She pulled over.

"Now what are you doing?" Earl's tone betrayed his frustration.

Aimee ignored him and turned off the engine.

Earl shoved the gun so deep into her ribs that the pain exploded around her. She bit the tip of her tongue but didn't cry out.

"Why'd you stop?" he hissed.

"I . . . I can't go on."

"You don't have a choice. Now, drive." He waved the gun in front of her face.

Aimee glared at him and something burned inside her. She threw the car door open, leaped out, and looked around. Emerald Bay spread out before her. Several yards from her, the cliff stood some fifty to sixty feet above the icy water. As though hypnotized, she moved toward the cliff's edge, and stopped only when she recognized the spot. There, as a little girl, she stood and watched her father's boat explode. Now she had returned, and once again, horror surrounded her. The cool, evening air caressed her body, and a hawk soared above.

A strong hand grabbed her arm.

Earl said, "Don't make me do it." He blinked several times and rearranged his features. "I have no idea what you hope to accomplish, but whatever it is, you'd better forget it. Get back in the car and drive to the airport. No more stalling." His grip hardened to the point where Aimee felt pain. "I'll hurt you if I have to."

His harsh tone left no doubt in her mind. She raised her hands. "Relax, you don't have to shoot me. I don't know what happened. I just snapped, but I'm okay now." She took a deep breath. "I guess the fresh air helped to calm me down."

With the gun, he motioned toward the car. "Then get--"

The loud squealing of tires interrupted his sentence. They both turned toward the noise. Rich's car came to an abrupt stop beside the Pontiac.

* * *

Rich scrambled out of the passenger's side and stumbled down to where Earl and Aimee stood. His hands were pressed against his left side, just below the ribs. His light gray shirt had turned a soggy red. Blood drenched the top of his blue jeans.

"Let her be!" Rich swayed but caught his balance.

Aimee gasped. She took a step toward Rich, wanting to help him but cursing him for placing his life in danger.

Her efforts abruptly stopped when Earl twisted her right arm back and pushed it up high behind her back. Aimee sucked in her breath as the pain soared through her arm. Fear replaced anguish. Earl shoved the cool metallic gun barrel against her temple. She knew he would use it.

"You're a fool, Rich," Earl said. "I should've finished you back there."

A fourth voice said, "It's over, Son. Put that gun down."

Aimee looked toward the source of the voice. Grandma Louise had gotten out of Rich's car and advanced toward them.

"Damn it. Why the hell did you bring her?" Earl inched a few steps back, dragging Aimee along with him.

Rich took several deep breaths and shuffled toward Earl. Rich blinked several times in rapid succession as though attempting to focus his eyes.

Aimee squirmed, but Earl's grip only

tightened around her. Her mind screamed. *Please, Rich, hang on.*

"Let her--" Rich's knees folded under him and he tumbled, face down, to the ground.

Grandma Louise said, "Son, he needs help. Let Aimee tend to him."

"No!" He shuffled his feet, moving backwards as he did.

Aimee strained to glance behind her. A couple more feet and they would reach the edge of the cliff. She held her breath.

Rich pushed himself up, swayed, and looked at Aimee through glazed eyes. He tumbled back down. With his right arm he reached up, grabbed hold of the earth, and pulled himself a few feet.

Earl smirked. "Do you know what people do to wounded animals?" He took the gun from Aimee's temple and aimed at Rich.

Aimee threw her head back as hard as she could. She couldn't tell if the explosion she felt was from hitting Earl's face or the gun going off.

"Bitch!" Earl yanked her arm.

Aimee cried out in pain.

"That was stupid. Now I'll have to kill you, too--after I finish him off." Earl once again pointed the gun at Rich.

Grandma Louise stepped in front of Rich's inert body. "No, Son. Too many people have died. It's time we do the right thing." She took a step forward.

Earl took two steps back. He relaxed the tension on Aimee's arm, but his grip remained firm. Aimee had no choice but to also creep back.

"The two of us." Grandma Louise advanced. "Together. We're from the same pod."

Earl took several more steps back. By now both Earl and Aimee perched at the edge of the cliff. Straight below them, nearly sixty feet down, the water churned. Aimee shivered in silent fear.

Rich stirred and Aimee's shoulder blades contracted. The pulse in her temples started to throb. She ransacked her mind for a possible solution. Earl loved his mother and would do anything to protect her. *Anything.* A theory sprang in her mind. "Grandma Louise, you killed Lauri, didn't you?"

Earl swung Aimee's arm back and pulled it up with so much force that she gasped. She heard him hiss, "I did. You hear that? I did."

Aimee shut her mouth tightly to keep from screaming. She nodded.

A veil of sadness covered Grandma Louise's face. "It's no use, Son. It's time for the truth to come out. You're right, Aimee. I killed Lauri."

Grandma Louise's words exploded in Aimee's mind.

Earl noticed Aimee's reaction. "Mom, hush."

"What's the use? She knows."

"Thing is, she didn't, but that doesn't matter.

Listen to me, Mom." He spoke quickly as though he was out of breath. "Nobody else knows--not even Burley. We'll tell the world I did it."

Grandma Louise sighed, dropped her eyes, and shook her head. She looked like an old, defeated woman. "I can't--"

"I've killed five women. What difference does one more make?"

She nodded and pointed with her eyes at Aimee. "What about her?"

"She'll have to die."

Aimee's body went limp in Earl's arms. He leaned forward to prevent her from falling. As he did, Aimee kicked him hard on the shin. He heaved like a weight lifter and dropped the gun.

Aimee threw herself to the ground and at the same time rolled over so that now she was facing him. She kicked him once more. This time her foot buried itself in his groin.

Her kick was more powerful than she had anticipated, as adrenaline surged through her veins. The impact pushed him backwards. For a few seconds he wavered, desperately trying to regain his balance. He clawed at the air and tumbled backwards, screaming all the way down like a man on the verge of madness.

Grandma Louise picked up the cocked gun and pointed it at Aimee.

Chapter 63

Aimee snapped her eyes shut and tightened her features. She waited for the blackness to close in. It never came. Hesitantly, she opened her eyes. The haunting, hollow expression in Grandma Louise's face renewed Aimee's fear.

The elderly woman spoke in a flat, lifeless tone. "You killed my son." Despair washed all color from her face. "I still have Burley, but it's not the same."

"Grandma Louise, I--" Sobs choked her words. *I killed Earl. My God, I killed Earl.* Tears streamed down her cheeks. She took a deep breath, silently counted to five, and swallowed the lemon-size lump in her throat. "Why did you kill Lauri?"

Grandma Louise's chin quivered, but she held her head high. "I'll tell you what happened, not because you deserve to hear it, but because I need to tell it." Grandma Louise's voice wavered. "Lauri came over that night to blackmail my son."

Grandma Louise's features took on a glassy look, making it seem as if her mind had traveled to the time of Lauri's death. Aimee thought she could rush her and take the gun away. How much of a struggle could an old woman offer?

Aimee stood up.

Grandma Louise continued with her narrative, "I told her we had no money, but she insisted Earl could get it. She said he had killed enough old ladies to stash a hefty amount. She demanded that I give her at least half of the money Earl had inherited. Can you imagine that?"

"She was doing it for her sister."

Grandma Louise's glare pierced Aimee's soul. "She threatened to go to the police." Grandma Louise took three steps toward the edge and looked down.

Aimee inched toward her and she caught the movement. "Don't do anything stupid."

Aimee nodded and stopped but didn't move back. She wasn't about to give up the yard she had gained. "Then what happened?"

"You've got to understand that Earl's my first born, and I love him. I had no choice. I had to lie to Lauri. I told her Earl buried the money in the forest. We'd have to dig it up. She believed me. Why not? She was still a child, and she trusted me." Her voice cracked, but she remained still, a picture of strength carved from granite.

"We went out and I found a deserted area. I told her to dig. At first we both dug, but after a few minutes of that, I told her I was too old to dig. She'd have to do it herself. She did and while she concentrated on her task, I took out the knife and--" A tight grimace tugged at her mouth. She continued, "I never meant for her to suffer. I liked Lauri, I really did. You believe me, don't you?"

Aimee nodded.

Grandma Louise looked relieved and almost smiled, but before the smile blossomed, it faded. "When I left, I thought she was dead. When I found out she survived for several hours, I almost went crazy. I kept hearing her screams, over and over again. Day in. Day out. In fact, the night before I went to visit you, I swear I heard her again. It was so real, I actually believed that I hadn't killed her. Someone else had. Someone, like maybe Gary.

"At times, the grief--the guilt--took hold of me and I said and did stupid things--like telling you about Earl's marriages." She let out a long sigh. "Other times I was strong, but at all times, deep down, I think I knew the truth." She looked at Aimee. "I suppose that's why I went to you. At first I thought I could manipulate you into finding Gary guilty. Then later, I wanted to be caught. I wasn't meant to be a killer. I was trying to protect my son the only way I knew." A tear ran down her cheek. "And now, he's gone. All this for nothing."

The hollowness in Grandma Louise's voice sent Aimee a warning signal. She inched a foot closer to her.

Grandma Louise raised the gun. Her

features set, hard and firm, but her hand shook and her face crumpled. She lowered the gun. "I can't shoot you." She pointed toward Rich. "He needs you. I hope it's not too late."

Relief filled Aimee's heart, momentarily. Her eyes traveled toward Rich, who lay without moving. "Rich!" she screamed.

Chapter 64

Aimee's face streaked with tears as she knelt down beside Rich. She reached for him, but he didn't respond. *Oh, God, no! Please, Rich, hang on.*

Aimee looked up and spotted Grandma Louise. She stood with her head bowed and shoulders hunched over, staring down at the bottom of the cliff. She sighed and cried out for her son.

Then Aimee listened to another sound in the distance, barely discernible at first, but rapidly growing louder--the wail of an approaching siren. She ran to the road to wave the car down. She put her hand above her eyes and squinted, barely able to make out the flashing red lights.

Hurry. Please, hurry.

A sharp crack erupted around her and Aimee jumped. Her heart caught in her throat. She pivoted toward the direction of the sound. She stood, unmoving, absorbing every detail. It took a few seconds for Aimee to see it all, nausea welled up and she looked away, the image seared in her brain.

The impact of the bullet exploded the top of Grandma Louise's head, scattering bits of brain and skull fragments everywhere. Aimee looked away and forced the bile down.

Behind her, a car screeched to a halt. Tom and Marie came running toward her with their pistols drawn. "Are you all right?" Marie asked.

Tom scanned the area.

"Call an ambulance!" Aimee pointed toward Rich. "Please help him."

"It's on the way, should be right behind us."

Aimee stood, numb. "How did you know where to find me?"

"You weren't at Grandma Louise's and you weren't home. Two of your neighbors reported gunshots. A passer-by called us. He said a man was holding a woman at gunpoint at Emerald Bay. I called an ambulance--just in case." Tom knelt down beside Rich and felt for a pulse. He studied the wound. "Rich's lost a lot of blood, but he's still got a pulse."

Off in the distance another siren announced its emergency. Tom removed his shirt, wadded it up, and applied pressure to the wound. "What happened here?"

Aimee opened her mouth to speak, but nothing came out. She focused on Grandma Louise's almost headless body.

Rich stirred, and Aimee wrapped her hand around his. "He'll be okay, won't he?"

"I'm not a doctor, Aimee." Tom grabbed Aimee's hand and placed it on the pressure point. "Keep pushing down until the paramedics arrive." He stood up and joined Marie, who searched the area close to Grandma Louise's body.

"Find anything?"

"Just the gun."

Tom looked down at the body. "How did this happen?"

Aimee's mind groped haphazardly, trying to refocus itself, trying to come up with the logical place to begin. She bit her tongue and glanced away from Grandma Louise. "Earl tried to shoot Rich. I couldn't allow that to happen."

"Earl?" Tom dropped into a semi-crouch. Marie raised her gun and looked around.

"He's dead. Over the cliff."

Marie stole a quick glance over the edge and saw Earl's mangled body crumpled among the rocks. "You did that?" She put the gun away.

Aimee nodded and began to shake. Tears ran down her cheeks as she looked at Rich.

Tom placed a reassuring hand on her shoulder. "You know the ambulance is on the way."

Aimee nodded and looked toward the road. Where is it? The minutes dragged as she applied the pressure and spoke softly to Rich. Her head perked up when she heard the screeching of tires as the ambulance driver brought the vehicle to a stop.

Tom rushed toward the two paramedics who were getting down from the ambulance. Marie stood between Aimee and the paramedics.

They took out the stretcher and ran toward

Rich and Aimee.

* * *

Aimee stood with her hand plastered over her mouth as she watched the vanishing ambulance. *Be okay. Please be okay. God, please let him be okay.*

"I'll take you to the hospital," Tom said.

She jumped in his car and wrung her hands, looking down the road as Tom and Marie barked orders to the detectives who had arrived shortly after the ambulance. "I'll get back as soon as possible," he told Marie.

Tom started the engine, flipped on the siren, and hit the gas. "Tell me how Earl and Grandma Louise ended up dead."

Aimee looked out the window. All the trees seemed to fuse into one. "It was an accident, but it was also self-defense. He dragged me to the edge of the cliff while Grandma Louise tried to talk him into giving up."

They had reached the part of the road that consisted mostly of curves. Tom slowed down. "Why was Earl holding you hostage?"

"Earl claimed he killed Lauri."

Tom shot Aimee a quick glance. "Earl killed Lauri?"

"No, actually Grandma Louise did."

Tom frowned and shook his head. "Tell me about it."

"Earl is the Truckee man and--"

"What's a Truckee man?"

Aimee explained about Rich's story and how that had led them back to Earl. "Somehow Lauri found out. She went to Grandma Louise and demanded money, which she planned to give to her mom for her sister's operation."

Tom pursed his lips and slowly nodded. He resumed speed as the road straightened. "You'll have to come in and give an official statement."

"I know," she mumbled and thought of Rich. She wanted to be with him, hold him, and let him know he had to live. Her mind stretched to the limits of space. She wished she could shout and scream.

"Don't you think so?" Tom waited for an answer.

Aimee shook herself, her eyes opened wide. "I'm sorry. What did you say?"

"Nothing." Tom returned his attention to the road. "Just tell me about the connection between the Truckee man, Earl, and Lauri's death."

Aimee did. A pause followed. "There's something else I want to tell you."

"What's that?"

"I have information which will help you solve an eighteen-year-old murder case."

Tom tightened his grip on the steering wheel. "Your mom?"

"Yes."

"Who did it?"

"My father." Nice and loud. Just stating a fact.

They reached the hospital and Tom drove around to the Emergency Entrance as the paramedics unloaded Rich's motionless body strapped to the gurney.

Aimee bolted out of the car, mumbling a quick *thanks*.

Epilogue
A Few Days Later

Aimee picked up the phone, punched the first number, and hesitated. She stared at the phone. The next number was two. She pushed it, frowned, and slammed the phone down.

Now was the time to apply for a job at one of the big-name newspapers. The editors would recognize her name. A week from now, she would be old news. As it was, she had already waited too long. Her name wouldn't mean as much.

Yet, she couldn't bring herself to dial those numbers, not while Rich lay in the hospital because of her. Just the thought of him warmed her. She longed to be by his side.

He had risked so much for her. The least she could do was put her dream on hold--at least temporarily. Later, when he was well, they would discuss the various issues facing them. Later for sure, but not now.

She turned her attention to her task at hand, creating a bouquet of flowers made out of newspapers. She arranged the bouquet and wondered how Rich would react to receiving a bouquet of newspaper flowers. She shrugged, retrieved the car keys, and drove down

Highway 50 to Barton Hospital.

* * *

Tom, Marie, Robert, and Dolphine gathered around Rich's hospital bed. Aunt Rachel stood next to them. When Aimee walked in, they were laughing at a joke of some kind.

"There she is," Robert said, "the world-renowned mystery solver." He stretched his arm toward Aimee.

Dolphine and Rich cheered. The pride in Aunt Rachel's face showed in her smile. Tom and Marie clapped.

"Stop it, you guys." Blood rushed to her face. "Besides, Dolphine deserves a lot of credit."

Everyone turned and clapped for Dolphine. She took an exaggerated bow. "Now that that's over, I'm really curious. How did you know?"

"About Lauri?"

Dolphine nodded.

"Remember the night Lauri supposedly ran away? I remember Karen telling me that as soon as Lauri walked out, she went to the window to see which direction Lauri went. She waited for a long time and never saw her. She thought maybe she had missed her because she was fussing with the baby. Then, it occurred to me that maybe Lauri never left the apartment building, at least not at that time. If so, there's only one place she would have gone."

"To Grandma Louise's." Marie tapped her

forehead.

Aimee nodded. "Right. The only other place she would have gone was to see Gary, and according to Karen, Lauri was eager to keep her date with Gary. But Gary denied making such plans. That's when I realized she intended to visit Grandma Louise all along."

For a few seconds everyone remained silent. Then Aimee snapped her fingers. "Oh, I almost forgot. I've got great news."

"What's that?" Rich asked.

"While I was making these flowers," she pointed to the paper bouquet, "Karen called. Her baby had just come out of surgery. She's going to be okay!"

Another round of thunderous cheer spread throughout the small, crowded hospital room.

"We've got news of our own." Marie looked up at Tom. He nodded. She continued, "We've apprehended the drug dealers who were after Charles, so he was able to be reunited with Karen and the baby without fearing for their lives."

"From what we've gathered," Tom said, "Charles got to the hospital in time to be with his wife throughout the operation. She was shocked and angry to see him. But the relief overcame her anger."

Marie's face lit up with a smile. "And another bit of good news is that Charles said he had no qualms about testifying."

Aimee briefly glanced at Rich. "I'm glad they were able to get together after all that's happened."

"Let's just hope they can stay together," Marie said.

All heads swiveled to look at her.

"Why wouldn't they?" Dolphine asked.

Tom cleared his throat. "Karen will have to face reckless endangerment charges. Remember, she gave the lawyers consent to use her own daughter to trap the senator."

"But the lawyers lied to her." Dolphine waved her opened hands to emphasize her point.

"And speaking of lawyers," Tom said, "Karen was smart enough to hire one. I heard he's working with the prosecutor on a plea deal for a minimal sentence."

The room grew quiet. "We're wishing her the best. But at least she'll have Charles and the baby to give her strength." Marie rubbed her temples. "Sometimes this job . . . "

Robert glanced at his watch. "Oh, oh, I promised Dolphine a fantastic meal, and if we don't take off pretty soon, the restaurant will get too crowded."

"Wait," Aunt Rachel said. "Before you go, there's something I've always wanted to know." She stared at Dolphine.

"Shoot," she said.

"I absolutely love your name. It's so unusual.

What's its origin?"

Dolphine smiled. "When my mom was pregnant, she knew I was going to be a boy. Grandpa Adolph was thrilled and told her he'd give her one hundred dollars if she named me after him. Then I was born and surprise, I'm a girl."

"Your poor mom," Aunt Rachel said. "I bet she hated to see that money fly away."

"You don't know my mom. A simple fact like that wasn't going to stop her. She, my dad, and the nurse brainstormed and they decided to add *-ine* to the end to make it feminine. Through the years, I lost the *A* and my name became Dolphine, but my real name is Adolphine."

Robert plastered both of his hands to his face and shook his head. "What a story." He looked at Dolphine and his eyes twinkled. "I'm sure glad you weren't a boy."

Dolphine's eyes returned the spark. "Me, too." They stared at each other's eyes until Dolphine broke the spell by stepping away from Robert. "We better get going."

"You can't leave yet," Aunt Rachel said. "You didn't finish the story. What happened to the hundred dollars?"

Dolphine smiled. "Mom got the money."

A round of clapping and cheering followed them out the room.

Tom reached for Marie's hand. "We don't have a fancy dinner planned, but we do have a ton and a half of paperwork waiting for us at the station."

Marie rolled her eyes. "Great. Something to look forward to."

Tom wrapped his arm around his wife and led her out. He paused at the door and turned around. "Aimee, we have an all points bulletin out on your father. So far, nothing's turned up, but I'll keep you posted."

Aimee swallowed hard. "Thanks."

The O'Days stepped out, and Aunt Rachel gave Aimee a kiss and squeezed Rich's hand. "I better go. Don't be strangers, either of you."

"We won't." Aimee opened the door for her and slowly closed it behind her. She turned to face Rich.

"I don't want to break the trend. I also have some news for you." He reached for the side drawer and groaned.

"Are you okay?"

"Yes. It just hurts when I move."

"Well, then don't move." Both laughed. "Let me get it for you. What am I looking for?"

"Inside that drawer--" Rich pointed to the roll-away tray, "--there's a folded piece of paper."

Aimee opened the drawer, retrieved the paper, and handed it to Rich.

"Keep it. It's for you. It proves I've been busy. I haven't been just resting, you know."

"Yeah? So what have you been doing?"

"Making all sorts of phone calls."

Aimee hesitated. "What kind of calls?"

For a moment Rich remained silent. "You'll see. It's all on that paper." His eyes focused on the newspaper flowers Aimee had made. "Are those for me?" His face lit up in amusement.

"Yeah, I wasn't sure what to get you, so I decided that your gift would be a combination. You'd get a bouquet of flowers, and if you didn't like looking at them, you could read them."

"Hmmm . . . maybe you should take up cooking."

Aimee smiled.

Rich smiled. "These are by far the most beautiful flowers I've ever received. Not that I've received many flowers, but that's beside the point." He opened his arms.

Aimee hesitated for a moment before leaning down and hugging him. She could feel his warmth and the longing for old times filled her heart.

"I did something for you," Rich said.

"What's that?"

He pointed to the folded paper she held in her hand. "Read it."

Aimee eyed it. "What does it say?"

"It's about making your dream come true. You broke two major stories--well, actually three. You're the one who solved my Truckee mystery. Anyway, I contacted several of the country's leading newspapers. What you hold in your hand are their answers."

Aimee's hands trembled as she unfolded the paper. The *Los Angeles Times* wanted to interview her. So did the *Chicago Tribune* and the *Dallas Morning News*. She held back a sigh. How could she leave Rich?

"I haven't heard from several other places, including the *New York Times*, but I'm willing to bet that they'll be interested too."

Aimee cradled the paper to her chest and turned. "If I accept one of these offers, I'll have to quit this job."

For a long time, silence filled the room. Aimee considered turning around to face Rich. He took a deep breath. "I promised that I wouldn't hold you back."

She turned and met his eyes, wanting to see his reaction. "What about us?"

Rich closed his eyes and let out his breath. "I've given it a lot of thought lately. I knew that if I made those calls, the newspapers' editors would want you to work for them. I realize that means losing you, but I also realize that you would want to make those calls yourself but because of me, you wouldn't. It's wrong for me to stand in your way, and besides, I had made you a promise." Holding onto his side, he sat up on bed. He signaled for Aimee to join him.

She sat beside him, and he wrapped his arm around her. "If you don't grasp this opportunity, some day down the road--it may be a year from now or ten years--you might come to resent me."

His voice trailed off.

Tears stung Aimee's eyes. "Rich, I wouldn't do that."

"You won't mean to, but you will."

"Rich, I--" She stopped. She didn't know how to answer. Dammit. Why did he have to be right? She looked down and a tear escaped her eye.

Rich turned her face toward his. He kissed her gently on the lips. "Oh, Aimee, you have no idea how much I want to beg you to stay, but if I did, and if you stayed, you'd be giving up your dreams. I won't allow that to happen."

Silence filled the room and in that silence, Aimee found the answer. "You're right, Rich, but it isn't just a dream anymore. That is something I want you to understand. It's now an obligation."

"I don't follow."

"You know my father killed my mother."

Rich nodded.

"I plan to accept a job with a big-time paper that will give me time to find my father and bring him to justice."

"I'm not sure such a job exists."

"Doesn't matter. I will find the money somehow."

"You are determined to do this."

"Yes," Aimee answered even though Rich hadn't asked a question. "I have vengeance in my heart."

"Then go," Rich said, "and may God bless

you."

"Rich?"

He looked tenderly into her eyes.

She read his pain. "I can't make it alone. I'll need your strength."

"You'll do fine without me. You've always been a survivor." He raised her head with his index finger. "But I'll expect you to come home for Christmas and vacations."

"And you'll come visit me?"

"Wherever you are." He kissed her.

About the Author

Highly acclaimed author L. C. Hayden is the creator of the popular Harry Bronson series, which includes *When the Past Haunts You*, a Watson Award Finalist, and *Why Casey Had to Die*, an Agatha Award Finalist for Best Novel.

Her non-mysteries include *Angels Around Us*, which rose to the Kindle Angels # 1 Best Seller List.

Besides being an accomplished author, Hayden is a popular speaker who is often in demand. She has done workshop and school presentations, has spoken to clubs and organizations, and works for several major cruise lines where she speaks about writing while cruising all over the world.

From October 2006 to October 2007, Hayden hosted Mystery Writers of America's only talk show, *Murder Must Air*.

You can reach her at www.lchayden.com

75680307R00227

Made in the USA
Columbia, SC
23 August 2017